M.W. Carr

Seven Pagodas

M.W. Carr

Seven Pagodas

ISBN/EAN: 9783337385538

Printed in Europe, USA, Canada, Australia, Japan

Cover: Foto ©Andreas Hilbeck / pixelio.de

More available books at **www.hansebooks.com**

𝔇escriptive and 𝔥istorical 𝔓apers

RELATING TO

THE SEVEN PAGODAS

ON THE

COROMANDEL COAST.

BY

WILLIAM CHAMBERS, ESQ.; J. GOLDINGHAM, ESQ.;
BENJAMIN GUY BABINGTON, ESQ., M.D., F.R.S.;
REV. G. W. MAHON, M.A.; LIEUTENANT JOHN BRADDOCK;
REV. W. TAYLOR; SIR WALTER ELLIOT, K.C.S.I.;
CHARLES GUBBINS, ESQ.

EDITED BY
CAPTAIN M. W. CARR,
Madras Staff Corps.

MADRAS:
PRINTED FOR THE GOVERNMENT OF MADRAS,
BY GRAVES, COOKSON AND CO., MOUNT ROAD.

1869.

EDITOR'S NOTE.

THE papers contained in this volume, descriptive of the Sculptures, Inscriptions and Monolithic temples known as the SEVEN PAGODAS, have been reprinted in a collected form, under the orders of the Government of Madras, with a view to promote the intelligent study and examination of these interesting relics of a bygone age. They have been selected as conveying valuable information on the subject, recorded by various competent observers at different times, but so scattered through the published transactions of learned Societies as to be rarely accessible to any one person visiting the spot.[*]

The origin of the European appellation "Seven Pagodas" cannot satisfactorily be traced. The name may have been given, as stated by Dr. Graul's guide, to the five *Rathas*, the Ganesa temple and the Shore temple.[†] The story of "magnificent pagodas swallowed up by the sea" is as apocryphal as the legend of the submerged city of Bali.

A matter of greater interest and importance, the age of the Sculptures and Inscriptions at Mávalivaram, has not, it is to be regretted, been definitely ascertained. No date has—if the record of such exist—been found in any one of the Inscriptions,

[*] Proceedings of the Madras Government, 1st May 1885

[†] Reise nach Ostindien, Vol. III., p. 212

Mr. Fergusson, writing of the *Raths*, states as his opinion that they were "carved by the Hindus, probably about 1300 A. D."[*] The researches of Sir Walter Elliot led him to fix the era of the oldest Tamil Inscription on the rocks of Mâvalivaram at the latter part of the 11th century, and that of the rock inscription at *Sâluvan* Kuppam at the commencement of the 12th century.[†]

The Sanscrit Inscriptions are doubtless anterior in date to those in the Tamil language. The Rev. Mr. Taylor conjectures that the excavations and sculptures, together with these older Inscriptions, were accomplished in the 16th or 17th century. Sir Walter Elliot, on the other hand, is of opinion that they could not have been made later than the 6th century.

The following observations of Mr. Fergusson explain the style of the monolithic *Raths* :—

" Although these *Raths*, as they are called locally, are comparatively modern, and belong to a different faith, they certainly constitute the best representations now known of the forms of the Buddhist buildings * * and make their external forms more intelligible than they could otherwise do; inasmuch the more internal copies of them which alone we possess [elsewhere] in the rock-cut examples. There are no essential differences which cannot be accounted for by the consideration that the sacred caves of the Buddhists were designed for a well-understood purpose—the Chaityas as temples, the Viharas as residences—which was the invariable rule in Buddhist times. When their successors the Hindus, began to follow their example, they copied blindly and unmeaningly. * * This * explains many points in the architecture [of the South of India] which without this would be perfectly unintelligible. The Raths are, in fact, transition specimens, and do well link the two styles together, the one serving to explain the peculiarities of the other."[‡]

[*] History of Architecture, Vol. II., p. 502.
[†] See p. 140 f., infra
[‡] History of Architecture, Vol II, p. 505

Some notes, corrective and explanatory, have been added by the Editor; these are distinguished by brackets [ ]. The orthography of Indian names occurring in these papers has been revised, and a uniform system of transliteration adopted.

In the Appendix will be found, among other matters, copies of the Sanscrit Inscriptions made by Mr. Arthur Burnell of the Madras Civil Service. Also a description of the Pagodas by Kávali Lakshmayya, printed in the original language from the Mackenzie MSS. in which it has lain for the last sixty odd years. This document gives a more detailed account of the antiquities at Mâvalivaram than is contained in any of the other papers on the subject; its translation, with Braddock's description, will probably be found the most useful guide to a traveller visiting the spot. An Index to the whole has been added.

The English letter press and illustrations have been executed by the Foster Press. The Devanâgarí printing was performed at the Press of the Society for the Promotion of Christian Knowledge.

A sketch map, carefully executed by the Revenue Survey Department, accompanies the volume. It contains ground plans of the monolithic temples and principal excavations.

MADRAS, September 1869.

CONTENTS.

I.—Some account of the Sculptures and
Ruins at Mâvalipuram, a place a few
miles north of Sadras, and known to
Seamen by the name of the Seven
Pagodas. By WILLIAM CHAMBERS, Esq. 1

II.—Some account of the Sculptures at
Mahâbalipuram; usually called the
Seven Pagodas. By J. GOLDINGHAM,
Esq. 30

III.—An account of the Sculptures and Inscriptions at Mahâmalaipûr; illustrated by Plates. By BENJAMIN GUY
BABINGTON, M.B., F.R.S., Sec. R.A.S. 44

IV.—A Guide to the Sculptures, Excavations,
and other remarkable objects at Mâ-
maRaipûr, generally known to Europeans as "The Seven Pagodas," by
the late Lieutenant JOHN BRADDOCK,
of the Madras Establishment. To
which are added some Archæological
Notes, by the Reverend WILLIAM
TAYLOR, and a Supplementary account

PAGE

of the remains at Sáluvan Kuppam,
by Sir WALTER ELLIOT, K.C.S.I., of
the Madras Civil Service.—Communicated to the Madras Journal of
Literature and Science by the Reverend
GEORGE WILLIAM MAHON, A.M., Garrison Chaplain, Fort St. George . . 63

V.—On the Inscription near the Varáhasvámi Temple, at Mâmallaipuram or
the Seven Pagodas, with a transcript
and translation. By Sir WALTER
ELLIOT, K.C.S.I. 132

VI.—Notes on the Ruins at Mahábalipuram
on the Coromandel Coast. By
CHARLES GUBBINS, Esq., Bengal Civil
Service 146

Appendix 173

The Sthalapurâna 173
Description of the Pagodas, &c. at
Mâvalivaram, written in the Telugu
language by Kâvali Lakshmayya in
1803. With a translation . . . 186
Sanscrit sloka 220
The Inscriptions 221
Arjuna's penance 225
Death of Mahishâsura 227
Bibliographical List 230

Index 232

ILLUSTRATIONS.

		PAGE
PLATE I.	Arjuna's Penance	47
II.	(1) Do. (2) Krishna Mandapa	48
III.	(1) Kailâsa (2) Nârâyana	49
IV.	Death of Mahishâsura	49
V.	Varâha Avatâra	50
VI.	Vâmana Avatâra	50
VII.	(1) Mahishâsura (2 & 3) Others	50
VIII.	(1) Devî (2) Dwârapâla	50
IX.	Excavated Temple	50
X.	(1) ? Durgâ (2) ? Durgâ (3) ? Vishnu	50
XI.	(1) Dolotsava Mandapa (2) Shore Temple	51
XII.	Vishnu	51
XIII.	Alphabet of Ancient Tamil	54
XIV.	Ganesa Temple Inscription	57
XV.	Inscription on buried Siva Temple	59
XVI.	Figures on Dharmarâja's Ratha	60
XVII.	Inscriptions on Dharmarâja's Ratha	61
XVIII.	Ancient Sanscrit Alphabets	68
XIX.	The five Rathas	108
XX. & XXI.	Plan of Mâmallaipûr	110
XXII.	The Shore Temple	186
XXIII.	Sketch of Mahâbalipuram	172
XXIV.	Buried Siva Temple at Sâduvankuppam	225

THE SEVEN PAGODAS.

I.—*Some account of the Sculptures and Ruins at Mávalipuram, a place a few miles north of Sadras, and known to seamen by the name of the Seven Pagodas.* By WILLIAM CHAMBERS, Esq.

[From the Asiatic Researches, Vol. I. 1788.]

AS amidst inquiries after the histories and antiquities of Asia at large, those of that division of it
in which this society* resides, may seem on many
accounts to lay claim to a particular share of its
attention, a few hints put down from recollection,
concerning some monuments of Hindu antiquity,
which, though situated in the neighbourhood of
European settlements on the Coromandel Coast, have
hitherto been little observed, may it is conceived, be
acceptable, at least as they may possibly give rise
hereafter to more accurate observations, and more
complete discoveries on the same subject. The
writer of this account went first to view them in
the year 1772, and curiosity led him thither again
in 1776; but as he neither measured the distances
nor size of the objects, nor committed to writing at
the time the observations he made on them, he

[* The Asiatic Society of Bengal.]

hopes to be excused if, after the lapse of so many
years, his recollection should fail him in some respects, and his account fall far short of that precision
and exactness, which might have been expected, had
there then existed in India so powerful an incentive
to diligent inquiry, and accurate communication, as
the establishment of this society must now prove.

The monuments he means to describe, appear to
be the remains of some great city, that has been
ruined many centuries ago; they are situated close
to the sea, between Covelong and Sadras, somewhat
remote from the high road, that leads to the different
European settlements. And when he visited them
in 1776, there was still a native village adjoining
to them, which retained the ancient name, and in
which a number of Brahmans resided, that seemed
perfectly well acquainted with the subjects of most
of the sculptures to be seen there.

The rock, or rather hill of stone, on which great
part of these works are executed, is one of the principal marks for mariners as they approach the coast,
and to them the place is known by the name of the
Seven Pagodas, possibly because the summits of the
rock have presented them with that idea as they
passed : but it must be confessed, that no aspect
which the hill assumes, as viewed on the shore,
seems at all to authorize this notion ; and there are
circumstances, which will be mentioned in the sequel,
that would lead one to suspect, that this name has
arisen from some such number of Pagodas that formerly stood here, and in time have been buried in
the waves. But, be that as it may, the appellation
by which the natives distinguish it, is of a quite
different origin : in their language, which is the

Tamil, (improperly termed *Malabar*,) the place is called Mávalipuram, which, in Sanscrit, and the languages of the more northern Hindus, would be Mahábalipura, or the City of the great Bali. For the Tamulians, (or Malabars,) having no *h* in their alphabet, are under a necessity of shortening the Sanscrit word *maht*, great, and write it *má*.* They are obliged also, for a similar reason, to substitute a *v* for a *b*, in words of Sanscrit, or other foreign original that begin with that letter; and the syllable *am*, at the end, is merely a termination, which, like *um* in Latin, is generally annexed to neuter substances.† To this etymology of the name of this place it may be proper to add, that Bali is the name of a hero very famous in Hindu romance; and that the river Mávaligangá, which waters the eastern side of Ceylon, where the Tamil language also prevails, has probably taken its name from him, as, according to that orthography, it apparently signifies the Ganges of the great Bali.

The rock, or hill of stone, above mentioned, is that which first engrosses the attention on approaching the place ; for, as it rises abruptly out of a level plain of great extent, consists chiefly of one single stone, and is situated very near to the sea-beach, it is such a kind of object as an inquisitive traveller would naturally turn aside to examine. Its shape is also

---

* They do indeed admit a substitute [maya], but the abbreviation is most used.

† This explains also, why the Sanscrit word *Veda*, by which the Hindus denominate the books of the law of their religion, is written by the Tamulians *Vedam*, which is according to the true orthography of their language, and no mistake of European travellers, as some have supposed ; while the same word is called *Bed* by the Bengalis, who have in effect no F in their alphabet.—See Dow, Vol. I. Dissert. p. 41.

singular and romantic, and, from a distant view, has an appearance like some antique and lofty edifice. On coming near to the foot of the rock from the north, works of imagery* and sculpture crowd so thick upon the eye, as might seem to favour the idea of a petrified town, like those that have been fabled in different parts of the world by too credulous travellers.† Proceeding on by the foot of the hill, on the side facing the sea, there is a pagoda rising out of the ground, of one solid stone, about sixteen or eighteen feet high, which seems to have been cut upon the spot out of a detached rock, that has been found of a proper size for that purpose.‡ The top is arched, and the style of architecture, according to which it is formed, different from any now used in those parts. A little further on, there appears upon an huge surface of stone, that juts out a little from the side of the hill, a numerous group of human figures in bas relief, considerably larger than life, representing the most remarkable persons, whose actions are celebrated in the Mahábhárata, each of them in an attitude, or with weapons or other insignia, expressive of his character, or of some one of his most famous exploits.§ All these figures are, doubtless, much less distinct than they were at first; for, upon comparing these and the rest of the sculptures that are exposed to the sea air, with others at the same place, whose situation has afforded them

* Among these, one object, though a mean one, attracts the attention, on account of the grotesque and ridiculous nature of the design; it consists of two monkeys cut out of one stone, one of them in a stooping posture, while the other is taking the insects out of his head.

† See Shaw's Travels, p. 155, et seq.

[‡ The Ganesa temple appears to be referred to.]

[§ Arjuna's penance.—cp. Braddock, infra.]

protection from that element, the difference is striking; the former being every where much defaced, while the others are fresh as recently finished. This defacement is no where more observable, than in the piece of sculpture which occurs next in the order of description. This is an excavation in another part of the east side of the great rock, which appears to have been made on the same plan, and for the same purpose that choultries are usually built in that country; that is to say, for the accommodation of travellers. The rock is hollowed out to the size of a spacious room, and two or three rows of pillars are left, as a seeming support to the mountainous mass of stone which forms the roof. Of what pattern these pillars have originally been, it is not easy now to conjecture; for the air of the sea has greatly corroded them, as well as all the other parts of the cave. And this circumstance renders it difficult to discover, at first sight, that there is a scene of sculpture on the side fronting the entrance. The natives, however, point it out, and the subject of it is manifestly that of Krishna attending the herds of Nanda Ghosha* the Admetus of the Hindus; from which circumstance, Krishna is also called Gopala, or the cowherd, as Apollo was entitled Nomius.

The objects which seem next to claim regard, are those upon the hill itself, the ascent of which, on the north, is, from its natural shape, gradual and easy at first, and is in other parts rendered more so, by very excellent steps cut out in several places, where the communication would be difficult or impracticable without them. A winding stair of this sort leads to a kind of temple cut out of the solid rock, with some

[* The cowherd Nanda, the foster and putative father of Krishna.]

figures of idols in high relief upon its walls, very well
finished, and perfectly fresh, as it faces the west, and
is therefore sheltered from the sea air.* From this
temple again there are flights of steps, that seem to
have led to some edifice, formerly standing upon the
hill; nor does it seem absurd to suppose, that this
may have been a palace, to which this temple, as
a place of worship, may have appertained. For,
besides the small detached ranges of stairs that are
here and there cut in the rock, and seem as if they
had once led to different parts of one great building,
there appear in many places small water-channels
cut also in the rock, as if for drains to an house; and
the whole top of the hill is strewed with small round
pieces of brick, which may be supposed, from their
appearance, to have been worn down to their present
form, during the lapse of many ages. On ascend-
ing the hill by its slope on the north, a very singular
piece of sculpture presents itself to view. On a
plain surface of the rock, which may once have served
as the floor of some apartment, there is a platform
of stone, about eight or nine feet long, by three or
four wide, in a situation rather elevated, with two
or three steps leading up to it, perfectly resembling
a couch or bed, and a lion very well executed at the
upper end of it by way of pillow, the whole of one
piece, being part of the hill itself. This the Brahmans,
inhabitants of the place, called the bed of Dharmarája, or Yadhishthira, the eldest of the five brothers,
whose fortunes and exploits are the leading subject in
the Mahábhárata. And at a considerable distance from
this, at such a distance, indeed, as the apartment of
the women might be supposed to be from that of

[* Cp. Braddock, No. 9.]

the men, is a bath excavated also from the solid rock, with steps in the inside, which the Brahmans call the bath of Draupadi, the wife of Yudhishthira and his brothers. How much credit is due to this tradition, and whether this stone couch may not have been anciently used as a kind of throne rather than a bed, is matter for future inquiry. A circumstance, however, which may seem to favour this idea is, that a throne in the Sanscrit, and other Hindu languages, is called *simhásana*, which is composed of the words *simha*, a lion, and *ásana*, a seat.

These are all that appear on that part of the upper surface of the hill, the ascent to which is on the north ; but, on descending from thence, you are led round the hill to the opposite side, in which there are steps cut from the bottom to a place near the summit, where is an excavation that seems to have been intended for a place of worship, and contains various sculptures of Hindu Deities. The most remarkable of these, is a gigantic figure of Vishnu, asleep on a kind of bed, with a huge snake wound about in many coils by way of pillow for his head ;[*] and these figures, according to the manner of this place, are all of one piece, hewn from the body of the rock.

But though these works may be deemed stupendous, they are surpassed by others that are to be seen at the distance of about a mile, or a mile and an half, to the southward of the hill. They consist of two[†] Pagodas, of about thirty feet long by twenty feet wide, and about as many in height, cut out of the solid rock, and each consisting originally of one

[* Cp. Braddock, No. 19. *infra*.]
[† There are five, the five *Mathas*.]

single stone. Near these also stand an elephant full
as big as life, and a lion much larger than the natural size, but very well executed, each hewn also out
of one stone. None of the pieces that have fallen
off in cutting these extraordinary sculptures are now
to be found near or any where in the neighbourhood
of them, so that there is no means of ascertaining
the degree of labour and time that has been spent
upon them, nor the size of the rock or rocks from
which they have been hewn, a circumstance which
renders their appearance the more striking and singular. And though their situation is very near the
sea-beach, they have not suffered at all by the corro-
sive air of that element, which has provided them
with a defence against itself, by throwing up before
them a high bank, that completely shelters them.
There is also great symmetry in their form; though
that of the Pagodas is different from the style of
architecture, according to which idol temples are now
built in that country. The latter resembles the
Egyptian; for the towers are always pyramidical,
and the gates and roofs flat, and without arches; but
these sculptures approach nearer to the Gothic taste,
being surmounted by arched roofs or domes, that are
not semi-circular, but composed of two segments of
circles meeting in a point at top. It is also observable
that the lion in this group of sculptures, as well as
that upon the stone couch above mentioned, are perfectly just representations of the true lion; and the
natives there give them the name, which is always
understood to mean a lion in the Hindu language,
to wit, *simha*; but the figure, which they have made
to represent that animal in their idol temples for centuries past, though it bears the same appellation, is

a distorted monster, totally unlike the original; insomuch that it has from hence been supposed that
the lion was not anciently known in this country, and
that *simha* was a name given to a monster that existed only in Hindu romance.   But it is plain that
that animal was well known to the authors of these
works, who, in manners as well as arts, seem to have
differed much from the modern Hindus.

There are two circumstances attending these monuments, which cannot but excite great curiosity, and
on which future inquiries may possibly throw some
light.   One is, that on one of the Pagodas last mentioned, there is an inscription of a single line, in a
character at present unknown to the Hindus.*   It
resembles neither the *Devanagari*, nor any of the
various characters connected with or derived from it,
which have come to the writer's knowledge from any
part of Hindostan.   Nor did it, at the time he viewed
it, appear to correspond with any character, Asiatic
or European, that is commonly known.   He had not
then, however, seen the alphabet of the *Páli*, the
learned language of the Siamese, a sight of which has
since raised in his mind a suspicion, that there is a
near affinity between them, if the character be not
identically the same.   But as these conjectures, after
such a lapse of time, are somewhat vague, and the
subject of them is perhaps yet within the reach of
our researches, it is to be hoped that some method
may be fallen upon of procuring an exact copy of
this inscription.

The other circumstance is, that though the out-
ward form of the Pagodas is complete, the ultimate
design of them has manifestly not been accomplished,

[* Since deciphered by Dr. Babington, see *infra.*]

but seems to have been defeated by some extraordinary convulsion of nature. For the western side of the most northerly one is excavated to the depth of four or five feet, and a row of pillars left on the outside to support the roof; but here the work has been stopped, and an uniform rent of about four inches breadth has been made throughout the solid rock, and appears to extend to its foundations, which are probably at a prodigious depth below the surface of the ground. That this rent has happened since the work began, or while it was carrying on, cannot be doubted; for the marks of the mason's tools are perfectly visible in the excavated part on both sides of the rent, in such a manner as to show plainly that they have been divided by it. Nor is it reasonable to suppose that such a work would ever have been designed, or begun, upon a rock that had previously been rent in two.

Nothing less than an earthquake, and that a violent one, could apparently have produced such a fissure in the solid rock : and that this has been the case in point of fact, may be gathered from other circumstances, which it is necessary to mention in an account of this curious place.

The great rock above described is at some small distance from the sea, perhaps fifty or an hundred yards,* and in that space the Hindu village before mentioned stood in 1776. But close to the sea are the remains of a Pagoda, built of brick,† and dedicated to Siva, the greatest part of which has evidently been swallowed up by that element ; for the door of the innermost apartment, in which the idol is placed, and

[* Would be more correctly estimated as half a mile.]
[† A mistake: it is built of stone.]

before which there are always two or three spacious
courts surrounded with walls, is now washed by the
waves; and the pillar used to discover the meridian
at the time of founding the Pagoda*† is seen standing
at some distance in the sea.   In the neighbourhood of
this building there are some detached rocks, washed
also by the waves, on which there appear sculptures,
though now much worn and defaced. And the natives
of the place declared to the writer of this account,
that the more aged people among them remembered
to have seen the tops of several Pagodas far out in
the sea, which being covered with copper (probably
gilt) were particularly visible at sunrise, as their
shining surface used then to reflect the sun's rays,
but that now that effect was no longer produced, as
the copper had since become incrusted with mould
and verdigris.‡

These circumstances look much like the effects of
a sudden inundation; and the rent in the rock above
described makes it reasonable to conjecture that
an earthquake may have caused the sea to overflow
its boundaries, and that these two formidable enemies
may have joined to destroy this once magnificent city.
The account which the Brahmans, natives of the place,
gave of its origin and downfall, partly, it should seem,
on the authority of the Mahábhárata, and partly on
that of later records, at the same time that it countenances this idea, contains some other curious particulars, which may seem to render it worthy of attention.   Nor ought it to be rejected on account of that

---

* See Voyage du M. Gentil, Vol. I., page 156.

[† More probably a flag-staff, *dhwajastambha*. It has been taken
by some for a *lingam*, which is manifestly an error.—cp. Bp. Heber's
Journal and Bruce's Scenes and Sights in the East.]

[‡ Cp. Gubbins, *infra.*]

fabulous garb, in which all nations, but especially
those of the East, have always clad the events of
early ages.

"Hiranyáksha (said they) was a gigantic prince,
"that rolled up the earth into a shapeless mass, and
"carried it down to the abyss, whither Vishnu fol-
"lowed him in the shape of an hog, killed him with
"his tusks, and replaced the earth in its original
"situation.   The younger brother of Hiranyáksha
"was Hiranyakasipu, who succeeded him in his king-
"dom, and refused to do homage to Vishnu.   He
"had a son named Prahláda, who at an early age
"openly disapproved this part of his father's conduct,
"being under the tuition of Sukráchárya.   His father
"persecuted him on this account, banished him, and
"even sought to kill him, but was prevented by
"the interposition of heaven, which appeared on the
"side of Prahláda.   At length, Hiranyakasipu was
"softened, and recalled his son to his court, where,
"as he sat in full assembly, he began again to argue
"with him against the supremacy of Vishnu, boasted
"that he himself was lord of all the visible world,
"and asked what Vishnu could pretend to more.
"Prahláda replied, that Vishnu had no fixed abode,
"but was present everywhere.   Is he, said his father,
"in that pillar?   Yes, returned Prahláda.   Then let
"him come forth, said Hiranyakasipu ; and, rising
"from his seat, struck the pillar with his foot ; upon
"which Vishnu, in the Narasinha Avatára, that is
"to say, with a body like a man, but an head like a
"lion, came out of the pillar, and tore Hiranyakasipu
"in pieces.   Vishnu then fixed Prahláda on his
"father's throne ; and his reign was a mild and vir-
"tuous one, and as such was a contrast to that of

"his father. He left a son named Namuchi,* who
"inherited his power and his virtues, and was the
"father of Bali, the founder of the once magni-
"ficent city of Mahábalipura, the situation of which
"is said to be described in the following verse, taken
"from the Mahábhárata :—

मञ्जावा: दक्षिणे भागे योजनानां शतद्वयं ।
पञ्चयोजनमात्रेण पूर्वाम्भेदेन पश्चिमे ॥

The sense of which is literally this :—

"South of the Ganges two hundred yojanas,
"Five yojanas† westward from the eastern sea."

Such is the Brahman account of the origin of this
place. The sequel of its history, according to them,
is as follows :—

"The son of Bali was Bánásura, who is repre-
"sented as a giant with a thousand hands. Aniruddha,
"the son‡ of Krishna, came to his court in disguise,
"and seduced his daughter ; which produced a war,
"in the course of which Aniruddha was taken prisoner,
"and brought to Mahâbalipura ;§ upon which Krishna
"came in person from his capital Dvâraka, and laid
"siege to the place. Siva guarded the gates, and
"fought for Bánásura, who worshipped him with

[* An error : Virochana was the son of Prahláda, and father of Bali ;
Namuchi was the son of Viprachitri by Sinhiká, sister of Hiranyakasipu.—See the Vishnupurána.]

† The yojana is a measure often mentioned in the Sanscrit books,
and, according to some accounts, is equal to nine, according to others
twelve English miles. But at that rate the distance here mentioned,
between this place and the Ganges, is prodigiously exaggerated, and
will carry us far south of Ceylon. This, however, is not surprising
in an Hindu poem ; but, from the second line it seems pretty clear
that this city, at the time this verse was composed, must have stood
at a great distance from the sea.

[‡ Aniruddha was the grandson, not the son, of Krishna.]

[§ Sonitapura, according to the Vishnupurána—cp. Wilson's trans.,
Book V. chap. 33.]

"his thousand hands ; but Krishna found means to
"overthrow Siva, and having taken the city, cut off
"all Bánásura's hands, except two, with which he
"obliged him to do him homage.   He continued in
"subjection to Krishna till his death ; after which a
"long period ensued, in which no mention is any
"where made of this place, till a prince arose, whose
"name was Malécheren,* who restored the kingdom
"to great splendour, and enlarged and beautified
"the capital.   But in his time the calamity is said
"to have happened by which the city was entirely
"destroyed ; and the cause and manner of it have
"been wrapped up by the Brahmans in the following
"fabulous narration.   Malécheren, (say they,) in an
"excursion which he made one day alone, and in dis-
"guise, came to a garden in the environs of the city,
"where was a fountain so inviting, that two celestial
"nymphs had come down to bathe there.   The Rájá
"became enamoured of one of them, who condes-
"cended to allow of his attachment to her ; and she
"and her sister-nymph used thenceforward to have
"frequent interviews with him in that garden.   On
"one of those occasions, they brought with them a
"male inhabitant of the heavenly regions, to whom
"they introduced the Rájá ; and between him and
"Malécheren a strict friendship ensued ; in conse-
"quence of which he agreed, at the Rájá's earnest
"request, to carry him in disguise to see the court
"of the divine Indra, a favour never before granted
"to any mortal.   The Rájá returned from thence
"with new ideas of splendour and magnificence, which
"he immediately adopted in regulating his court, and
"his retinue, and in beautifying his seat of govern-

[* The same as Mallésuda ? cp. Taylor, infra.]

"ment. By this means Mahábalipura became soon
"celebrated beyond all the cities of the earth ; and
"an account of its magnificence having been brought
"to the gods assembled at the court of Indra, their
"jealousy was so much excited at it, that they sent
"orders to the God of the Sea to let loose his billows,
"and overflow a place which impiously pretended to
"vie in splendour with their celestial mansions. This
"command he obeyed, and the city was at once over-
"flowed by that furious element, nor has it ever
"since been able to rear its head."

Such is the mode in which the Brahmans choose to
account for the signal overthrow of a place devoted
to their wretched superstitions.

It is not, however, improbable, that the rest of
this history may contain, like the mythology of
Greece and Rome, a great deal of real matter of fact,
though enveloped in dark and figurative representations. Through the disguise of these we may dis-
cern some imperfect records of great events, and of
revolutions that have happened in remote times ; and
they perhaps merit our attention the more, as it is
not likely that any records of ancient Hindu history
exist but in this obscure and fantastic dress. Their
poets seem to have been their only historians, as
well as divines ; and whatever they relate, is wrapped up in this burlesque garb, set off, by way of
ornament, with circumstances hugely incredible and
absurd, and all this without any date, and in no other
order or method, than such as the poet's fancy suggested, and found most convenient. Nevertheless,
by comparing names and grand events, recorded by
them, with those interspersed in the histories of other
nations, and by calling in the assistance of ancient

monuments, coins, and inscriptions, as occasion shall offer, some probable conjectures, at least, if not important discoveries, may, it is hoped, be made on these interesting subjects. It is much to be regretted, that a blind zeal, attended with a total want of curiosity, in the Muhammadan governors of this country, has been so hostile to the preservation of Hindu monuments and coins. But a spirit of inquiry among Europeans may yet perhaps be successful; and an instance, which relates to the place above described, though in itself a subject of regret, leaves room to hope that futurity may yet have in store some useful discoveries. The Kāzī of Madras, who had often occasion to go to a place in the neighbourhood of Mahābalipura, assured the writer of this accouut, that within his remembrance a ryot of those parts had found, in ploughing his ground, a pot of gold and silver coins, with characters on them which no one in those parts, Hindu or Muhammadan, was able to decipher. He added, however, that all search for them would now be vain, for they had doubtless been long ago devoted to the crucible, as, in their original form, no one there thought them of any value.

The inscription on the Pagoda mentioned above, is an object which, in this point of view, appears to merit great attention. That the conjecture, however, which places it among the languages of Siam, may not seem in itself chimerical, the following passages from some authors of repute are here inserted, to show that the idea of a communication having formerly subsisted between that country and the coast of Coromandel, is by no means without foundation; nay, that there is some affinity, even at this day,

between the Páli and some of the Hindu languages: and that the same mode of worship seems
formerly to have prevailed in the Deccan, which is
now used by the Siamese.

Monsieur de la Loubère, in his excellent account
of Siam, speaks thus of the origin of the Páli language:—

"The Siamese, says he, do not mention any coun-
"try where the Páli language, which is that of their
"laws and their religion, is at present in use. They
"suppose, indeed, on the report of some among them,
"who have been on the Coast of Coromandel, that
"it bears some resemblance to some of the dialects
"of that country; but they at the same time allow,
"that the character in which it is written is not known
"but among themselves. The secular Missionaries
"settled at Siam believe that this language is not
"entirely a dead one; because they have seen in
"their hospital a man from the neighbourhood of
"Cape Comorin, who mixed several Páli words in
"his discourse, declaring that they were in use in his
"country, and that he himself had never studied nor
"knew any other than his mother-tongue. They at
"the same time mention, as matter of certainty, that
"the religion of the Siamese comes from those parts;
"as they have read in a Páli book, that Sommona
"Kodam,* the idol of the Siamese, was the son of a
"king of Ceylon."†‡

[* The Siamese form of Sramana Gautama, a name applied to
Buddha, signifying 'Gautama the ascetic.']

[† Buddha, according to tradition, was the son of Suddhodana, the
king of Kapilavastu, a city and State on the borders of Nepal.]

‡ "Les Siamois ne nomment aucun Pais, ou la langue Bali qui est
"celle de leurs loix et de leur religion, soit aujourdhuy en usage.
"Ils soupçonnent à la verité, sur le rapport de quelques-uns d'entre
3

The language of the man mentioned in this passage, who came from the neighbourhood of Cape Comorin, could be no other than the Tamil; but the words here alluded to may very possibly have been derivatives from the Sanscrit, common to both that and the Páli.

In another part of the same work, where the author treats of the history of Samana Kodam at large, on the authority of the Páli books, he says :—

"The father of Samana Kodam, according to the "same Páli book, was a king of Teve Lanká, that "is to say, of the famous Ceylon."*

Here it is observable, that, while the country of Siam seems to be utterly unknown, both to the natives of Ceylon and Hindostan, Ceylon should nevertheless be so well known to the Siamese, and under the same appellation it bears in the Sanscrit. An epithet is also here prefixed to it which seems to be the same as that used by the Hindus in speaking of that island; for they also call it, in Sanscrit, Deva Lanká, or the Sacred Lanká. From several passages in the same work it also appears, that the Sanscrit word mahá, which signifies "great" is constantly used

---

* "eux, qui ont été à la côte de Coromandel, que la langue Balie a quel-
"que ressemblance avec quelqu'un des dialects de ce pais là: mais
"ils conviennent en même temps que les lettres de la langue Balie
"ne sont connues que chez eux. Les Missionaires séculiers à Siam
"croyent que cette langue n'est pas entièrement morte; parcé qu'ils
"ont vu dans leur hôpital un homme des environs du Cap de Como-
"rin, qui savoit plusieurs mots Balis dans son langage, assurant
"qu'ils étoient en usage en son pais, et que luy n'avoit jamais étudié,
"et ne savoit que sa langue maternelle. Ils donnent d'ailleurs pour
"certain que la religion des Siamois vient de ces quartiers là, parce
"qu'ils ont lu dans un livre Balie que Sommonacodom que les Sia-
"mois adorent, etoit fils d'un Roy de l'isle de Ceylone."

* "Le pere de Sommonacodom etoit, selon ce mesme livre Bali, un
Roy de Tere Lanca, c'est a dire un Roy de la célèbre Ceylan."

in the Páli language in the same sense. And the names of the days of the week are most of them the same in Sanscrit and in Páli, as may be seen in the following comparison of them :—

Sanscrit.	Páli.*	
Aditya-vára,	Van Athit,	Sunday.
Soma-vára,	Vant Tchân,	Monday.
Mangala-vára,	Van Angkaan,	Tuesday.
Budha-vára,	Van Pout,	Wednesday.
Brihaspati-vára,	Van Prahout,	Thursday.
Sukra-vára,	Van Souc,	Friday.
Sani-vára,	Van Sâon,	Saturday.

The same author gives, in another place, an account of a pretended print of a foot on a rock, which is an object of worship to the Siamese, and is called Prábát, or the venerable foot. For prá, in Páli he says, signifies "venerable," which agrees with *parápara* and *parameshtha* in Sanscrit; and *bát* in the same tongue is a foot, as *páda* in Sanscrit. After which he goes on to say :—

"We know that in the island of Ceylon, there "is a pretended print of a human foot, which has "long been held in great veneration. It represents, "doubtless, the left foot; for the Siamese say that "Samana Kodam set his right foot on their Prábát "and his left foot at Lanká."†§

From Knox's History of Ceylon it appears, that the impression here spoken of is upon the hill called,

[* The names given are Siamese.]

† Here one Hindu word is substituted for another; for Chând in Hindustani, and Chandra in Sanscrit, signify the moon as well as Soma.

‡ "On sait que dans l'isle de Ceylan, il y a un prétendu vestige de "pié humain, que depuis long temps y est en grande vénération. Il "représente sans doute le pié gauche; car les Siamois disent que "Sommonocodom pose le pié droit à leur prabat, et le pié gauche à "Lanck."

[§ Op. Spence Hardy's Manual of Budhism, p. 212.]

by the Singhalese, "Hamalell;" by Europeans,
"Adam's Peak;" and that the natives believe it to be
the footstep of their great idol Buddou, between the
worship of whom, as described by Knox, and that of
Samana Kodam, as related by M. de la Loubère,
there is a striking resemblance in many particulars,
which it may be proper here to enumerate.

1st.—Besides the footsteps above mentioned, there
is a kind of tree (which, from description, appears to
be the Pipal tree* so well known in India) which the
Singhalese hold sacred to Buddou, and the Siamese
to Samana Kodam; insomuch that the latter deem
it meritorious to hang themselves upon it. The
Singhalese call it Bogahah;† for gahah, in their
language, signifies a tree: and bo seems to be an
abbreviation of Bod or Buddou;‡ and the Siamese
call it, in Pāli, Pruuk Mabd Dend, which according
to La Loubère's interpretation, signifies the tree of
the great Pout.§ This he supposes to mean Mercury; for he observes that Pout, or Poot, is the name
of that planet in the Pāli term for Wednesday; and
in another place, he says, Pout is one of the names
of Samana Kodam. It is certain that Wednesday is
called the name of Bod, or Budd, in all the Hindu
languages, among which the Tamil, having no b,
begins the word with a p, which brings it very near
the Pāli mode of writing it. It is equally certain

[* From religious, called by Buddhists the Bodhi tree, "the tree
of wisdom," because under it Gautama became Buddha "the
Enlightened."—Cp. Bigandet's life of Gaudama, p. 85.]

[† The 'bo-tree.']

[‡ Fo, Bod, Buddou, Budd, Booth, Pood, &c., are some of the
numerous modes in which Gautama's appellative, Buddha, has been
spelt.—See Manual of Budhism, p. 354.]

§ In vulgar Siamese they call it Ton-pō.

that the days of the week, in all these languages, are called after the planets in the same order as with us; and that Bod, Budd, or Pood, holds the place of Mercury. From all which it should appear that Pout, which, among the Siamese, is another name for Mercury, is itself a corruption of Buddou, who is the Samana Kodam of the Greeks. And it is singular that, according to M. de la Loubère, the mother of Samana Kodam is called, in Páli, Maha-mania,* or the great Mania, which resembles much the name of Maia, the mother of Mercury. At the same time that the Tamil termination *an*, which renders the word Poodan, creates a resemblance between this and the Woden of the Gothic nations, from which the same day of the week is denominated, and which, on that and other accounts, is allowed to be the Mercury of the Greeks.†

2ndly.—The temples of Samana Kodam are called Pihan; and round them are habitations for the priests, resembling a college; so those of Boddou are called Vihar, and the principal priests live in them as in a college. The word Vihar,‡ or, as the natives of Bengal would write it, Bihar, is Sanscrit; and Ferishtah, in his History of Bengal, says, that this name was given by the Hindus to the Province of Behar, because it was formerly so full of Brahmins, as to be, as it were, one great seminary of learning, as the word imports.

[* Mahámáyá, Mahámáyádeví, Máyá, or Máyádeví.]

[† "Much erroneous speculation has originated in confounding Budha, the son of Soma, and regent of the planet Mercury, 'he who knows,' the intelligent, with Buddha, any deified mortal, or 'he by whom the truth is known.'—Wilson's Vishnu Purána." Spence Hardy, Manual of Budhism, p. 354 n.]

[‡ Vihára.]

3rdly.—The Siamese have two orders of priests, and so have the worshippers of Buddou. Both the one and the other are distinguished by a yellow habit, and by another circumstance, which must be mentioned in the words of the respective authors. Knox says of the Buddou Priests, "They have the "honour of carrying the Tallipot* with the broad "end over their heads foremost, which none but the "king does." And M. de la Loubère says of the Siamese priests, "To defend themselves from the "sun they have the Talapat, which is their little "umbrella, in the form of a screen."†

The word here used is common to most of the Hindu languages, and signifies the leaf of the Palmyra tree. M. de la Loubère mentions it as a Siamese word, without seeming to know its origin or primary signification.

4thly.—The priests of Buddou, as well as those of Samana Kodam,‡ are bound to celibacy, as long as they continue in the profession; but both the one and the other are allowed to lay it down and marry.

5thly.—They both eat flesh, but will not kill the animal.

6thly.—The priests of either nation are of no particular tribe, but are chosen out of the body of the people.

These circumstances plainly show that this is a system of religion different from that of the Vedas; and some of them are totally inconsistent with the

[* Tàlapàt, "palm-leaf."]
† " Pour se garentir du soleil ils ont la Talapat, qui est leur petit "parasol en forme d'écran."
[‡ The same persons: Samana Kodam (Sramana Gautama) was the Buddha, i. e. the "Enlightened." (Max Müller.) See note * at p. 17.]

principles and practice of the Brahmans. And, indeed, it is manifest, from Knox's whole account, that the religion of the Singhalese is quite distinct from that which prevails at this day among the Hindus, nor does it appear that there is such a race of men as that of the Brahmans among them. The only part in which there seems to be any agreement is in the worship of the Devatas, which has probably crept in among them from their Tamil neighbours; but that is carried on in a manner very different from the Brahmanical system, and appears to be held by the nation at large in very great contempt, if not abhorrence. Knox's account of it is this: "Their temples "(i. e. those of the Devatas) are, he says, called "Kóvils," which is the Tamil word for Pagoda. He then goes on to say, "A man piously disposed, "builds a small house at his own charge, which is the "temple, and himself becomes priest thereof. This "house is seldom called God's House, but most "usually Yakko,* the Devil's." But of the prevailing religion he speaks in very different terms, and describes it as carried on with much parade and splendour and attended with marks of great antiquity. "The "pagodas, or temples of their gods, says he, are so "many that I cannot number them. Many of them "are of rare and exquisite work, built of hewn stone, "engraven with images and figures; but by whom, "and when, I could not attain to know, the inhabi-"tants themselves being ignorant therein. But sure "I am, they were built by far more ingenious artifi-"cers than the Chingelays† that now are on the land. "For the Portuguese, in their invasions, have defaced "some of them, which there is none found that hath

[* Yakha.]   [† Singhalese.]

"skill enough to repair to this day." In another
place, he says, "Here are some ancient writings,
"engraven, upon rocks, which puzzle all that see
"them. There are divers great rocks in divers parts
"in Cande Uda,* and in the northern parts. These
"rocks are cut deep with great letters for the space
"of some yards, so deep that they may last to the
"world's end. Nobody can read them, or make any-
"thing of them. I have asked Malabars and Gen-
"toos, as well as Chingelays and Moors, but none of
"them understood them. There is an ancient temple,
"Goddiladenni in Yattanour, stands by a place where
"there are of these letters." From all which the
antiquity of the nation and their religion is sufficiently evident ; and from other passages it is plain,
that the worship of Buddou, in particular, has been
from remote times a very eminent part of that religion ; for the same author, speaking of the tree at
Anurodgburro,† in the northern part of the island,
which is sacred to Buddou, says, "The due perform-
"ance of this worship they reckon not a little meri-
"torious ; insomuch that as they report, ninety
"kings have reigned there successively, where, by
"the ruins that still remain, it appears they spared
"not for pains and labour, to build temples and high
"monuments to the honour of this god, as if they
"had been born to hew rocks and great stones, and
"lay them up in heaps. These kings are now happy
"spirits, having merited it by these labours." And
again he says, "For this god, above all other, they
"seem to have an high respect and devotion," &c.

And from other authorities it will appear, that this
worship has formerly been by no means confined to

[* Kandy.]   [† Anuradhapura.]

Ceylon, but has prevailed in several parts of India
prior to that of the Brahmans; nay, that this has
been the case even so late as the ninth and twelfth
centuries of the Christian Æra.

In the well-known* Anciennes Relations, translated from the Arabic by that eminent orientalist
Eusebius Renaudot, the Arabian traveller gives this
account of the custom of dancing-women, which
continues to this day in the Deccan, but is not known
among the Hindus of Bengal, or Hindustan Proper.

" There are in India public women, called women
" of the idol, and the origin of this custom is this :
" when a woman has made a vow for the purpose of
" having children, if she brings into the world a pretty
" daughter, she carries it to Bod, (so they call the
" idol which they adore,) and leaves it with him."†

This is a pretty just account of this custom, as it
prevails at this day in the Deccan ; for children are,
indeed, devoted to this profession by their parents,
and when they grow up in it they are called, in
Tamil,‡ *Devadasi*, or female slaves of the idol.   But
it is evident they have changed their master since
this Arabian account was written, for there is no idol
of the name of Bod now worshipped there.   And
the circumstance of this custom being unknown in
other parts of India, would lead one to suspect that
the Brahmans, on introducing their system of religion

---

* Anciennes Relations des Indes et de la Chine, de deux voyageurs
Mohametans, qui y allèrent dans le neuvième siècle.   Paris, 1718. 8vo.

† " Il y a dans les Indes des femmes publiques, appellées femmes
" de l'idole : l'origine de cette coustume est telle: Lorsqu'une femme a
" fait un voeu pour avoir des enfans, si elle met au monde une belle
" fille, elle l'apporte au *Bod*, c'est ainsi qu'ils appellent l'idole qu'ils
" adorent, auprès duquel elle la laisse, &c.   Anc. Rel. p. 109.

[‡ The word is Sanscrit, and common to the vernacular languages.]

into that country, had thought fit to retain this part
of the former worship, as being equally agreeable to
themselves and their new disciples.

The same Arabian travellers give us an account of
a very powerful race of Hindu kings, according to
them, indeed, the most powerful in India, who then
reigned on the Malabar Coast with the title of Bal-
hára.* Their dominion appears to have extended over
Guzerat, and the greatest part, if not the whole, of
the ancient kingdom of Vijayapúr. For the Arabian
geographer quoted by M. Renaudot makes Nahel-
várah the metropolis of these princes, which is, doubtless, Nahervalah, the ancient capital of Guzarat;
though M. Renaudot seems not to have known that
place; and the rest of the description sufficiently shows
the great extent of their dominion southward.   M.
D'Anville speaks of this race of kings on the authority
of the Arabian geographer Edrisi, who wrote in the
twelfth century, according to whom it appears that
their religion was, even so late as that period, not the
Brahmanical, but that of which we are now speaking.
M. D'Anville's words are these : " Edrisi acquaints
" us with the religion which this prince professed in
" saying, that his worship was addressed to Bodda,
" who, according to St. Jerome and Clemens Alexan-
" drinus, was the founder of the sect of the Gym-
" nosophists, in like manner as the Brahmans were
" used to attribute their institution to Brahmá."†

<hr/>

[* Cp. Sir H. M. Elliot's History of India, as told by its own Historians, pp. 86—89.]

† " L'Edrisi nous instruit sur la religion que professoit ce Prince, en
" disant que son culte s'adressoit à Bodda, qui selon St. Jerome and
" St. Clement d'Alexandrie, avoit été l'instituteur des Gymnoso-
" phistes comme les Brachmanes rapportoient à Brahma leur institut."
Ant. Geog. de L'Inde, p. 94

The authority of Clemens Alexandrinus is also cited on the same subject by Relandus in his 11th Dissertation, where, treating of the language of Ceylon, he explains the word Vihâra, above spoken of, in these terms :—

"Vihâra signifies a temple of their principal god "Buddou, who, as Clemens Alexandrinus has long "ago observed, was worshipped as a god by the "Hindus."[*]

After the above quotations, the following extract from the voyage of that inquisitive and ingenious traveller M. Gentil, published in 1779, is given as a further and very remarkable illustration of this subject :—

"This system is also that of the Brahmans of our "time; it forms the basis of that religion, which "they have brought with them into the southern "parts of the Peninsula of Hindustan into Madura, "Tanjore, and Mysore.

"There was then in those parts of India, and "principally on the Coast of Coromandel and "Ceylon, a sort of worship, the precepts of which we "are quite unacquainted with. The god, Baouth, "of whom at present they know no more in India "than the name, was the object of this worship; but "it is now totally abolished, except that there may "possibly yet be found some families of Indians "who have remained faithful to Baouth and do not "acknowledge the religion of the Brahmans, and who "are on that account separated from, and despised "by the other castes.

---

[*] Vehar, templum dei primarii Buddæ &c. quem Indos ut Deum venerari jam olim notavit Clemens Alexandrinus. Strom. lib. 1. p. 223. Rel. Diss. pars tertia, p. 65.

" I have not, indeed, heard that there are any such
" families in the neighbourhood of Pondichurry ;
" but there is a circumstance well worthy of remark,
" which none of the travellers that have treated of
" the Coast of Coromandel and Pondicherry seem to
" have noticed. It is this, that at a short league's
" distance to the south of this town, in the plain of
" Virapatnam, and pretty near the river, we find a
" statue of granite very hard and beautiful. This
" statue, which is from three feet to three and a half
" in height, is sunk in the sand to the waist, and
" weighs doubtless many thousand weight ; it is, as
" it were, abandoned in the midst of this extensive
" plain. I cannot give a better idea of it, than by
" saying, that it exactly agrees with, and resembles
" the Samana Kodam of the Siamese ; its head is of
" the same form, it has the same attitude, its arms
" are in the same attitude, and its ears are exactly
" similar. The form of this divinity, which has
" certainly been made in this country, and which
" in no respect resembles the present idols of the
" Gentoos, struck me as I passed this plain. I made
" various inquiries concerning this singular figure,
" and the Tamilians, one and all, assured me that
" this was the god Baouth, who was now no longer
" regarded, for that his worship and his festivals had
" been abolished ever since the Brahmans had made
" themselves masters of the people's faith." *

* " Ce système est aussi celui des Brames de nos jours ; il fait la
" base de la religion qu'Ils ont apportée dans le sud de la presqu'île
" de l'Indostan, le Madure, le Tanjaour, et le Maïssour.
" Il y avoit alors dans ces parties de l'Inde, & principalement à la
" Côte de Coromandel & à Ceylan, un culte dont on ignore absolument
" les dogmes · le Dieu Baouth, dont on ne connoit aujourd'hui, dans
" l'Inde, que le nom, étoit l'objet de ce culte ; mais il est tout-a-fait

M. Gentil then goes on to say a good deal more upon this subject, in the course of which he supposes that this deity is the Fo of the Chinese, whose worship by their own accounts, was brought from India. And, indeed, the abridgement of the name Pout, mentioned in a note of this paper, which the vulgar Siamese reduce to the single syllable Po, seems to countenance this opinion. But as this is foreign to our present purpose, and the above passages, it is hoped, are sufficient to establish what was proposed, it seems high time to take leave of this subject, with an apology for that prolixity which is inseparable from this kind of discussion.

17th June, 1784.

"aboll, si on n'est qu'il se trouve encore quelques familles d'Indiens
"séparées & méprisées des autres castes, qui sont restées fidèles à
" Baouth, & qui ne reconnoissent point la religion des Brames.

" Je n'ai pas entendu dire qu'il y ait de ces familles aux environs de
" Pondichery ; cependant, une chose très digne de remarque, & à
"laquelle aucun des voyageurs qui parlent de la Côse de Coromandel
" & de Pondichery, n'ont fait attention, est que l'on trouve à une
" petite lieue au sud de cette Ville, dans la plaine de Virapatnam,
" assez près de la rivière, une statue de Granit très dur & très beau :
" cette statue, d'environ trois pieds a trois pieds & demi de hauteur,
" est enfoncée dans le sable jusqu'à la ceinture, & pose sans doute
" plusieurs milliers ; elle est comme abandonnée au milieu de cette
" vaste plaine ; je ne peux mieux en donner une idée, qu'en disant
" qu'elle est entièrement conforme & ressemblante à Baouth même
" des Siamois ; que la même forme de tête, de même les oreilles tirées
" dans le visage, c'est la même attitude dans les bras, & les oreilles
" sont absolument semblables. La forme de cette divinité, qui cer-
" tainement a été faite dans le pays, & qui ne ressemble en rien aux
" divinités actuelles des Gentils, m'avoit frappé lorsque je passai dans
" cette plaine ; je fis diverses informations sur cette figure singulière,
" les Tamoults m'assurèrent tous que c'étoit Baouth qu'on ne regar-
" doit plus ; que son culte & ses fêtes etoient cessés depuis que les
" Brames s'étoient rendus les maîtres de la croyance du peuple."

II.—*Some account of the Sculptures at Mahábali-puram; usually called the Seven Pagodas.* By
J. Goldingham, Esq.

(From the Asiatic Researches, Vol. V. 1798.]

THESE curious remains of antiquity, situate near
the sea, are about thirty-eight English miles
southerly from Madras. A distant view presents
merely a rock, which, on a near approach, is found
deserving of particular examination. The attention,
passing over the smaller objects, is first arrested by a
Hindu pagoda, covered with sculpture, and hewn
from a single mass of rock : being about twenty-six
feet in height, nearly as long, and about half as broad.
Within is the *lingam,** and a long inscription on the
wall, in characters unknown.

Near this structure, the surface of the rock, about
ninety feet in extent, and thirty in height, is covered with figures in bas-relief. A gigantic figure of
the god Krishna is the most conspicuous, with
Arjuna his favourite, in the Hindu attitude of prayer ;
but so void of flesh, as to present more the appearance of a skeleton than the representation of a living
person. Below is a venerable figure, said to be

[* This temple now contains an image of Ganesa.—Cp. Babington,
infra.]

the father of Arjuna;* both figures proving the
sculptor possessed no inconsiderable skill. Here
are the representations of several animals, and of
one which the Brahmans name *simha*, or lion ; but
by no means a likeness of that animal, wanting the
peculiar characteristic, the mane. Something intended to represent this is, indeed, visible, which
has more the effect of spots. It appears evident,
the sculptor was by no means so well acquainted
with the figure of the lion as with that of the elephant and monkey, both being well represented in
this group. This scene, I understand, is taken from
the Mahábhárata, and exhibits the principal persons
whose actions are celebrated in that work.

Opposite, and surrounded by a wall of stone, are
pagodas of brick, said to be of great antiquity.
Adjoining is an excavation in the rock, the massy
roof seemingly supported by columns, not unlike
those in the celebrated cavern in the Island of Elephanta, but have been left unfinished. This was
probably intended as a place of worship. A few
paces onward is another, and a more spacious, excavation, now used, and I suppose originally intended,
as a shelter for travellers. A scene of sculpture
fronts the entrance, said to represent Krishna attending the herds of Ananda.† One of the group represents a man diverting an infant, by playing on a flute,
and holding the instrument as we do.‡ A gigantic
figure of the god, with the *gopis*, and several good
representations of nature, are observed. The columns

---

†* A Brahman on the spot states that this figure represents Droná-
cháryya, the preceptor of the Kauravas and Pándavas.]

[† Nanda.*]   [‡ Krishna.]

supporting the roof are of different orders : the base
of one is the figure of a Sphynx.   On the pavement
is an inscription, (see Inscript.) Near is the almost
deserted village, which still retains the ancient name
Mahábalipuram.   The few remaining Brahmans visit
the traveller, and conduct him over the rock.

In the way up the rock a prodigious circular stone
is passed under, so placed, by nature on a smooth
and sloping surface, that you are in dread of its
crushing you before you clear it.   The diameter of
this stone is twenty-seven feet.   The top of the rock
is strewed with fragments of bricks, the remains, as
you are informed, of a palace standing on this site.
A rectangular polished slab, about ten feet in length,
with the figure of a *simha* couchant, at the south
end, is shewn you as the couch of the Dharmarája.
A short way further, the bath used by the females
of the palace is pointed out.   A tale I suspect
fabricated by the Brahmans to amuse the traveller.
That some of their own caste had chosen this spot,
retired among rocks, and difficult of access, to reside
in, and that the bath, as it is called, which is only a
rough stone hollowed, was their reservoir for water,
would have an air of probability.   The couch seems
to have been cut from a stone accidentally placed in
its present situation, and never to have made a part
of the internal furniture of a building.   The *simha*,
if intended as a lion, is equally imperfect with the
figures of the same animal before mentioned.

Descending over immense beds of stone, you
arrive at a spacious excavation ; a temple dedicated
to Siva, who is represented, in the middle compartment, of a large stature and with four arms ; the
left foot rests on a bull couchant ; a small figure of

Brahmá on the right hand; another of Vishnu on the left; where also the figure of his goddess Párvatí is observed. At one end of the temple is a gigantic figure of Vishnu, sleeping on an enormous cobra-da-capella with several heads, and so disposed as to form a canopy over the head of the god.* At the opposite end is the goddess Siva with eight arms, mounted on a *simha*. Opposed to her is a gigantic figure with a buffalo's head and human body. Between these is a human figure, suspended with the head downwards. The goddess is represented with several warlike weapons, and some armed dwarf attendants; while the monster is armed with a club. In the character of Durgá, or protector of the virtuous, the goddess is rescuing from the Yamarája† (the figure with the buffalo's head) the suspended figure fallen improperly into his hands. The figure and action of the goddess are executed in a masterly and spirited style. Over this temple, at a considerable elevation, is a smaller, wrought from a single mass of stone. Here is seen a slab, similar to the Dharmarája's couch. Adjoining is a temple, in the rough, and a large mass of rock, the upper part roughly fashioned for a pagoda. If a conclusion may be drawn from these unfinished works, an uncommon and astonishing perseverance was exerted in finishing the structures here; and the more so, from the stone being a species of granite, and extremely hard.‡

The village contains but few houses, mostly inhabited by Brahmans, the number of whom has, how-

---

[* Sesha, "the king of the serpent race as a large thousand-headed snake, at once the couch and canopy of Vishnu, and the upholder of the world, which rests on one of his heads."—Wilson.]

[† Should be Mahishásura.]   [‡ Cp. Gubbins, *infra*.]

5

ever decreased of late, owing to a want of the means
of subsisting. The remains of several stone edifices
are seen here ; and a large tank, lined with steps of
stone. A canopy for the pagoda attracts the attention, as by no means wanting in magnificence or elegance.* It is supported by four columns, with base
and capital, about twenty-seven feet in height ; the
shaft tapering regularly upwards is composed of a
single stone, though not round, but sixteen-sided ;
measuring at bottom about five and a half feet.

East of the village, and washed by the sea, which,
perhaps, would have entirely demolished it before
now but for a defence of large stones in front, is a
pagoda of stone, containing the *lingam*, and dedicated to Siva. Besides the usual figures within, one
of a gigantic stature is observed stretched out on the
ground, and represented as arranged in that position.†
This the Brahmans tell you was designed for a Rájá,
who was thus secured by Vishnu ; probably alluding
to a prince of the Vishnu caste having conquered the
country, and taken its prince. The surf here breaks
far out over, as the Brahmans inform you, the ruins
in the city, which was incredibly large and magnificent. Many of the masses of stone near the shore
appear to have been wrought. A Brahman, about
fifty years of age, a native of the place, whom I
have had an opportunity of conversing with since
my arrival at Madras, informed me his grandfather
had frequently mentioned having seen the gilt tops of

[* The Dolotsava Mandapam, 'porch of the swinging festival,'
where the image of the god used annually to be brought out and
swung before the people.]

[† It is an image of Vishnu, in a recumbent position. The folds
of his garment were apparently mistaken for fetters.—Cp. other
notices, *infra*.]

five pagodas in the surf, no longer visible. In the account of this place by Mr. William Chambers, in the first volume of the Asiatic Researches, we find mention of a brick pagoda, dedicated to Siva, and washed by the sea ;* this is no longer visible ; but as the Brahmans have no recollection of such a structure, and as Mr. Chambers wrote from memory, I am inclined to think the pagoda of stone mentioned above to be the one he means. However, it appears from good authorities that the sea on this part of the coast is encroaching by very slow, but no less certain steps, and will perhaps in a lapse of ages entirely hide these magnificent ruins.

About a mile to the southward are other structures of stone, of the same order as those north, but having been left unfinished, at first sight appear different : the southernmost of these is about forty feet in height, twenty-nine in broadth, and nearly the same in length, hewn from a single mass : the outside is covered with sculpture, (for an account of which see Inscriptions :) the next is also cut from one mass of stone, being in length about forty-nine feet, in breadth and height twenty-five, and is rent through the middle from the top to the bottom ; a large fragment from one corner is observed on the ground. No account is preserved of the powerful cause which produced this destructive effect. Beside these, are three smaller structures of stone. Here is also the *sinha*, or lion, very large, but, except in size, I can observe no difference from the figures of the same animal northerly. Near the *sinha* is an elephant of stone about nine feet in height, and

[* See page 19, *supra.*]

large in proportion. Here, indeed, we observe the true figure and character of the animal.

The Brahman before mentioned informed me that their Puránas contained no account of any of the structures here described, except the stone pagodas near the sea and the pagodas of brick at the village, built by Dharmaríja and his brothers. He, however, gave me the following traditional account : That a northern prince (perhaps one of the conquerors) about one thousand years ago was desirous of having a great work executed, but the Hindu sculptors and masons refused to execute it on the terms he offered. Attempting force I suppose, they, in number about four thousand, fled with their effects from his country hither, where they resided four or five years, and in this interval executed these magnificent works. The prince at length discovering them, prevailed on them to return, which they did, leaving the works unfinished as they appear at present.*

To those who know the nature of these people, this account will not appear improbable. At present we sometimes hear of all the individuals of a particular branch of trade deserting their houses, because the hand of power has treated them somewhat roughly ; and we observe like circumstances continually in miniature. Why the Brahmans resident on the spot keep this account secret, I cannot determine ; but am led to suppose they have an idea, the more they can envelope the place in mystery the more people will be tempted to visit and investigate, by which means they profit considerably.

[*Cp. Gubbins, infrn.]

The difference of style in the architecture of these structures, and those on the coast hereabouts, (with exceptions to the pagodas of brick at the village, and that of stone near the sea, both mentioned in the Puráṇas, and which are not different,) tends to prove that the artists were not of this country ; and the resemblance of some of the figures and pillars to those in the Elephanta cave, seems to indicate they were from the northward.[*] The fragments of bricks, at the top of the rock, may be the remains of habitations raised in this place of security by the fugitives in question. Some of the inscriptions, however, (all of which were taken by myself with much care,) may throw further light on this subject.

INSCRIPTIONS AT MAHABALIPURAM.[†]
On the lower Division of the Southern Structure and the Eastern Face.

This inscription is above a figure apparently female, but with only one breast, (as at the cave in *Elephanta* Island.)[‡] Four arms are observed ; in one of the hands a battle-axe, a snake coiled up on the right side.

[* " There is nothing here of which the prototype cannot be traced in the caves of the north. In plan and design they resemble the Hindu series at Ellora, though many of their details are only to be found at Ajunta and Salsette."—Fergusson, Jour. R. A. S. Vol. VIII, p. 88.]

[† Cp. Babington, *infra.*]

[‡ Arddhanárísa, a form of Síva, half male, half female.]

Above a male figure with four arms.

Northern Face.

Above a male figure with four arms; a battle axe in one of the hands.

Southern Front.

Above a male figure, with four arms.

Above a male figure.

On the Middle Division, Eastern Face.

ꢂꢂꢂꢂ

Above a male.

ꢂꢂꢂꢂ

Above a male, bearing a weapon of war on the left shoulder.

Northern Face.

ꢂꢂꢂꢂ

Above a male with four arms, leaning on a bull ; the hair plaited, and rolled about the head : a string across the left shoulder, as the Brahmans' string of the present day.

Above two figures, male and female. The former has four arms, and the string as above; is leaning on the latter, who seems to stoop from the weight. The head of the male is covered with a high cap, while the hair of the female is in the same form as that of the female figures at Elephanta.

Above two figures, male and female. The former has four arms, and the string.

Above a male figure, with four arms, and the Brahmanical string.

Southern Face.

Above a male figure, with four arms.

Above a male figure, with four arms, leaning on a female, seeming to stoop under the weight.

Above a male, with four arms. A sceptre appears in one hand. This inscription being very difficult to come at, is perhaps not quite correct.

Above a male figure, with four arms.

West Front.

ప ఱు ఒ ౧ ౼ ౿:
ఒ ౧ ఐ||

Over a male.   The string over the left shoulder,
and a warlike weapon on the right.

Another figure on this face, but no inscription
above it.

On the Upper Division.

Each front of this division is ornamented with
figures, different in some respects from those below :
all, however, of the same family.

On the Eastern front is a male figure, (two arms
only.)   He has two strings or belts ; one crossing
the other over the shoulder.

Over him is the following inscription, the only one
on this division.

ఱ ఆ ఘ ఋ ఱు ఒ ఙ ౿ ఒ ఇ ఘ ఙ ||

ఇ ౩ 8 ఒ:

The characters of this inscription bear a strong resemblance to those of the inscription in the stone pagoda, near the village mentioned in the first part of the account of the place.

This inscription* is on the pavement of the choultry near the village, very roughly cut, and apparently by different artists from those who cut the former.

[* A scrawl in the modern Telugu character.—Cp. Babington, *infra.*]

III.—*An account of the Sculptures and Inscriptions at Mahámalaipúr; illustrated by Plates.* By BEN-JAMIN GUY BABINGTON, M.D., F.R.S., Sec. R.A.S.

[From Transactions of the Royal Asiatic Society, Vol. II. 1830.]
Read July 19th, 1828.

THE remains of ancient sculpture, called by Euro-peans the Seven Pagodas, on the Coromandel Coast, thirty-five miles south of Madras, have long attracted the attention of those who feel an interest in Hindu Archæology ; and, so long ago as the year 1788, formed the subject of a paper in the first volume of the Asiatic Researches. The author, Mr. William Chambers, wrote from memory, after an interval of twelve years from the period at which he had visited the scene which he described. His account, unaccompanied as it was by drawings or fac-similes of the inscriptions, could therefore scarcely be expected to be sufficiently minute to answer any further purpose than that avowed by himself, of exciting public attention, and "giving rise to more accurate observations, and more complete discoveries on the same subject." In the fifth volume of the Asiatic Researches, published in 1798, there is a more descriptive account of these temples and excavations, written by Mr. Goldingham, a gentleman of well-known talent, on whose observations, as they were recorded on the spot, we may with confidence rely.

Mrs. Graham is indeed a later writer on the subject: but her remarks are desultory, and her information imperfect, as might be expected from the opportunities presenting themselves to a casual and hasty visitor. In Bishop Heber's narrative, three pages are devoted to a notice of Mahábalipúr. (Pages 216—218, vol. iii.) But the author merely follows the legends of the place, and evidently aims at nothing more than a record in his journal of his impressions on a cursory visit. The testimony, however, which this lamented prelate bears to the degree of skill displayed in these sculptures must, from his acknowledged taste, be looked upon as peculiarly valuable ; and it is gratifying to one who has taken much interest in them to find, that he considered "some of the porticos, temples and bas-reliefs as very beautifully executed," and pronounced "the general merit of the work as superior to that of Elephanta."*

With these notices already before the public, it would be superfluous to occupy the attention of the Society with another detailed description of those monuments, and I shall therefore content myself with a reference to Mr. Goldingham's paper, as far as may be necessary to accomplish the objects which I have at present in view. These are, first, to convey a just notion of the merits of the principal sculptures, by means of drawings made on the spot by Mr. Andrew Hudleston and myself, several years since ; and, secondly, to throw some light upon the inscriptions found among these temples.

To the legendary accounts of the Brahmans at

[* Op. Ferguson's "Rock-cut Temples of India," London, 1864. Introduction p. xiii.]

Mahâmalaipûr, which are given at such length by Mr. Chambers and Mrs. Graham, I attach little value, because I find that they have not even preserved the memory of the language and character of the inscriptions which here abound ; and because this place, in being accounted the work of the five sons of Pându, only shares a tradition common to all the antiquities of unexplained origin in the south of India. So far from believing in the tales of these Brahmans, who are obviously interested in connecting wonderful stories with the remains which they gain a livelihood by shewing to strangers, I even doubt whether Mahâmalaipûr was ever, as asserted by them, the site of a great city, now partly covered by the sea ; and still more, whether the gilded summit of one of the five pagodas, said to be so covered, was visible two generations ago. Several circumstances lead me to be sceptical on these points : first, the absence of all remains of buildings,* walls, mounds of rubbish, or broken pottery, such as I have invariably found surrounding the site of other ancient cities ; secondly, the fruitless attempts made by the late Mr. Ellis and Colonel Mackenzie to ascertain the existence of sunken buildings by careful soundings made off the shore ; thirdly, the silence of tradition on other parts of the Coromandel Coast regarding so vast an encroachment of the sea,† and consequent loss of land, as must necessarily have taken place to effect the submersion of lofty pagodas still remaining erect, and that too since the formation of the present system of

* The small ruined brick edifice on the top of the rock can hardly be considered an exception.

[† Op. Newbold's Summary of the Geology of Southern India. Journ. R. A. S. Vol. viii. p. 250.]

Hindu mythology, to which the existing sculptures obviously relate ; fourthly, the circumstance that the authenticity of the legend must mainly depend on the name of the place as connected with the history of Mahábali ; whereas it will be shewn, when considering the inscriptions, that Mahábalipúr is not its ancient designation ; lastly, the omission of all mention of Mahábali in the inscriptions, and of any reference to him in the sculptures.*

Although I thus reject the account of the Brahmans on the spot, I have nothing certain to offer in its room. If a conjecture however may be hazarded regarding the origin of this place, I should be inclined to believe that its sequestered situation and the picturesque position of the rocks and caves induced certain Brahmans to obtain royal grants for founding an Agrahára† here, and that, in order to increase the sanctity of their temples, they from time to time employed stone-masons (several families of whom reside at Mahámalaipúr, and appear to have worked the quarries of granite time immemorial) to ornament the rocks with the excavations and sculptures which we now find.

Plate I. represents the sculptured rock, which has been described by Mr. Goldingham in his second paragraph, as occupying a surface about ninety feet in extent and thirty in height, and covered with figures in bas-relief. This subject has been represented in Mrs. Graham's Journal by an etching copied from an outline belonging to Colonel Mackenzie, the inaccuracy of which will be sufficiently apparent on

[* The Asura Bali is probably represented by one of the figures in plate VI.]

[† A village granted to Brahmans.]

comparing it with my drawing, which was executed with much care and labour by my companion.

During our visit to the Seven Pagodas, we caused the earth to be removed from the lower part of this rock to its base, and thus exposed to full view some figures (see plate II., No. 1), of which the heads alone were before visible.

Not far from the rock last mentioned is the spacious chamber called the Krishna Mandapam, described by Mr. Goldingham in his third paragraph. Of the scene sculptured on the rock facing the entrance, Mr. Hudleston and myself made a joint drawing (see plate II., No. 2); and as this rock is going fast to decay, owing to a spring of water from above, which keeps its surface constantly wet, it is not improbable that in the course of a few years it will be entirely decomposed; it is the more desirable therefore that some record of its subject should be preserved. Several interesting particulars regarding the ancient Hindus may be gathered from this pastoral scene. The dress of the females resembles that now worn by the Neyris* and Tiyyattis† of Malabar, who are uncovered above the waist. The men, it appears, wore turbans, and the women very large ear-rings, with bangles on their hands and feet. The peculiar practice of carrying the infant on the hip, which cannot fail to attract the notice of Europeans at the present day, was then in use; and even the vertical arrangement and method of tying together the three earthen vessels here represented, is recognized by all

[* Náyar (Nair) women appear to be referred to, but the word is incorrect.]

[† Females of the Tiyyar (Tier) caste.]

PLATE IV

Hindu visitors as being universally adopted by the modern Gopálas.* The execution of this work is coarse, and the design rude; and though particular parts have much merit, yet the limbs of the principal figures are clumsy and ill-proportioned, the attitudes forced, and the countenances without expression.

Greatly superior is the skill displayed by the artists employed in the excavation described by Mr. Goldingham in his fifth paragraph ;† but even here, under the same roof, there is much inequality in the execution of the different subjects. The central compartment (see plate III., No. 1), and that on the left on entrance (see plate III., No. 2) are tame performances, compared with the very spirited representation of Durgá seated on her lion, and attacking Mahishásura, which occupies the right compartment.‡ (See plate IV.) I have no hesitation in pronouncing this to be the most animated piece of Hindu sculpture which I have ever seen; and I would venture to recommend that a cast of it should, if possible, be taken for this Society. In the meantime, a tolerably just notion may be formed of its merits from the excellent and accurate delineation of Mr. Hudleston.

The smaller temple, which Mr. Goldingham mentions as placed at a considerable elevation above that just alluded to, and wrought out of a single mass of rock, is so rich in sculpture and ornament, and occupies so picturesque and sequestered a spot, that it is surprising he should have passed it over with so slight a notice. This excavation is in form a parallelogram, open on one of the longer sides, where it is supported on two columns. It contains four large

[* Cowherds.]   [† P. 32-33, supra.]   [‡ Cp. Braddock, infra.]

compartments or panels of sculpture : namely, one at each end, and one on each side of the central recess opposite the entrance ; besides two niches occupied by Dwárapálás.* The Varáha Avatára represented in plate V., is placed at the left end of the chamber. Plate VI., the subject of which seems to be some incarnation of Vishnu,† fills the compartment at the opposite end. On the right of the recess a female deity‡ appears, surmounted by an umbrella (see plate VII., No. 1) ; whilst on the left is a female figure§ seated on a lotus throne, and attended by damsels who bear water-pots, to be discharged in turn over her head by the elephants seen in the background (see plate VIII.) The position of the Dwárapálás will be seen in plate VIII., No. 2. Of the columns which support the front of the excavation, as well as of the side pilasters, I have thought it worth while, on account of their beauty and singular order, to furnish drawings (plate VII., Nos. 2 and 3) ; while the general appearance of the cave-temple will be best understood by reference to plate IX.¶

There are several other pieces of sculpture contained in small temples among the rocks, not noticed either by Mr. Chambers or Mr. Goldingham ; and of these, plate X., Nos. 1, 2, 3, are examples.

The Dolotsava Mandapam,‖ seen in the centre of the village, is remarkable for the lightness and elegance of its construction. It is of granite, and is

[* Door-keepers.]

[† The dwarf incarnation, Vámana Avatára.]

[‡ Bhadrakálí, a form of Párvatí.]

[§ Párvatí, as Deví.—Cp. plates 30 and 33 in Moor's Hindu Pantheon.—But the Vaishnavas call the figure Gaja Lakshmí.]

[¶ The writer has omitted to mention that the ceiling is painted.]

[‖ See note * p. 34, supra.]

N° 3

N° 2

supported on four columns, which rise from a platform elevated by three steps. (See plate XI., No. 1.)
The shafts of the columns with the base are hewn
from a single stone, and, including the capital, are
twenty-seven feet in height.

The stone pagoda on the sea-shore, which serves
as a land-mark for shipping, and is erroneously stated
by Mr. Chambers to be built of brick,* is delineated
in plate XI., No. 2; and the gigantic figure lying
stretched on the floor in one of its recesses, in plate
XII. At the time when this drawing was made, the
figure was enclosed in a small chamber; but on a
subsequent visit I found that the walls had given
way, thus leaving it exposed to the open air. As a
record therefore of the state of this pagoda and figure,
I regard these drawings as not without value in the
collection now presented to the Society; for such is
the dilapidated condition of this structure, that the
period cannot be far distant when it will no longer
exist. The effects of the salt-water spray add much
to those of time in hastening its decay.†

Whether this pagoda was dedicated to Vishnu or to
Siva, I regard as doubtful: tradition favours the
former supposition. At all events, the pillar which
stands before it amid the spray of the sea is certainly
not a *lingam*, as some suppose, but merely the *stambha*
or post, which is found, I believe, fronting all Hindu
temples of consideration.‡ That this pillar is now
near the high-water mark is by no means a convincing

[* P. 10, *supra*.]

[† The writer greatly under-estimated the strength of this building.
There is no probability of its disappearance.]

[‡ See note † p. 11, *supra*.—The Brahmans say it is a lamp-post,
Dîpastambha.]

proof that the sea has encroached here, for I see no
reason why such a spot should not have been originally selected for its erection.   If it be a fact, as mentioned by Bishop Heber, that the sea is receding
from most other parts of the Coromandel Coast, it is
difficult to conceive why it should advance in this
place; such a local encroachment could only be effect-
ed by a change in the position of the land, and as the
primitive rocks here appear on the surface, this cannot be admitted as a probable occurrence, unless under
some violent convulsion of nature.   Had the coast
been of an alluvial formation at this spot, high tides
might have advanced upon it with greater facility.

The five monolithic temples, situated about a mile
to the southward of the village, have justly attracted
the attention of all who have visited Mahámalaipúr.

They are called on the spot रथ: *Rathas*, or
sacred vehicles: but it is obvious, that they were
never meant as imitations of those enormous wooden
structures, which are so conspicuous in certain Hindu
processions.   They were probably intended to serve
the purpose of temples; but bear evident marks of
having been left in an unfinished state; for though
highly ornamented on the outside, they have not
been excavated within, being merely solid masses of
sculptured granite remaining in their original posi-
tions.*   For the general view of these Rathas, I
would refer to Mrs. Graham's plate, which, together
with Mr. Goldingham's description, will serve to

[* " The Brahmans found a group of granite boulders lying on the
sea-shore, and have carved them into the form of temples, having all
the appearance of structural edifices with the advantage of monolithic
durability."—Fergusson, Rock-cut Temples of India.   London, 1861.
Intro., p. xviii.]

convey a notion of these curious remains of antiquity. Several of the basso relievo figures with which they are ornamented are represented in plate XV., and will be further noticed when I come to speak of the inscriptions which are placed over them.

OF THE INSCRIPTIONS.

Exclusively of a scrap of modern Telugu, very incorrectly designed and rudely sculptured on the floor of the Krishna Mandapam, and in consequence erroneously copied as ancient by Mr. Goldingham (see Asiatic Researches, vol. v, page 80),* I noticed three kinds of inscriptions at Mahámalaipúr, two of which have hitherto remained undeciphered. It is also highly probable that three other kinds, which I shall have occasion to mention, are to be met with in this neighbourhood.

First. An ancient Tamil inscription is seen on a face of rock by the side of the inner entrance to the Varihasvámi pagoda, which is still in use. This would be legible throughout, were it not that a wall, which projects from the rock, cuts off a considerable portion of each line; on this account I did not consider it worth while to take a copy.† From what remains visible, it is certain that the inscription records a grant to the Varihasvámi pagoda of a quantity of land, the boundaries of which are very minutely defined, both as respects the property of others, and the cardinal points. The act of donation is attested by numerous witnesses, and the name of the donor is also mentioned. A perfect copy of this inscription might easily be made, if the wall which I have noticed were removed; and as the

[* P. 43, supra.]   [† Cp. Sir Walter Elliot's copy, infra.]

date might possibly thus be ascertained, I would suggest that the Madras Literary Society be recommended to take measures for effecting this object. In order to facilitate the task of deciphering this and similar records, I have drawn out an alphabet (see plate XIII.) from a careful collation of several ancient Tamil inscriptions.*

As it seems probable, from a passage in another ancient inscription hereafter noticed, that Mahámalaipúr was a Siva-sthala, I am inclined to consider the Varáhasvámi pagoda as quite distinct, and probably of a different era from the antiquities,

---

* The changes which time has produced are in some letters very great; and where characters are so simple as those of the Tamil language, even slight alterations in form give rise to perplexity. I may adduce, as an example, the letter ka, the most ancient form of which was a Latin cross †. In the course of time a top was added to the left side, and the cross bar was curved thus. The next alteration was the addition of a perpendicular line falling from the left extremity of the top. The top was then extended to the right, and by prolonging the extremities of the curved line, the modern letter has at length been formed, or in a still more complicated manner as in the Grantha thus. In its modern form it might easily be confounded with the which, though it now has a tail, was anciently written without one, thus. Other examples might be given, but they suggest themselves on an inspection of the alphabet itself.

I cannot touch on the subject of ancient Tamil characters without remarking, that their extreme simplicity seems one among many circumstances, which indicate that the language is of very high antiquity. The Sanscrit of the south of India is written in characters (the Grantha) derived from the Tamil, but they are much more complicated, and therefore probably posterior in point of antiquity. The peculiar structure of the Tamil language, wholly dissimilar from the Sanscrit, its deficiency in aspirated consonants, its

properly so called, which belong to this place. The difference of language in the inscription, and the circumstance that the pagoda is a built structure projecting from the face of the rock, and not an excavation, increase the probability of this conclusion. It is not unlikely, however, that there may exist in the sanctuary a subordinate sculpture representing the Varáha Avatára like that of Krishna and the Gopálas in the Krishna Mandapam, and of equally ancient date, and that a roof and walls may have been thrown out from this rock, and a temple thus formed.* The Brahmans on the spot did not permit me to enter the sanctuary to ascertain this point.

Throughout this Tamil inscription the place is called Mahámalaipûr, which signifies the city of the great mountain, evidently with reference to the rocky eminence in the vicinity. This indeed cannot be called a great mountain on account of its size : but the word mahá may refer to greatness of sanctity, or renown, with equal propriety.

To designate the village Mahâbalipuram, the native name at the present day, is therefore an error, which has led to the assumption that this was the capital of that renowned giant Mahá Bali, whose kingdom, if it ever actually existed, was on the

possession of letters and sounds not found in Sanscrit, its division into dialects, one of which contains but few words of Sanscrit derivation; and lastly, its locality at the southern extremity of India, would seem likewise to indicate an independent origin, and one of at least equal antiquity with the Sanscrit itself; but this is a subject foreign to that now under consideration, and deserving a more lengthened discussion than the limits of a note will allow.

[* This supposition is correct; a temple has been built round an ancient sculpture on the face of the rock, representing the Varáha Avatára.]

western coast of India, where he is still honoured
by an annual festival.

A second kind of character found at Mahámalaipûr is in a small monolithic pagoda,* now dedicated
to Ganesa,† and situated on the north side of the
hill. It is contained in an inscription (see plate
XIV.) of considerable length, but is so faintly out,
and on such rough granite, that the fac-simile which
I have furnished, however imperfect, cost me several
days' labour to trace.‡ One of the Jain Brahmans,
in the employ of Colonel Mackenzie, had such a
knowledge of ancient characters somewhat similar to

---

* Mrs. Graham gives an engraving of this small pagoda, which she
says is called the Tir of Arjuna, and she explains the word Tir (properly Têr), to mean a place of religious retirement. The explanation
is erroneous, as the word Têr signifies, in Tamil, a car or sacred
vehicle, corresponding with the Sanscrit Ratha.

† When Mr. Goldingham wrote his account, this pagoda contained a
lingam (see his first paragraph [p. 30 supra]), so that it has passed from
the Saivas into the possession of the Vaishnavas since that period.§
Brahman families of both sects reside on the spot.

‡ In this character there are two forms of affix for long á, used in-
differently as convenience may suggest. Thus, in the first stanza,
we find the syllable (கா) ká in the word kírosum (காரசு) made

thus ⌀; while in the eighth stanza the same syllable in the word

kíma (கீம) is made thus ⌀. The letters p (ப) and s (ஸ) seem
similar in form; but perhaps some slight difference may have
escaped my observation. In modern Grantha, an inflection in the
middle of the character makes the difference between s and p, thus

⌀ ⌀. So also in the ancient character, the inflection may
have been greater in the s than in the p, thus ⌀ and ⌀; but I
have not upon this supposition felt authorised to depart from the
copy which I made on the spot.

[§ An old Vaishnava Brahman tells a different tale : he states that
the Lingam was taken away, (with an image of Hanumán,) by Lord

this, that on visiting the spot with me, he succeeded
in deciphering a great part of this inscription, the
language of which is Sanscrit. The following is a
translation of the ten slokas which were intelligible,
while about two verses at the end were left undeciphered :—

1. May the cause of creation, existence, and
destruction, which is itself without cause,
the destroyer of Manmatha (desire), be propitious to the desires of the world.

2. May he who is united with Umá, of many
kinds of illusion, without quality, the destroyer of evil dispositions, of incorruptible
wealth, the Lord of Kubera, be counted
excellent.

3. May that deity (Siva) protect us all, who is
the seat of prosperity, and by whose means
Kailása disappeared and descended to Pátála, yielding by its weight, which he caused
on account of its being with (supported
by) the ten-faced (Rávana).

4. May he who bears Siva in his mind engrossed
by devotion, and the earth on his shoulders,
with as much ease as if it were an ornament, long prevail.

5. By that king of satisfied wishes, with crowds
of conquered enemies, who is known by
the name of Jayarasa Stambha, this building was made.

Hobart (?) and sent to England, Lady H. giving 20 pagodas to the
villagers as a consideration! Lord Hobart was Governor of Madras
from Sept. 1794 to February 1798. Mr. Goldingham's account was
published in the latter year.]

6. May that fear-inspiring, good-giving, desire destroying Siva, to whom the earth, space, the moon, fire, the sun, &c., are a body, be victorious.

7. The good-faced among nations (the beauty of the world) sprung from a mother bringing forth heroes, remains without doubt in a place of lotuses, full of sacred waters, and is adorned with all sorts of precious stones.

8 and 9. Siva, the beautiful, sits in the broad lake Sirns which teems with (*lit.* is a mine of) lotuses resembling variegated gems, and is full of water for sprinkling the fortunate and much-loved Kámarája, who puts down the pride of his enemies, who is the source (receptacle) of glory, and is earnest in worshipping Siva.

10. He (Kámarája) who dwells on the heads of kings, caused this temple of Siva, which resembles the temple on Kailâsa, to be erected for the happiness of the earth.*

I have lately received from Madras two ancient inscriptions purporting to be from the neighbourhood of Mahámalaipúr, and two also have been kindly furnished me by Colonel De Havilland. Of these four, two appear to be identical, which reduces the number to three. Their precise localities I have not the means of knowing, with the exception of one, entitled by Colonel De Havilland, "Sanscrit inscription engraven on the north side of the verandah of a pagoda excavated out of the solid granite, two miles north of Mahábalipuram." All

[* See Appendix.]

No. 1. No. 2.

writing, whereof two (plate XIV. and plate XV.,
No. 1.) are, in my opinion, ancient forms of the
Grantha, or that character in which Sanscrit is
invariably written in the south of India, and in
which alone I was able to procure books for study
at Madras. The other two will probably be considered as species of ancient Devanágarí. (See
plate XV., Nos. 2 and 3.)

This variety of character, with identity of matter,
leads me to think it probable that the inscription
itself was a kind of general proclamation sculptured
in different places, and modified, as in my inscription, to render it applicable to local circumstances.
Whether it will throw light upon the history of
Mahámalaipúr, containing as it does the name of the
sovereign who founded the temples to which it has
been affixed, is a question which I must leave to be
examined by those who have studied the ancient
dynasties of the south of India.

A third kind of character at Mahámalaipúr, or a
sixth kind, if we reckon those received from Madras
and from Colonel De Havilland, is to be found in
the inscriptions over the basso-relievo figures which
ornament the monolithic pagodas already mentioned as situated to the southward of the village, and
of which several are represented in plate XVI.
Neither the Jain Brahman employed by Colonel
Mackenzie, nor any other native of India who had
seen these inscriptions, was able to decipher them,
or to offer any conjecture as to the language in which
they were written ; and even the learned Mr. Ellis,
after repeated visits to this place, was equally unsuc-
cessful in his endeavours. Mrs. Graham, indeed,
states that Colonel Mackenzie had found a Brah-

ORIGINAL	THE SAME IN DEVANAGARI	ENGLISH TRANSLATION
	कामलक्षित प्रमेयसाय: सकलकल्याण:	*(faded)*
	श्रीनरसिंह अप्रनिहतशासन: भुवनभाजन: श्रीमेघ:	*(faded)*
	स्थिरभक्ति:मदनाभिराम:	The form in fact ...
	विधि	The Apsa ...
	विश्रान्त:	*(faded)*
	विधि:	The Apsa ...
	श्रीनिधि:	*(faded)*
	निरन्तर:	*(faded)*
	तयत मतोद्ध: सर्वतोभद्र:	*(faded)*
	लक्षित	The Lovely
	सत्यपराक्रम:	*(faded)*
	श्री नरसिंह:	*(faded)*
	? ? भार:श्रीभर:	*(faded)*
	भुवनभाजन:	*(faded)*
	परावर:	*(faded)*
	भयात्र	*(faded)*
	वाम:	*(faded)*
	अतिमान.	*(faded)*
	श्री प्रसन्नकामपप्रवर्धन निहारभोजन:	*(faded)*

man who read the character so as to pronounce
the sounds, but did not understand the language
they express. Whether any person did actually
thus impose on that gentleman, or whether Mrs.
Graham has confounded these inscriptions with the
last, I cannot determine, but it is quite certain that,
if any person had been able to decipher the character, he would, without any difficulty, have discovered the language to be Sanscrit. It was by assuming
this to be the case, that I succeeded in deciphering
these inscriptions.*

I beg now to lay them before the Society, together
with a transcript in Devanágari, and a translation.
(See plate XVII.)

It is to be regretted that these inscriptions,
instead of containing general information respecting
the origin or date of the sculptures, are merely
epithets applicable to the figures, over which they
are placed. At the same time we should remember
that their brevity and position, having led to the
assumption that they were names of deities, thus
rendered the task of deciphering them somewhat
less difficult. Unimportant as they are in themselves, a knowledge of them may lead to the acquire-
ment of useful or curious information to be drawn
from other sources, and I trust that the Society will
indulgently consider the utility of this research, not

---

* There is one instance, as will be seen on a reference to plate
XVII., in which the characters are of the same kind as those in the
inscription of the Ganesa pagoda, a proof that both were in use at
the same period. It is probable therefore that one was the round,
and the other the square form, analogous to the two varieties of Páli
and Ariyam.†

[† Áryam is the round, modern Malayálam character.]

so much with reference to the information actually obtained, as to its general subserviency to the purposes of history.

There are certainly no historical monuments in India more decidedly authentic than the copper and stone inscriptions found in such abundance in many parts of the country, and it is advancing one step to have determined that these, however different the characters in which they are sculptured from those in use at the present day, are all in the Sanscrit language, in which so little change has taken place in the lapse of ages, that, when once we have succeeded in the task of deciphering, all difficulty is at an end, and the record of a remote antiquity is placed intelligibly before us.

These inscriptions, and those at Kenorah in the island of Salsette, one of which, with the modern Sanscrit, and a translation, I laid before the Society on a late occasion, are perhaps the most ancient, at least the most dissimilar from characters at present in use, which I have met with; and I think myself therefore warranted in concluding that there are no inscriptions of Hindu origin to be found in India which may not, by attentive study, be deciphered, and by the assistance of learned natives, afterwards interpreted.

With a view to rendering the characters of those deciphered inscriptions generally applicable, I have added two tables (plate XVIII.): the one containing all the characters found in the inscription in the Ganesa pagoda; the other, those met with over the basso-relievo figures on the Rathas.

IV.—*A Guide to the Sculptures, Excavations, and other remarkable objects at Mâmallaipûr, generally known to Europeans as " the Seven Pagodas," by the late* Lieutenant JOHN BRADDOCK, *of the Madras Establishment. To which are added some Archæological Notes, by the* Reverend WILLIAM TAYLOR, *and a Supplementary account of the remains at Sâluwan Kuppam, by* WALTER ELLIOT, ESQ.,* *of the Madras Civil Service.—Communicated by the* Reverend GEORGE WILLIAM MAHON, A.M., *Garrison Chaplain, Fort St. George.*

[From the Madras Journal of Literature and Science, Vol. XIII. 1844.]

IN the month of June 1840, I accompanied a small party of friends on a visit to the remarkable remains at Mâmallaipûr. As our excursion, from its necessary brevity, was likely to prove one of amusement rather than of antiquarian research, and the large quartos of the Asiatic Society are somewhat cumbrous, we borrowed from our friend Mr. Braddock a little pamphlet published by him some years before, which at once served as a guide to what was worth seeing, and explained to such of us as were but slightly acquainted with Hindu Mythology, the subjects and allusions of the various sculptures.

(* Now Sir Walter Elliot, K.C.S.I.)

On our return I expressed to Mr. Braddock a desire that he should undertake a fuller account of the place, and suggested that it should combine the useful and entertaining properties of a Guide Book with the more important lucubrations of the scholar. As topics for the latter I named a more satisfactory account of the Inscriptions, and some information, if obtainable, as to the history of Mâmallaipûr and the origin of the excavations and sculptures. With his habitual modesty he seemed to doubt his competency to deal with the latter subjects, but promised to revise and dilate his former paper. I then suggested that he should solicit the assistance of his old and valued friend, the Rev. W. Taylor, in ascertaining something of the history of the place. This gentleman, so well known as an accomplished oriental linguist, having been recently engaged in the examination of the Mackenzie MSS., might, I thought, have discovered amongst them some information tending to throw light on so interesting a subject. Mr. Taylor, it will be seen, has responded with equal good feeling and ability to the request so made to him; and his notes, appended to Mr. Braddock's paper, must be considered as a most valuable addition to it.

As Mr. Braddock proceeded with his work he forwarded the rough sheets for my perusal, with a request that I should suggest any alterations which my more recent visit to the place might enable me to do. The paper was scarcely completed, no time had been granted for revision, I had not even seen its concluding sheets, when the amiable and talented writer was hurried away by one of those rapid attacks which disease sometimes makes on European

constitutions in this climate : and I was called on, all
but unexpectedly, to perform the last sad offices for
one whom I had so recently seen usefully and actively
employed.   A marble tablet erected in the Church at
Vepery by public subscription, serves to perpetuate
the memory of this worthy man ; and at the same
time to evince the general sense of his Christian
virtues, of his scientific acquirements, and of his
constant readiness to employ them for the public
good.

Some months after Mr. Braddock's death, I was
requested by his family to revise and prepare for
publication his papers on Mámallaipúr ; a task which
I have undertaken not without great . diffidence.
Had my lamented friend survived, he would, I
doubt not, have made many emendations in them,
which cannot on many accounts be done by another
hand.

It will be seen that neither Mr. Braddock nor Mr.
Taylor has treated of the *Inscriptions* at Mámallaipúr, otherwise than incidentally.   Those who wish
for some account of them, may be referred to the
valuable article by Dr. Babington in the 2nd Volume
of the Transactions of the Royal Asiatic Society.
He says that he noticed three kinds of inscriptions at
" Máhámalaipúr," two of which have remained undeciphered, and that it is highly probable that there are
other kinds to be met with in the neighbourhood.
The first he alludes to is an ancient Tamil inscription
on a face of rock, by the side of the inner entrance
to the Varáhasvámi pagoda (No. 29 in the Map.)*
He gives no copy of it, but states that "it records

* Plate XX.

a grant to the Varáhasvámí pagoda of a quantity of
land."* The language of this inscription renders it
doubtful whether it is of earlier or later date than
some of the others, which are in Sanscrit. Dr. Babington says that throughout this Tamil inscription the
place is called "Mahámalaipúr," which he translates
"city of the great mountain," adding that the word
Mahá may imply "greatness of sanctity or renown."
This if correct might be adduced as proof of the more
recent age of the inscription ; for the hill is by no
means remarkable, otherwise than for the "sanctity
or renown" which the sculptures may have procured
for it. It will be seen, however, that the Rev. W.
Taylor speaks of two inscriptions, in which the place
is called Mánmallaipúr, with two l's, and if this orthography is correct, which he seems to think it is, the
translation of Dr. Babington is of course overthrown,
since *mallai* does not mean "hill." The present
name of the place in common use appears to be
Mávalavaram, and not Mahábalipuram, as some
have stated. The latter mistake can scarcely be
regretted, however, by those who have perused the
pleasing fiction which the poetical talent of Southey
has embodied in his "Curse of Kehama."

The second kind of inscription mentioned by Dr.
Babington appears in the temple dedicated to Ganesa,
situated near the north end of the hill, and described in its order by Mr. Braddock. By the assistance
of his Jain Brahman in deciphering the characters,
Dr. Babington was enabled to translate this inscription ; and as it appears that much of the substance
of it is repeated in some other inscriptions which he

[* Vide Sir Walter Elliot's translation of this inscription, *infra*.]

subsequently examined, it may prove interesting to copy his translation in this place. It consists of ten slokas deciphered, and there remains undeciphered about as much as would make two slokas more.

Translation by Dr. Babington and his Jain Brahmins of the ten first slokas in the Sanscrit Inscription found in the Ganesa Pagoda at Mámallaipúr.

" 1. May the cause of creation, existence, and destruction, which is " itself without cause, the destroyer of Manmatha (desire) be propi- " tious to the desires of the world.

" 2. May he who is united with Umá, of many kinds of illusion, " without quality, the destroyer of evil dispositions, of incorruptible " wealth, the Lord of Kubera, be counted excellent.

" 3. May that deity (Siva) protect us all, who is the seat of pros- " perity, and by whose means Kailása disappeared and descended to " Pátála, yielding by its weight, which he raised on account of its " being with (supported by) the ten-faced (Rávana).

" 4. May he who bears Siva in his mind engrossed by devotion, " and the earth on his shoulders, with as much ease as if it were an " ornament, long prevail.

" 5. By that king of satisfied wishes, with crowds of conquered " enemies, who is known by the name of Jayaraya Stambha, this " building was made.

" 6. May that fear-inspiring, good-giving, desire-destroying Siva, " to whom the earth, space, moon, fire, the sun, &c., are a body, be " victorious.

" 7. The good-deed among nations (the beauty of the world) sprung " from a mother bringing forth heroes, remains without doubt in a " place of lotuses, full of sacred waters, and is adorned with all sorts " of precious stones.

" 8 and 9. Siva the beautiful, who in the tank lake Siva, which " teems with (is a mine of) lotuses, resembling vanquished gems, and " is full of water for sprinkling the fortunate and much-loved " Kámaraja, who puts down the pride of his enemies, who is the " source (receptacle) of glory, and is earnest in worshipping Siva.

" 10. He (Kámaraja,) who dwells on the heads of Kings, caused " this temple of Siva, which resembles the temple on Kailása, to be " created for the happiness of the earth."

Three additional inscriptions were sent to Dr. Babington by some Madras friends; one by Colonel

De Havilland from the "north side of a verandah of
"a pagoda (No. 30 in the Map)* excavated out of the
"solid granite, two miles north of the place." Of
these Dr. Babington says, "all these inscriptions
"differ in character from each other, but agree pre-
"cisely in matter; and it is remarkable that the
"slokas of which they are composed, are, with the
"exception of the last, contained, though in different
"order, in the inscription copied by me from the wall
"of the Ganesa pagoda. My inscription is in a
"character differing again from any of the rest.
"The other inscriptions consist of five slokas only,
"with some undeciphered portions. The first
"three slokas in my inscription are not found in the
"others; my fourth sloka is the same as theirs. The
"fifth, sixth, and seventh slokas of my inscription are
"wanting in the others. My eighth and ninth slokas
"are their first and second, and my tenth is their
"third. Their fifth sloka I have ascertained after a
"very careful comparison, to be quite different from
"the undeciphered portion of my inscription. Its
"translation is as follows:—

"Atiramachanda (he who in battle is very furious) Lord of Kings
"built this place, called Atiramachandesvara. May Siva the beloved,
"accompanied by the daughter (Pārvati) of the snowy mountain, by
"Kārtikeya, and their suite of deities, be present in it for ever."

The third kind of inscription is found over the
figures on the monolithic temples to the south of the
village. So completely have these characters become
obsolete, that none of the learned natives consulted
were able to decipher them. After considerable trouble, Dr. Babington himself succeeded in doing so.

It might reasonably have been expected that these

[* Plate XXI.]

inscriptions would have thrown some light on the origin or probable age of the sculptures, excavations, and themselves. They afford no very precise information at all. The appellations given to the prince or princes who "caused the erections," are mere epithets, by which no individual can with certainty be identified, (vide Mr. Taylor's note *d*); and were it possible to do this, the chronology must still be in a very great degree theoretical. I perfectly agree in opinion with Mr. Taylor that there is little in the sculptures themselves, if we except the Rathas, the Váráhasvámí Pagoda, the Ganesa temple and the temple at Sáluvan Kuppam, to justify the supposition of their very great antiquity. Most of them are in the most perfect preservation, and present a freshness of appearance which creates an involuntary idea of their almost recent execution. The subjects of the sculptures too are an evidence that they are not of very remote antiquity. They are representations of various personages and incidents in Hindu mythology, and are chiefly borrowed from the famous poem, the Mahábhárata. This and the language of the inscriptions which is Sanscrit, or Tamil with Sanscrit derivatives, mark the presence of the Brahmanical faith. Now it appears from Mr. Taylor's researches, that previous to the seventh century of the Christian era, the whole of the district in which Mámallaipúr stands was occupied by the Kurumbas, a half-civilized people of the Jaina religion; and it was about that period or probably later that, under the auspices of Adondai, a prince whose capitals were Conjeveram and Tripati,[*] the Brahmans were intro-

duced into this part of the country. The extent of
the works, and the labor and expense bestowed on
them seem to indicate a long established Brahmanical influence; and it will be seen from Mr. Taylor's
note (c) that an historical paper amongst the Mackenzie MSS. affords grounds for supposing that at least
some of these excavations, &c., were executed so
lately as the seventeenth century by a prince denominated Sinhamanáyudu. The supplementary paper
by Walter Elliot, Esq., relating to the remains at
Sáluvan Kuppam, serves to suggest a much earlier
date than the latter for certain of these remarkable
productions which he therein specifies.

Works of this nature have been executed in all
parts of the world during the earlier stages of civilization. Rocky caves formed by nature offer a con-
genial shelter for the gloomy rites of a dark super-
stition, a ready defence from the attacks of enemies
or the inclemency of the weather, and supplied
appropriate receptacles for the remains of the dead.
In the most ancient times the Holy Scriptures speak
of caves as places of residence and refuge, as well as
of sepulture. Many of these natural recesses were
greatly enlarged and rendered more commodious
or better adapted for the purposes of shelter and
defence by human labor and art. This may still be
traced in several countries of the East. Maundrell
has described a cave near Sidon, whose sides contain
two hundred smaller caverns. Sir R. K. Porter has
given an interesting account of a cavern or labyrinth
in the mountain of Kerofto, in Eastern Kurdistan.
Similar excavations are found according to the same
authority at Maraga in Media; in the mountains
near the lake Sivan, and near the site of Artaxata,

the ancient capital of Armenia. The sepulchral caves of Egypt have been admirably illustrated by Belzoni. Sir Alexander Burnes has given an interesting account of the sculptures and caves at Bamecan. Those at Elephanta and Ellora are well known in India: and such as are interested in these remarkable records of past times should not overlook the description and beautiful sketches of Petra by Laborde. Amongst the savages of North-Western Australia, Captain Gray has discovered sculptured rocks and painted caverns. In this way nature appears to have suggested to mankind the earlier efforts of art.

The Rathas, or monolithic temples to the south of the village, are probably the most ancient of the remains at Mâmalhaipûr. Their inscriptions are in a character so completely obsolete, that the most learned natives, according to Dr. Babington, are unable to decipher them. This species of sculpture is remarkable, and much more rare than mere excavations. It was, however, practised by the ancient Egyptians, and Herodotus (Lib. ii. cap. 155) has given a short description of a monolithic temple of Latona, which stood at Buto, near the Sebennytic mouth of the Nile. He says it measured 40 cubits or 60 feet in height, breadth, and width: and its roof consisted of a separate stone, four cubits high. This temple, which must have been conveyed to its site, must have weighed on the lowest computation upwards of 5,000 tons. At the 175th chapter of the same book, he describes another monolithic temple at Sais, which had been brought thither by King Amasis from Elephantine, the island opposite Syene, immediately below the first cataract; a distance of twenty days' sail, or of 700 miles by land. The outside measure-

ment of this monolith he states to be—length, 21
cubits; breadth, 14; and height, 8; the inside measure-
ment was—length, 13 cubits and 1 pygon; breadth,
12 cubits; and the height, 3 cubits. Taking the cubit
in round numbers at 1 foot 6 inches and the pygon at
1 foot 3 inches, the temple must have been externally
31 feet 6 inches long, 21 feet broad and 13 feet high:
and internally 28 feet 3 inches long, 18 feet broad,
and 7½ feet high. This monolith then was inferior in point of mere size to the largest of those at
Mâmallaipûr; the dimensions of which externally,
according to Mr. Goldingham, are as follows:—length
49 feet, breadth 25 feet, and height 25 feet. But we
must remember that while these are *in loco naturæ*,
being cut in fact from large boulders or distinct
masses of granite, the monolith of Amasis had to be
conveyed to its site by manual labor; and Herodotus affirms that two thousand boatmen were occupied in its removal for a period of upwards of three
years. After all indeed it was not placed precisely
where the king had proposed; for which two reasons
are assigned. First, that the architect, weary of the
labor and time expended on the work, heaved a deep
sigh as the workmen were dragging it forward, which
Amasis interpreted as an unfavorable omen: and
secondly, that one of the workmen, having unfortunately fallen under the moving mass, was crushed to
death, and on this account it was allowed to remain
where it then was. Mr. Burton, in his excerpta (plate
41) gives a representation of a similar monolith said to
be of the same king, and found at Tel-et-mai. This
measures externally 21 feet 9 inches high, 13 feet
broad, and 11 feet 7 inches deep: and internally 19
feet 3 inches high, 8 feet broad, and 8 feet 3 inches deep.

The sculptured rocks at Mâmallaipûr, (on which is represented the penance of Arjuna,) are by no means without their parallel. This primitive application of the art of sculpture seems an obvious mode of perpetuating the memory of events, historical or mythological, and has been adopted from the earliest ages. On the rocks of the river Lycus, near Beirout in Syria, are still to be seen the figure in relief, and the name inscribed, of Rameses the great king of Egypt, who is supposed to have flourished about B. C. 1350, and was therefore contemporary with Ehud and Shamgar mentioned in the book of Judges : but early Egyptian chronology is so exceedingly uncertain, that the era of Rameses must always be conjectural. Not far from this is another sculpture of a Persian king, and an inscription in the arrow-headed character, which not having been yet deciphered affords likewise no conclusive evidence as to its age. Copies of these have been made by Bonomi. No Christian can have forgotten the exclamation of Job, " Oh that my words were now written ! Oh " that they were printed in a book ! That they were " graven with an iron pen and lead in the rock for " ever !" (Chap. xix., 23, 24.) And from some remains in the wady Mokatteb, and in other valleys near the mountains of Sinai, it would seem that the art of " engraving" on rocks is in those regions of great antiquity. Figures of men and animals accompany these inscriptions ; the characters of the latter are for the most part unknown in the present day. These inscribed rocks extend in one place for about three hours march, and are mentioned by Burkhardt, Laborde, and other travellers.

At Be-Sitoon, near Kermanshah in Persia, is a

stream above whose fountain-head is a projecting rock containing the remains of an immense piece of sculpture. The great antiquity of this interesting relic is evidenced by the successive mutilations it has suffered, to afford room for subsequent inscriptions, as well as by the ordinary operations of time upon both it and them. By Mr. Macdonald Kinnier this bas-relief has been supposed identical with one spoken of by Diodorus Siculus, on the authority of Ctesias; who certainly had peculiar advantages for obtaining accurate information connected with Persian tradition and history. He says, " We are informed by Diodorus Siculus that Semiramis, in her march to Ecbatana, encamped near a mountain called Bagistan, in Media. She cut out a piece of the lower part of the rock, and caused her image to be carved upon it, and a hundred of her guards that were lancetters, standing round her; she wrote likewise in Assyrian letters on the rock, that Semiramis ascended from the plain to the top of the mountain, by laying the packs and fardles of the beasts that followed her one upon another." There are many points of resemblance between the mountain of Be-Sitoon and that of Bagistan described by Diodorus Siculus; and supposing Mr. Kinnier to be right in his conjectures, we have here the remnants, for they are unfortunately no more, of a bas-relief executed at the lowest computation 800 years before the Christian era. Throughout ancient Media and Persia sculptured rocks, of various ages, repeatedly occur: a great many of these bas-reliefs, however, appear to belong to the Sassanian era: (from A. D. 226 to A. D. 632.)

These introductory notes have, I fear, already become too long and tedious; it only remains, there-

fore, that I acknowledge my obligations to Walter
Elliot, Esq., of the Madras Civil Service, to whose
friendly kindness I am indebted for the very valuable
supplementary paper on the remains at *Sáluvan Kuppam*, as well as for a map of Mámallaipúr drawn
in 1808 by Colonel Mackenzie. The latter I have
reduced, and by numbering the several objects both
in it and in Mr. Braddock's description, I have
endeavoured to render the whole a more useful guide
to those who may dedicate a few spare hours to a
visit to this interesting spot. The sculptures are for
the most part such as do mark no very advanced
state of art. They possess none of that finished elegance and refined taste, and but little of that purer
poetic spirit which characterize the productions of
Europe. Still they are highly deserving attention
as the best specimens of native skill to be met with,
I believe, in Southern India; and will not be under-
valued by those who are capable of comprehending
the extent to which art, even in its earliest infancy,
has contributed to the civilization of mankind.

G. W. M.

Fort St. George.

---

*Lieutenant Braddock's Guide to the Sculptures,
Excavations, &c., at Mámallaipúr.*

I shall commence my account of these curious
sculptures and ruins with a small dilapidated temple
built within fifty yards of the northern termination of the hill. (No. 1.)[*]   It is a rectangular building

[* The Nos. in this paper refer to plates XX. and XXI.]

of plain hewn stone devoid of ornament : 24 feet
long, 15 feet broad, and about 12 feet high.   It has
two apartments, the innermost of which contains a
black stone lingam, neatly executed and in good
preservation, notwithstanding that from the absence
of roofing it is exposed to the weather.   This temple
is completely overshadowed with trees, which have
taken root in the walls, and whose branches forcing
their way through the joints of the stones have contributed much to its dilapidation and present ruinous
appearance.

At a short distance to the eastward of this pagoda
lies the *Group of Monkeys* (No. 2) spoken of in the
Asiatic Researches, in an account of this place written in 1784.*   The group, now much buried in the
sand, consists of a male, a female, and a young one.
The male monkey with a laudable love of cleanliness
is studying the head of its partner with the most
friendly attention, and the young one is satisfying
its hunger.   At a little distance lies a mutilated
figure of Ganesa or Pillaiyar, the Hindu God of high-
ways, &c., of whom I shall speak presently.

Looking towards the south, a *loose mass of rock*
(No. 3) will be seen resting on a slope of the hill,
apparently on so mere a point, that it seems as though
a small force would dislodge it and roll it headlong
on the plain.   Its circumference is 68 feet, and its
height about 25.‡   From the eastward it has a circular appearance ; from other points of view its figure
is irregular.

[* Cp. Chambers, p. 4, supra.]
[‡ Not found there now (1869).]
‡ Mr. Goldingham gives its diameter as 27 feet.

On the western face of the northern termination
of the hill, not far south of the pagoda just described, may be found, after a little search, a circular
cistern cut out of a solid stone.* It is 8 feet 6 inches
in diameter, and 4 feet deep, but cracked.

Near this cistern the face of the rock is carved and
ornamented to the extent of 29 feet in length by 14
feet in height. There are three *large excavated niches*
(No. 4) with a flight of four steps leading into each.
Figures are sculptured on each side the entrances.
The centre or principal niche contains a figure of
Mahádeva and four other figures cut on the back
wall. The other two niches contain a figure of
Vishnu and four others. This rock faces the north-
west, and to the right or south of it is an imperfect
representation of Durgá, eight-handed, and trampling
under foot the head of Mahishásura, whose story
will be told presently. On the eastern face of this
rock are carvings of a well-proportioned elephant five
feet high, and the heads of three smaller elephants:
with those of a monkey and of a peacock.† The
communication between the eastern and western faces
of this rock is through a cleft at the north end of it.

At a short distance in a south-westerly direction
from this place is an excavation in the solid rock
(No. 5) measuring 32 feet long, 9 feet 6 inches deep, and

[* Called the 'Gopís' churn' by the Brahmans, who have also
named the boulder on the slope of the rock 'Krishna's butter-ball.'—
Cp. Bruce's Scenes and Sights in the East, pp. 130—132.]

[† "The head of the elephant is admirably finished. Perched
above the elephant is a monkey, the figure and attitude of which are
exquisitely faithful to life. The flow of its tail is full of expression,
and is a study in itself. The whole face is marked by the anxious
and mischievous spirit so natural to this creature."—Bruce, p. 132.]

8 feet high. The top is supported by two plain, strong, square pillars. It contains a square niche, on each side of which is a figure, probably that of Párvatí, a goddess who will be introduced to the reader presently. This excavation is on the western face of the hill, which is a continuous range of granite masses.

Still keeping on the same side, at 100 or 150 yards southward from the last excavation we come to another (No. 6) containing five niches, with steps leading into three of them; and two rows of pillars, four in each. This excavation is 36 feet long, 16 feet deep, and nearly 10 feet high. The niches contain each a kind of recess, (intended probably for a group of figures,) and a circular trench, (intended probably for lingams.) A figure is carved on each side of all the niches at the entrance. Four steps lead into this temple which faces north-west, half-west.

Adjoining is a *rough excavation* 36 feet long, 10 deep, and 10 high. In the middle is a large niche, also rough. About 12 feet of the rock appear to have been cut away before sufficient height was obtained for the front. This occurs in other places also; and a platform or level space is thus formed in the rock in front.

About half a mile westward, at the western extremity of the Palmyra tope which is on the west of the hill, there are three small unfinished temples sculptured out of solid detached masses of stone, (No. 7): but as more elaborately finished and larger temples of the same description will be described hereafter, I shall not dwell on those smaller ones. I would now lead the reader back to the large stone before described as resting on the slope of the rock on the eastern side of the hill. (No. 3.)

Proceeding southerly from this stone, you presently arrive at *a temple* fashioned out of the rock, (No. 8,)[a] and ornamented according to a style of architecture wholly different from that of this part of India in the present day. The top is elliptical, and bears considerable resemblance to the gothic style. The pillars which support a verandah on the western side are, I think, similar to columns which I have seen in the sketches of Egyptian Ruins by M. Denon. This temple is 28 feet high, 20 feet long, and 11 feet 6 inches broad. On the western face, at what may be called the foundation, there is a rent in the rock, which causes the temple to incline a little out of the perpendicular towards the south-east. This handsome structure (if so it may be termed), has a verandah and a niche, the latter containing an image of Ganesa, which, blackened by smoke and ghee, is still an object of adoration to the people of the village. Their Brahmans, I was told, propitiate the stone deity every Friday with lustrations of ghee and cocoanut oil, and certain rites and prayers. The inner wall of the verandah, south of the niche, bears an inscription in the same kind of character as that hereafter noticed. According to Dr. Babington, (Transactions Royal Asiatic Society, Vol. 2, pp. 258-6,[b] and plate XIV.) this inscription consists of verses in praise of Siva.[c] I have stated that this temple contains an image of Ganesa, and as this is the second time that Ganesa has been mentioned, it may be right to state who and what he is.

[a] Called by the Brahmans 'Arjuna's Baths.'—See note * p. 56, *supra.*]
[b] Pp. 56, 57, *supra.*]
[c] See Dr. Babington's translation of this inscription in the introductory notes, [p. 67, *supra.*]   M.

Colonel Moor, in his Hindu Pantheon, says—that Ganesa* is the God of prudence and policy, and the reputed eldest son of Siva or Mahádeva and Párvatl. He is represented with an elephant's head; generally with four hands, but sometimes with only two, and sometimes with six or eight. He is said to be propitiated by Hindus of all sects in the outset of any business: if a house is to be built, a book written, or a journey commenced, Ganesa is invoked.

It is very common for Hindu authors to give different versions of the same tale, and there are different accounts of the manner and cause of Ganesa's possession of an elephant's head. One relates that Vishnu and Ganesa fought, and that Ganesa would have been triumphant, but that Siva (his father!) cut off his head: whereat his mother Párvatl, being very much distressed and offended, proceeded to revenge the act by performing such austerities as, had they continued, would have deranged the destinies of the universe. This alarmed the whole congregation of the gods, who intreated Siva to restore Ganesa to life. He consented to do so, but the severed head could not be found: it was determined therefore to place on the headless trunk the cranium of the first animal they met with, which proved to be an elephant. There is another story to this effect, that Mahádeva and Párvati quarrelled; their quarrel was followed by a reconciliation; and their reconciliation by the birth of Ganesa. On this joyful occasion all the gods came to congratulate Párvatl; but one of them,† whose name I have forgotten, kept his eyes cast

[* Lord (Isa) of a troop (gana); so called, because he is chief of the subordinate gods attendant upon Siva.—Wilson]

[† Sani (Saturn).]

D 1050

down and forebore to look up. The goddess observing this asked him the reason of it ; when he told her that he was doomed to injure whomsoever he looked upon, and therefore would not venture to look on the child. Párvatí would not believe that any injury could be done, and urged him to admire her beautiful Ganesa. But no sooner did he lift up his eyes, than the child's head vanished. This unexpected result astounded Párvatí, who had no sooner recovered from her first surprise, than she gave such passionate vent to her feelings, that Vishnu, apprehensive of the consequences, flew to the banks of the Ganges, and brought thence the head of an elephant, which he placed on Ganesa's shoulders.

Passing the north-western front of the temple just described, and following the foot-path which leads through a narrow acclivity formed by rocks and bushes on either side, we come to *an excavation* with a very pretty frontage, on the left hand. (No. 9.) It is hewn in the side of the hill, is 22 feet long, 11 feet deep, and 10 feet 6 inches high. Of this excavation and of the imagery within it, plates are given in the second Volume of the Royal Asiatic Society's Transactions.*

On the wall, at the right hand or south-west end, there is a group of figures representing the Vámana Avatára, or fifth incarnation of Vishnu, undertaken by him to punish pride and presumption. The story is this :

Mahábali, a prince who lived in the Treta yuga, or the second age, was so elated by his prosperity, that he omitted to perform the more essential sacrifices to the

[* See plates V. – IX., *supra.*]

ii

gods. This being highly offensive to them, Vishnu, determined to check so bad an example, became incarnate and assumed the form of a wretched Brahman dwarf. Mahábali was at that time in possession of the whole universe, having previously acquired this dominion in consequence of his signal piety, or punctual performance of certain austerities and rigorous acts of devotion. Vishnu, in the shape just mentioned, appeared before him, and asked as a boon so much of his wide possessions as he could pace in three steps. This the monarch readily undertook to grant, at the same time desiring him to ask something more worthy for a prince to bestow. The pretended Brahman, however, professed his content with what he had already requested, and the king proceeded to ratify his promise by pouring water into the petitioner's hand, which was, it would seem, the most solemn mode of confirming a grant. As he was doing this, the size of the dwarf grew larger and continued to expand until it filled the whole earth. Vishnu then discovering himself, deprived Mahábali in two steps of earth and heaven ; but in consideration of his previous virtue and general good conduct, he deprived him of no more, but left to his government the kingdom of Pátála, a lower or inferior world, said to be the abode of serpents. Some say that the water used in this transaction for the purpose of ratification fell from Vishnu's hand on the head of Siva, and flowing thence, formed the origin of the Ganges.

Vishnu in this character is sometimes called "Trivikrama," "the three-step taker." In this sculpture he is represented eight-handed, and in the act of stepping prodigiously : the right foot is on the

ground, and the left is raised sideways as high as his
head.   It looks, therefore, as it is, very unnatural,
for the articulation of the head of the thigh bone in
its socket would not admit of such a position.   The
subordinate figures do not appear to illustrate the
story, or at least the version above given of it.
Perhaps another circumstance should be related, and
the imagination may be allowed under some restric-
tion to be the interpreter : but even then only a part
of the figures seem to be connected with the tale.

It is said that Sukra, regent of the planet Venus
and guru of the Asuras, acting as mantri, or minister,[*]
of Mahábali, faithfully informed the king of the
deceit that was being practised upon him.   There is
a figure with a dog-like head speaking to another,
who seems to rest his chin on his right hand in deep
reflection.   These two figures occupy the upper part
of the sculpture on the left of Vishnu.   Below them
are two figures in human shape represented as falling.
Perhaps the former may represent Sukra and Mahábali at the moment when the prince was first made
acquainted by his counsellor with the true character
of the dwarf, but was too proud to withdraw his royal
pledge : and the latter the same after he had fallen
from his high estate : or the two falling figures may
imply that the two steps of Vishnu had deprived him
of the dominion of heaven and earth.   What the rest
of the figures may illustrate, I do not conjecture.[†]

On the wall of the opposite or north-eastern end
is a sculptured delineation in bas-relief of the Varáha

[* Priest and preceptor, not minister.]

[† Cp. the passages descriptive of the dwarf incarnation given in
Muir's Sanscrit texts, Part IV., pp. 114—131.]

Avatára. Among the legendary stories of the Hindus, several different accounts are given of Vishnu's reasons for taking on himself this incarnation, and particularly why he assumed the shape of a boar. Among others it is said that a Daitya, or evil spirit, named Hiranyáksha, gained from Brahmá by his scrupulous piety and the performance of penances of very great efficacy, a promise that he should have given to him anything he asked. Accordingly he desired universal dominion, and exemption from being hurt by the bite or power of any living creature. He enumerated all animals and venomous reptiles that bite or sting, except the boar, which was forgotten. His ambitious desires were no sooner obtained than he became exceedingly presumptuous, proud, and wicked ; and forgetting the great power of the gods, he ran away with the whole earth, and plunged it and himself into the depths of the sea ! This singular exploit made the interposition of the preserving power necessary ; and Vishnu changing himself into the form of a boar, plunged into the ocean ; fought a dreadful battle which lasted a thousand years ; at length slew the impious Daitya ; brought back the earth on his tusks, and restored it to its usual good order, peace, and tranquillity.*

The sculptures illustrative of the story appear to refer to a period subsequent to the battle, for the figures supply the imagination with the idea that the boar-headed deity is now solacing himself after the toils and dangers of his thousand years' conflict.

[* There appears to be confusion here between the story of Hiranyakasipu and the legend of the death of his brother Hiranyáksha.—Cp. Vishnupurána, Book I., chap. 4, Wilson's note (p. 62, Vol. I, 8vo. edn. by Hall) and chap. 17. Also Muir's Sanscrit Texts, Part IV., p. 89 ff.]

The principal figure, Vishnu (four-handed), is executed with considerable spirit. He stands firmly on the left leg. The right leg is raised, and the foot rests on the head of another figure. On the right knee sits a female; Vishnu's left hand grasps the small part of her right leg, and his right hand passes behind her, a little lower than the waist, while he regards her with interesting pig-headed gravity. His two remaining hands hold a conch shell and the chakra.* Below Vishnu's right leg is the upper portion of a figure with the hands raised as in prayer, its lower part being immersed in what may be supposed a representation of the waves of the sea, (the rock being here very rough and unfinished.) Another figure, rising out of this imaginary water, is also in a posture of supplication; and there are other accessories, but they do not appear to explain the story.

From the back wall of this excavated fane is a projection measuring 7 feet 9 inches broad and 3 feet 6 inches deep. It contains an empty niche, in which, however, may be traced the outlines of a deity, which the chisel of the workman has not brought into being. A flight of three small steps leads into the niche, and on either side its entrance, as well as at each end formed by the projection, is a figure in bas-relief, with the name, attributes, or office of which I am unacquainted.

Sculptured on the back wall between this niche and the north-east end of the excavation is a female figure, probably Devī or Pārvatī, the consort of Śiva, bathing. She is attended by her females and two

---

* The chakra is a circular piece of metal, not unlike our discus or quoit. M.

elephants, one of which is pouring a vessel of water over her, and the other is receiving another vessel from the hands of one of her attendants.*

On a similar space to the south of the niche is another female figure, which I take to be a representation of the same great personage ; in this, however, I am not positive.† On each side of the principal figures are two bulky little fellows, and a fourth figure of a more natural size. There are also two heads of animals, one somewhat similar to an antelope's, the other intended perhaps for that of a tiger.

The front of this excavation is supported by two columns and two pilasters of a handsome style of architecture. The ceiling is ornamented with flowery sculpture, but has several cracks in it running lengthways ; i. e. in a north-east and south-westerly direction.

About eighty yards west of this place, on the top of the hill, may be found, after a little research, the stone bed, with a lion for its pillow, which, in the account published in the Asiatic Researches already alluded to, is called the Dharmarája's lion-throne, (No. 10); and at a trifling distance S. W. of this, is the bath of Draupadí. The lion and bed measure in length 9 feet 6 inches, and in breadth 3 feet 6 inches ; the lion is 18 inches high, and stretching across the south end appears as if intended for a seat or pillow. The bed lies due north and south, and is hewn out and fashioned on the surface of the solid rock. There is not the least appearance of the place having once been an apartment of a palace, as intimated in that account : the top of the hill hereabout is indeed quite uneven and irregular, and abounds with immense blocks and masses of granite.

There is nothing more which merits notice on the surface of the hill, if we except numerous mortice holes, which may be seen running parallel to its western edge, and many small flights of steps cut in several parts of the rocks.

Leaving the top of the hill, and descending by the path in front of the temple last mentioned, at a few feet south-east of the pagoda which contains the image of Ganesa, will be found sculptured in bas-relief, on the eastern faces of two large rocks, the *story of the Tapas* (No. 11) or intense penance of Arjuna. These two rocks adjoin each other, being divided only by a fissure. They measure 84 feet in length, and about 30 feet in height.

In this group of sculptures, the principal figure, that of Arjuna, is not the largest. He is seen on the left of the fissure in the posture of penance; his arms are raised above his head, his right leg is lifted up. He is supposed to stand on the great toe of his left foot. His arms and right leg appear withered, but his left leg is of the natural size. His chest and ribs are prominent, but the stomach and abdomen sunken; the whole figure representing emaciation from long fasting. Besides this figure there is a multitude of others both of men and animals; and among the latter two well-proportioned elephants as large as life. The largest of them measures 17 feet from the proboscis to the tail, and 14 feet in height. The smaller is in height 10 feet, and in length 11. Under the belly of the larger elephant there is a small one, with the heads and trunks of two others, while the head of a fourth is seen between his proboscis and fore feet.   These figures of elephants are cut on the right hand rock on a level with the ground.   On the rock to the left, near the fissure, and below the figure of Arjuna, is a neat little temple,* with a niche and a figure† in it.   Just within the fissure itself is a figure like that of the Mermaid, but in the native languages it has a name purporting half-woman and half-snake.‡ Scattered over the face of both rocks there are many representations of men, ascetics, monkeys, lions (or what are meant for lions), tigers, antelopes, birds, satyrs and monstrous animals which it would puzzle a naturalist of the present age to nomenclate.§   The whole are executed with considerable spirit, and occupy a space of about 2,400 square feet.   A plate giving a representation of these sculptures is published in the 2nd Vol. of the Transactions of the Royal Asiatic Society of Great Britain and Ireland.¶

* At the south-east corner of this little fane, in a sitting and stooping posture, and entirely detached from the rock, is an admirable figure of an ascetic, miserably emaciated, which, though somewhat worn by exposure to the weather, bears evidence to the talent, skill, and anatomical knowledge of the artist.‖

[† Said to be Krishna.]

[‡ Nága, the name of demi-gods inhabiting the lower regions, the upper part of whose bodies is human, and the lower part that of a serpent.   There is the figure of a male Nága as well as that of a female, but the upper part of the body has fallen off and is lying in front of the rock.]

[§ On the north side of the crevice, at the foot of the rock, is the figure of a cat standing on its hind legs, with its fore-paws raised above its head in seeming imitation of Arjuna, performing penance— after eating part of Krishna's butter-ball—in order that the sea may dry up and she be thus able to devour all the fish!   Near the cat are rats, enjoying apparently their temporary immunity from persecution.]

[¶ See plate L and plate LI., No. 1, supra.]

[‖ Said to be Drona, (see note * p. 31, supra,) the figures, now headless, of whose pupils are in front, and somewhat below that of their preceptor.]

The story of the penance of Arjuna may be told as follows :—

The five sons of Pânḍurâja lost their dominions in play with their cousin Duryodhana; who, however, played unfairly and won through "guile and wicked stratagem."* The consequence was that they and their followers were banished for twelve years and upwards, and were doomed to wander in jungles, wilds, and solitudes. During this period the elder brother took counsel with the others, how they might repossess themselves of their patrimony after the term of banishment had expired : and in order to attain this it appeared desirable to gain the mantra Pâsupatâstra.† This mantra, or incantation, was of such wonderful efficacy, that if it was uttered while in the act of shooting an arrow, the arrow became inevitably destructive, and moreover possessed of the power of producing or generating other weapons, which not only scattered death on all sides, but were able to cause the destruction of the whole world.‡ This mantra could be obtained only from the god Îsvara, (a name of Siva) ; and Arjuna, as he was distinguished among his brethren for his prudence, fortitude, and valour, was employed to procure it.§

The hero of this story had to travel far to the north of the Himâlaya mountains, there to perform austere and rigid penance in order to propitiate the

[* See Wheeler's Hist. of India, Vol. I., chap. 7.]

[† The Pâsupata weapon, not mantra.]

[‡ Cp. Muir's Sanscrit Texts, Part IV., p. 196.]

[§ He went first to Indra by the advice of his grandfather Vyâsa, and afterwards, at the suggestion of Indra, to the Himâlaya, to obtain a sight of Mahâdeva.—Cp. Monier Williams' Indian Epic Poetry, pp. 102—104, and Muir's Sanscrit Texts, Part IV., p. 194 ff.]

17

god and obtain his favor : and as a preparatory measure he was instructed in all requisite mantras and
mystic ceremonies.   On reaching the appointed place
he found a delightful retreat; a grove or forest
abounding with streams and fruits and flowers, with
whatever could regale the senses or charm the eye.
Not only was the earth most bountiful, but the air
was filled with the strains of celestial melody.   In
this place Arjuna commenced and carried on his austerities by meditation, by prayer, and by ceremonial
purification.

During the first month he ate but once in four
days : during the second month, but once in seven
days : during the third month, only once in fourteen
days : and during the fourth month he did not eat at
all, but completed his penance by standing on the tip
of his great toe, the other leg being lifted from the
ground, and his hands raised above his head.*   This
is the period of the penance which the sculptor has
selected for illustration, in the curious work now
under notice.   The figure of Arjuna is exhibited in a
posture agreeing exactly with the story, the relation
of which, however, it seems necessary to continue a
little further, in order to explain the accessories, the
figures of men and animals, with which the whole
face of the rock is covered.

The nearest *Rishis,* (hermits or ascetics, who by
austerities and meditation may attain, as their object
is, riches, power, supernatural arms, or beatitude),
seeing the intense devotion of Arjuna, went and
reported it to the god Íswara, who was highly grati-
fied : but in order to try the constancy and courage

[* See the passage from the Mahábhárata given in the Appendix.]

of the hero, the deity assumed the form of a wild hunter.* One of his accompanying attendants was transformed into a wild boar,† and Arjuna preparing to shoot it was interrupted by the unknown deity, who forbade him to strike his game. Arjuna notwithstanding let fly a shaft, and so did the disguised hunter, and the boar fell lifeless. This occasioned an altercation, which brought on a personal combat; and when Arjuna had expended all his arrows on his antagonist without effect, he tore up rocks and mountains to hurl at him, but they too fell harmless at his feet. This so enraged our hero, that he attacked his foe hand to hand. Such was the daring audacity of this act, and the bold and determined courage of Arjuna, that all heaven was filled with surprise, and the beasts of the forest, and the inhabitants of the etherial regions, alike flocked to witness the contest, which was terminated by the god's revealing himself, and bestowing on his votary the boon he wished for, viz., the Pásupatástra.‡

This congregating of the inhabitants of the skies and of the forest, this mixture of men and brutes, makes probable the supposition that it is the second point or period of the story that has been selected by the artist for exemplification, as instanced by the particular postures and variety of the figures seen in this curious carving.

[* Kirâta.]

[† A Dánava (demon) in the form of a boar was about to attack Arjuna.]

[‡ The story is related in the Vanaparva of the Mahâbhárata.—Cp. Muir's Sanscrit Texts, Part IV., pp. 194—196. The combat between Arjuna and Siva, disguised as a Kirâta, is the subject of the poem Kirâtârjunîya, by Bhâravi.]

Adjoining the sculptured imagery of Arjuna, to the south, are the wide beginnings of an excavation (No. 12) having a front of 50 feet, and a depth at the north end of 40 feet, and at the south end of 35 feet. A large portion of the solid rock projects from the back of the excavation 25 feet, with a frontage of 23 feet, leaving deep recesses on either side, in which stone has been left rough cut for three pillars. The front of this excavation is supported by five octagonal columns,* whose bases are formed of figures of a grotesque horned animal: a sixth column originally existed, its base and capital still remain, but its shaft is removed. At a few feet within is a second row of six columns corresponding with those in front. The ground at the entrance is partly overgrown with bushes, and the cave now affords shelter to the village cattle.

A few yards south of this excavation, opposite to a street of the village is an open building, which from the sculptures it contains may very properly be denominated Krishna's Choultry (No. 13). These sculptures are executed on the back wall of the building, or rather that part of the solid hill which forms the back wall. They represent the exploit of Krishna supporting the mountain Govarddhana in order to shelter his followers from the wrath of Indra,†—the god that darts the "swift blue bolt," the

---

* The capitals of these columns are not unlike those of some of the pillars of the Indra Sabhá at Ellora, and of the cave temples of Elephanta. M.

[† See the Vishnupurána, Book V., chap. 11.—" It seems not unlikely that this legend has some reference to the caves or cavern temples in various parts of India. A remarkable representation of it occurs upon the sculptured rocks of Mahábalipúr." Wilson's note.—

"Sprinkler of genial dews, and fruitful rains
   Over hills and thirsty plains."*

This action is fabled to have been performed by
Krishna with one of his little fingers at the age of
seven.

"With one finger raised the vast Goverdhen;
   Beneath whose rocky burden,
On pastures dry, the maids and herdmen trod:
The Lord of thunder felt a mightier God."
                                        Sir W. Jones.

In the present sculpture, the attitude of the God
corresponds sufficiently with the story. He appears,
however, to sustain the mountain with the palm of
his left hand, instead of the little finger as in the
poetical version.† The only representation of the
supported mountain consists of a rough line running
above the whole of the figures. This line has been
formed by cutting away as much of the rock as would
answer the purpose of giving the requisite degree of
relief for typifying, in the above manner, the rugged
bottom of the mountain, torn up from its foundations,
and sustained aloft in the air. The whole group
looks clumsy; the proportions are bad; the countenances are destitute of expression; and little praise
is due to it either as a work of art or imagination.
So singular a deliverance from sudden destruction
ought to have supplied the artist with a subject
capable of being embodied with great spirit: but
here, instead, is an inanimate, meaningless group,
which, but for the principal figure, would not at all

The story is also given in the Bhágavataparána.—See Eastwick's
translation of the Prem Ságar, chap. XXVI.]

[* Sir William Jones,—Hymn to Indra.]

[† "With one hand," according to the Vishnupuráṇa; "on the little
finger of his left hand," according to the Prem Ságar.—See plate of
in Moor's Hindu Pantheon.]

have interpreted the story.   There are about twenty
figures of men, women, and children, and as many
heads of cows or bullocks.   There is one tolerable
figure of a brahmany bull, and another of a cow
licking its calf while in the act of being milked.   It
may be that the general quietude and repose of
the figures are intended to imply their security from
the terrible danger so recently, and still but for
the god's interposition, impending over them.   In
another part of the sculpture is a figure playing on a
flute or pipe; this may also represent Krishna, in
his character of Muralidhara, *the tuneful.* [*]   In this
form he is called Bâlakrishna, and is said to have amus-
ed himself by piping to the swains and damsels of
Govarddhana.[†]   This figure of Krishna is small, and
might be overlooked ; it is situated over the hinder
part of the cow and calf just mentioned.   At the
north end of this sculpture, raised 5 or 6 feet from
the floor, is a well executed figure of a brahmany
bull in full relief ; and at the south end are several
figures of beasts apparently intended for lions : one
of them, however, resembles the Sphynx,[‡] having a
human face with a body of a quadruped.

Krishna's Choultry extends in front 47 feet ; is 26
feet deep and 12 feet high.   The roof is made of
hewn stone, which is partially covered with earth ;
and is supported by three rows of columns, 4 in each.
The bases of those in the front row consist of grotesque figures of a nondescript animal, sitting on its

[* *Lit.* "the flute-holder."—Cp. plate 60, fig. 8, in Moor's Hindu
Pantheon.]

[† See Eastwick's Prem Sâgar, chap. XXII.]

‡ A similar figure is met with at Ellora.   M.

launches, having curved horns, and a long tail which is curled upon its back like the figure 8.

On the hill above this choultry is the *foundation of a rectangular building* (No. 14)[*] measuring 66 feet in length, and 42 in breadth. In the middle of this is a gateway 12 feet wide, running east and west; and in the gateway are two recesses, each 12 feet square, one on each side. Near the corners of these recesses in the gateway there are four large square stone pillars, 16 feet high, 3 broad and 2 thick, with flowery ornaments. This foundation corresponds with a similar one (No. 15) about a hundred yards[†] distant towards the east, in the plain below; and the two form nearly a straight line with a very ancient temple situated on the sea shore.

From the front of Krishna's Choultry, on looking towards the south-west, may be seen on the top of the hill, a small *dilapidated building* (No. 16) quite in ruins.

Beneath this is an *excavation*[‡] in the side of the hill (No. 17) of a rectangular shape, measuring 25 feet long, 18 feet deep, and 10 feet 6 inches high. The front is adorned by two neatly finished pillars and two pilasters. At each end are imperfect traces and outlines of a group of figures; and on each side of the excavation in front is a neatly finished niche, 3 feet high, 3 feet deep, and 2 feet 6 inches wide. In front of the whole is the skeleton of a verandah 48 feet long, 12 feet high, and 12 feet wide. Steps are cut in the side of the hill, at one end of the

[* It is said to be the commencement of a Gopuram.]

[† The distance is more nearly 800 yards.]

[‡ Called Râmânujaiyyar Mandapam. There is a short inscription on the floor.]

verandah, by which there is an easy ascent to the top of it.

At a few yards distance to the eastward, is a stone bed, with an elevation at the north end of it for a seat or pillow. The bed is 7 feet 3 inches long, and 3 feet 9 inches broad, and the pillow is 10 inches high.

On the eastern face of the easternmost of the detached rocks near this place, may be seen another group of sculptures, representing the same story of Arjuna ; but the figures are not so distinct as the former, nor equally numerous, and they appear to have suffered much more from the weather.

On the summit of the most southern eminence of the mountain is a *small ruined temple* of sculptured stone (No. 18) 22 feet in length, 16 feet in breadth, and 16 in height.* Its foundation, which is of brick, measures 30 feet by 26. There is no regular access to it : the roof has fallen in, and the temple is partially covered by an old banyan tree. There is a fine open view of the surrounding country from the top of its walls.

Directly beneath, and cut into the same rock on which this little fane is built, is an excavated temple (No. 19) 33 feet long, 13 feet high, and 17 feet deep. In front are four columns, (one of which is broken), and pilasters at each end. The excavation contains three niches, of which the centre one is the principal ; it has a sort of portal before it, and contains a group of figures representing Mahádeva, Párvatí,

[* Called by the Brahmans Arákkamei (ஜ்ரக்கெண்மெய்) temple, as one ollock (about 1½ gill) of oil used formerly to be expended daily for lighting it. This temple once, it is said, contained a lingam.]

their infant son Subrahmanya, five other figures and a bull, (Nandi).* The bull is in front of the principal figures, and on its back rests one of the feet of Mahádeva, and one of those of Párvatí. In the floor of this principal niche is a circular trench, 4 feet 6 inches in diameter, and about 3 inches deep, in the centre of which is a circular hole 16 inches in diameter, intended probably for the reception of a lingam. The other niches contain no sculptures. The portal before the centre niche projects from the back wall 8 feet 6 inches, and has a frontage of 11 feet. The front of this is sustained by two sculptured columns, and it has pilasters where it joins the wall.

This excavation, however, is chiefly remarkable for the sculptures executed on its side walls. These represent, the one, one of Vishnu's states of existence, and the other a celebrated conflict between Durgà and Mahishâsura.

I shall first speak of that on the south-western side representing Vishnu. Previously, however, it will be necessary to observe that considerable uncertainty attaches to Nárâyana,† or the state or mode of being in which Vishnu here appears. Hindu Mythology sometimes speaks of it as a mode of existence of Brahmâ, sometimes of Siva, and sometimes

_____

[* On Mount Kailâsa, the "residence of Kuvera, and favorite haunt of Siva."—Wilson.]

[† A name of Vishnu, but especially considered as the deity who was before all worlds. The word has several etymologies. That given by Manu is "he whose resting-place (ayana) was on the primeval waters (nárá)," so called because they are the offspring of Nara, the embodied deity. See Wilson's Sans. Dict. under Nárâyana, Goldstücker's Dict. under अयन, Muir's Sanscrit Texts Part IV., p. 26 ff., and Wilson's Vishnupurâna, 8vo. edn. by Hall, Vol. I. pp. 55—59.]

of Vishnu in the act of willing the creation.* Under this character Vishnu is represented lying on the lotus, as well as on the thousand-headed serpent Sesha.

The sculpture now spoken of is in bas-relief, and measures 13 feet in length and 8 in height. The figure of Vishnu is 9 feet 6 inches long, recumbent on the snake Sesha, which is ingeniously coiled for his support in several convolutions, forming together a couch 3 feet high from the base ; while five of its heads, (as many as could well be introduced,) form a kind of canopy over the head of the supposed deity.† Above the god are two small figures, male and female ; below him in front in a kneeling posture, three ; and at his feet erect, two. All these but the last are diminutive ; but the two at his feet are seven feet high, and one of them grasps a club. The village brahmans say that two of the figures in front repre-

[* See passage from the Náradiyapurána translated by Vans Kennedy,—Researches, p. 209.]

† This representation of Vishnu must be very similar to the following. "Hari is one of the titles of Vishnu, the deity in his preserving quality. Nearly opposite Sultan Ganj, a considerable town in the province of Bahar, there stands a rock of granite, forming a small island in the Ganges, known to Europeans by the name of the Rock Jehangiri, which is highly worthy of the traveller's notice for a vast number of images, carved in relief upon every part of its surface. Among the rest there is Hari, of a gigantic size, recumbent on a coiled serpent, whose heads, which are numerous, the artist has contrived to spread into a canopy over the sleeping god ; and from each of its mouths issues a forked tongue, seeming to threaten instant death to any whom rashness might prompt to disturb him. The whole lies almost clear of the block on which it is hewn. It is finely imagined and executed with great skill. The Hindoos are taught to believe, that at the end of every Calpa (creation), all things are absorbed into the deity, and that in the interval of another creation, he reposeth himself upon the serpent Sesha (duration)."—Wilkins' Hitopadesa. B.

sant cow-keepers, who had been ill-used by Mahishásura. These cow-keepers (husband and wife) had
come to complain to Vishnu. Before they did so,
however, they had inquired of the third figure, said
to be a "Sástrakáran," or sorcerer, as to the precise time when they might have a propitious opportunity. That while they were making the inquiry,
one of the attendants of Mahishásura, the figure bearing the club, came to carry them to his master, to
punish them for daring to appeal to Vishnu. The
other figure at the feet of Vishnu hereupon interposed,
and being one of Vishnu's attendants, drove from his
master's presence the presumptuous servant of the
wicked Mahishásura. The expression and postures
of the figures do certainly seem to correspond with the
story; but the tale itself suits ill the position and
circumstances of Vishnu Náráyana, which no doubt
is represented in this sculpture.

The sculptures on the opposite or north-eastern end
of the temple represent the conflict between Durgá,
(a personification* of active, not passive, virtue), and
Mahishásura, (a personification of wickedness.) These
figures merit particular description.

The recess in which they are sculptured is 12 feet

* The Devatás are represented as good beings, the Asurás as evil
ones, in so far only as there is any countenance to the fiction of
personified virtue and vice. That fiction is European. All that I
have ever read makes the Asuras blameable because of acquired
power; and power is subdued by superior skill or force. In some
instances the Asuras are described as cheated, injured, oppressed,
rebelling in consequence, and then subdued and destroyed. The
story of Durgá and Mahishásura is the subject of the Chandipátha of
the Skándapuránat; and is the great occasion of celebration at Calcutta in the Durgápújá feast, which is anything but virtuous. W. T.

(† The Chandipátha is a portion of the Márkandeyapuráne. See
note * p. 101, infra. Also Appendix.]

9 inches long and 8 feet high. To the left is seen Durgā, mounted on what is intended for a fierce lion. To the right is Mahishásura grasping a short thick club. The figure of Durgā is 5 feet high and eight-handed : two of her arms have greater relief than the others, a circumstance which imparts to the figure a much greater appearance of truth and nature than would otherwise be the case. The left principal arm is stretched at full length, and the hand grasps a bow : the right arm is drawn back, as if in the act of discharging an arrow : but we see neither the arrow nor the string of the bow. Her six remaining hands hold respectively, on the left, a bell, a sankha, and something not easily distinguishable ; and on the right, the fatal cord (pása,) a chakra (discus), and a sword. Mahishásura is represented with a buffalo's head and horns and a human body. He stands in a retiring attitude, resting on his left foot, the right being advanced. His figure measures 7 feet 9 inches, not perpendicularly, but according to the posture in which he stands. Above, below, and behind Durgā, may be seen her attendant warriors, armed with swords and bucklers : and also two domestics, one with a switch of hair* such as horsekeepers use, the other with a kittisal (or umbrella). Mahishásura has a similar attendant also. Durgā's attendants are all dwarfish, corpulent figures ; those of Mahishásura seem of more natural proportions. Durgā appears the assailant, Mahishásura on the defensive. Of three figures between the two principal personages, two are in active conflict,

[* Chámara (chaurī), the tail of the Yak (Bos grunniens or Poëphagus), used to whisk off flies, also as an emblem or insignia of princely rank.—Wilson.]

and the third is falling headlong.   One between the
legs of Mahishásura seems to have fallen ; and
another of the same party supports himself on his
left hand, two fingers of the right being held up to
indicate discomfiture and alarm.   The whole group
is executed with much skill and ability, and evinces
the talent of the artist.   The figure of Durgá in
particular is represented with much spirit, and is
graceful and easy.   The following from a paper by
Mr. Wilkins in the 1st Vol. of the Asiatic Researches, serves to illustrate the story.   "The evil
"spirit Mahishásura, in the disguise of a *buffalo* as
"the name imports, had fought with Indra and his
"celestial bands for a hundred years, defeated him
"and usurped his throne : the story is to be found at
"length in a little book called Chandí.*   The van-
"quished spirits being banished the heavens, and
"doomed to wander the earth, after a while assem-
"ble, and resolve to lay their grievances before
"Vishnu and Śiva.   Conducted by Brahmá they
"repaired into the presence of those deities, who
"heard their complaint with compassion, and their
"anger was so violent against Mahishásura, that a
"kind of flame issued from their mouths, and from
"the mouths of the rest of the principal gods, of
"which was formed a goddess of inexpressible beauty
"with ten arms, and each hand holding a different
"weapon.   This was a transfiguration of Bhaváni,

[* The Chandípátha, or Devímáhátmya, of the Márkandeyapurána,
" in which the victories of the goddess [Chandí, Deví, Kálí or Durgá]
over different evil beings or Asuras are detailed with considerable
power and spirit.   It is daily read in the temple of Durgá, and furnishes
the pomp and circumstance of the great festival of Bengal, the
Durgápújá."—Wilson, Preface to the Vishnupurána.   See also Muir's
Sanscrit Texts, Part IV., p. 370 ff.]

"the consort of *Siva*, under which she is generally
"called Durgá." She is sent against the usurper.
"She mounts her Lion, the gift of the mountain
"Himálayat (snowy), and attacks the monster, who
"shifts his form repeatedly : till at length the god-
"dess planteth her foot upon his head, and cuts it off
"with a single stroke of her sword. Immediately
"the upper part of a human body issues through
"the neck of the headless buffalo, and aims a stroke,
"which being warded off by the Lion with his right
"paw, Durgá puts an end to the combat, by piercing
"him through the heart with a spear." The reader
will observe that the latter part of this story does
not correspond entirely with the sculpture just
described, but this must not surprise us, for the
Hindu Poets, Sculptors, and Painters, seem to claim
the license of representing the same action in a
thousand different ways, and under a thousand
different versions.‡

I am tempted here to transcribe the following
lines, written by Sir William Jones, in reference to
this subject :—

> "§ O Durgá, thou hast deign'd to shield
> Man's feeble virtue with celestial might,

[* Bhavání, wife of Bhava (Siva) is the name given to Párvatí in
her pacific and amiable form, she being called Durgá in her terrific
form.—Wilson.]

[† The abode (álaya) of snow (hima), personified as Himavat the
mythical father of Umá or Durgá—hence her patronymic Haimavatí,
"daughter of Himavat," or Párvatí, "daughter of the mountain."]

[‡ Cp. plate 33 in Moor's Hindu Pantheon.]

§ It is now almost universally admitted that Sir W. Jones rallied
his great talents by writing hymns to Hindu gods. They all borrow
scriptural or classical ideas, and paint the personifications of India
with colors not their own. The leading idea in these lines is not
Hindu, but European. W. T.

Gliding from yon jasper field,
  And, on a lion borne, hast brav'd the fight ;
For, when the demon Vice thy realms defied,
  And arm'd with death each archod horn,
Thy golden lance, O goddess mountain-born,
  Touch but the pest—He roar'd and died,"

Marks of the workman's chisel may be seen on a large block of granite, opposite the front of this excavation; and also at a few yards to the north-east of it, on a rough hewn stone, intended for a bed, with an elevation at one end for a pillow. The bed measures 10 feet 6 inches by 4 feet 9 inches: the pillow is 2 feet broad and 12 inches high. There are two small steps at the foot of the bed.

On some of the rocks between this place and Krishna's Choultry may be seen the rude commencement of several designs, which have been abandoned. Amongst them, however, is a finished excavation 21 feet long, 17 deep, and 9 high. The roof is sustained by four strong pillars. There are three niches in this excavation, with the outlines of a figure on each side of the centre niche. There is also a long inscription on the south-west end, now almost illegible.

About a mile to the south of the village in a small palmyra tope is a cluster of monolithic temples. It consists of five,* each differing from the rest in shape and dimensions, and each fashioned out of a detached solid mass of rock.

The first I shall notice stands a little to the west of the others, (No. 20), and is in shape similar to a horse-shoe.† It is a neat piece of sculpture 18 feet

---

* At a second visit to the place I understood that the sculptor's idea was the construction of five dwellings for the five Pândavas. W. T.

[† Called by the Brahmans the Raths of Nakula and Sahadeva, the youngest two of the five Pândavas.]

in length, 11 feet in width, and about 16 feet in height. At the south end, that which is right-angled, is a roughly hewn niche, and a portal with two pillars.

The four other temples lie nearly in a straight line ; but before describing them I would notice an image of a lion* and another of an elephant, both as large as life, which stand between this small temple and the other four. That of the lion is cracked. It measures in length 7 feet, and round the neck 8 feet : it is sunk in the earth about knee deep ; nevertheless it has a noble appearance and its body is well proportioned. The elephant measures 14 feet in length and 12 feet in height. Its circumference in the largest part of its body is about 20 feet : round its head and throat, 14 feet ; and round the largest part of the proboscis, 7 feet. It appears somewhat unfinished, and is sunk a little in the earth.

On the eastern side of the temples, near the most northern one, is a colossal Brahmany Bull, (Nandi, the vehicle of Siva.) Its head and neck only appear above ground : the length of the former being 4 feet, and the distance between the roots of the horns 3 feet 3 inches.

Of the temples, the most northern (No. 21)† is a neat little structure about 16 or 18 feet high and 11 feet square. The top diminishes on all sides by a parabolic curve, till it ends in a ridge 3 or 4 feet long. It has a niche on the western side, in which is a group of figures said to represent Draupadi, the wife of Dharmarája.‡ My own idea is that it represents one

---

* Lion, the symbol of kingly power : elephant—that of great prosperity ; and in particular the vehicle of Indra, [called Airávata.] W. T.

[†Called Draupadi's Ratha.]   [‡ And of his four brothers.]

of the consorts of Vishnu or Siva. A female figure
is also sculptured on each side of the entrance to the
niche.

The temple next to this (No. 22)* towards the
south is of a pyramidal shape, and covered with
ornamental sculpture. It is about 11 feet in front,
16 in depth, and 30 in height. It is much cracked,
has a niche on the same face as the last, but there
are no figures within.

The largest temple in the group (No. 23)† stands
next in order ;‡ it was abandoned before the design
was completed and remains in an unfinished state.
Across the middle there is a large rent, in some parts
3 or 4 inches wide ; this has divided the body of the
temple, and caused the separation of a large piece of
the solid stone on the western side about the centre
of the verandah. Another large piece has fallen from
the south-western corner. Unfinished excavated
verandahs exist round the lower part : and above
them, on the outside, the body of the temple diminishes in width and length, so as to leave sufficient
space to walk round it. The verandah on the south-
eastern or sea-face of the temple is almost choked up
with sand ; but that on the opposite face retains its
original height, and in it a large block of the solid
stone projects from the back wall. The roof or top

[* The Brahmans have named this Arjuna's Ratha.]

[† Called Bhima's Ratha.]

‡ Mr. Braddock has by an oversight omitted to give the measurements of this temple. I therefore supply them from Mr. Goldingham's
account ; although I must here observe that in other measurements
as given by them respectively I find some trifling discrepancy. Mr.
Goldingham's says that the temple measures 42 feet by 25 feet, and
35 feet in height. M.

14

of this temple is elliptical, and the general design is
beautiful and elegant.

The last and most southern temple of the group
(No. 34)[*] is of a pyramidal shape : its base measures
28 feet by 27, and it is 34 feet in height. It is neatly
finished and much ornamented. In the two upper
stories on the north-western face are niches ; and on
the ground story of the same face is a portal with four
pillars, projecting from the body of the temple 4 feet.
Besides the ornaments which it possesses in common
with the rest, this temple has a profusion of figures
of various sizes, representing Vishnu and Siva, in
some of the many different characters which they
sustain in the mythology of the natives. These figures
are carved in recesses corresponding with their size ;
and over the majority of them are inscriptions, of
which and of the figures, lithographed sketches may
be seen in the transactions of the Royal Asiatic
Society before alluded to.

About 3 miles to the south of the village, on the
sea shore, are several granite rocks, one of which
inclining to the eastward projects about 40 feet above
the surface like a huge pillar. On another are sculptured various figures representing heads of fierce
horned animals, of the precise appearance of which
it would be difficult to give a written description.
Returning towards the village, about half a mile
north of the village choultry, we meet with a small
temple built of hewn stone, and resembling in its
ornaments those already described.[†] The entrance is
nearly filled with sand, and the walls are much

[* This is called Dharmarāja's Ratha.]
[† Said to be a Jain temple, and called Muknadantyār Kōvil.]

dilapidated by trees which grow out of them.　There
is nothing, I believe, inside.

The last of these ancient remains to be described,
are two temples (No. 26) built eastward from the
village close to the sea shore.　They are indeed so
near the sea that the surf dashes against the foundations of them.　They occupy a space of about
1,600 square feet and are becoming ruinous.　They
adjoin each other, being in some sense but one piece
of building; but the existence of their two spires
impresses one with an idea of their being two
separate temples.[*]　The more lofty structure I
imagine to be about 60 feet high.　This is the most
eastern of the two, and has, overlooking the sea,
a doorway 7 feet 6 inches high and 6 feet wide.
Within this temple will be found a large broken
black granite Lingam,[†] and a group of sculptures
representing Mahàdeva, Pàrvatî, and their son Kàrtikeya or Subrahmanya.[‡]　The smaller temple contains a similar group of figures.　The body of the
large temple is inclosed with a massive stone wall,
which as well as the temple itself bears the appearance of having been decorated with much ornamented
sculpture.　Small pieces of chunam still adhering to
the ornaments give rise to the conjecture that the
temples were either originally coated with it, or have
been so covered in subsequent repairs.　There can,

[* Cp. Guldana, infra.]

[† It is sixteen-sided, with a perimeter of 6 feet 9 inches.]

[‡ The latter name is that generally used in South India.　The son
of Siva is called Kàrtikeya because he was nursed by the Krittikâs,
the personified Pleiades, and Subrahmanya because he is the special
guardian of the Brahmanical order.　For the origin of another of his
names, Skanda, see Muir's Sanscrit Texts, Part IV., p. 296.]

I think, be no doubt that they were once elegant specimens of architecture; though they are now too much decayed to retain many traces of their original beauty.* The mineralogist might possibly form some idea of their age from an inspection of the several species of granite of which the walls are composed. Some kinds of this rock, it is known, are much more liable to decomposition than others, (gneiss especially); and the fact is here evident; some of the stones are very much decayed, while others appear as sound as on the day they were hewn. In a kind of passage of the larger temple is a large mutilated statue of Vishnu, now lying supine.†

These temples were formerly surrounded by an outer stone wall, part of which only is now standing. Two pillars also remain shewing the position of the western gateway.

Huge heaps of granite stones, on several of which are sculptured figures, lie in front and on each side of the eastern temple, and have tended greatly to protect it from the hostility of the sea, which has evidently encroached considerably. Many of these stones are of large dimensions, measuring from 6 to 10 feet long, 3 feet wide, and 1 foot thick; and on some of them are appearances of sculptured architectural ornaments, though the injuries of the weather, the action of the water, and the lapse of time have combined to deface them. About 65 feet in front of the eastern temple, and now standing in the sea, is a

[* "Mr. Fergusson, in his 'Ancient Architecture of Hindostan' declares it [the larger temple] to be with the single exception of the Pagoda at Tanjúr, the finest and most important Vimāna in the south of India."—Murray's Hand-Book of India, Part 1, p. 31.]

[† See p. 34, supra.]

square stone pillar, (a common appendage, I believe, to all the country pagodas), which measures 11 foot in height and is 22 inches square.*

At a few yards north of the temples, on a detached rock (No. 27) close by the sea, may be observed a gigantic figure of Mahishásura represented with the head of a buffalo.   On a similar detached rock to the south are figures of a horse and an elephant's head (No. 28).   These sculptures are considerably worn by the continual washing and action of the surf.†

There is no doubt in my mind that the sea has made considerable encroachments since the erection of these temples.   I cannot conceive, were it not so, why they should have been built on the shore, so close to the sea that the surf in the calmest weather dashes against the doorway ; while some of the well known appendages of such pagodas are actually at some distance in the waters.   The large quantities of stones lying about the temple, and others which partially appear buried in the sea, seem even to indicate that other buildings also have existed to the eastward of these, which are now destroyed and overwhelmed by the ocean.

I have now given an account of all the curious sculptures and buildings which came under my observation at three several visits to the Seven Pagodas, and I believe I have omitted nothing which merits notice.   I am fully aware that the account is imperfect : indeed, I hold it impossible to convey a correct idea of the remains of former ages by a written description, even if the account be per-

[* See note † p. 11, and note ‡ p. 51, supra. Also Gubbins, infra.]
[† There are a number of sculptured bulls (Nandi) lying among the rocks close to the temple on the south side.]

fectly accurate. Who could by such means form a just conception of the actual appearance of the ruins of ancient Persepolis, of Tadmor in the desert, of Pompeii, of the various temples in Italy, and the remains of classic elegance in Greece and the Isles of the Ægean Sea? We may indeed read of pillars, colonades, porticoes, rooms, baths, apartments, and a long list of architectural definitions ; but after all, the mind possesses but an imperfect image of the originals. Pictures and drawings help the description, but personal inspection is best of all. I therefore advise you, "gentle reader," if you have it in your power, to visit these singular vestiges of antiquity at Mämallaipur. I can promise you ample recompense for your trouble. If you have antiquarian curiosity, you may here satisfy it. If you have any disposition to moralize,—as a Christian should do,—on the end of human greatness, you will see that though here it has been attempted to "grave it in the rock for ever," it still passes away ; and you will turn your thoughts from these, amongst the most durable perhaps of mortal productions, to that heavenly city which is indeed eternal.

Remarks by the Rev. W. Taylor.

The author of the foregoing paper having done me the honor of transmitting it to me for perusal and remark ; and the few cursory observations made having called forth a fuller explanation of his wishes, —although I do not think myself fully able to meet them,—I offer the few following observations on the locality which is the subject of his interesting illustrations.

PLAN OF
MĀMALLAPUR

1. The Name.* This the people of the neighbourhood colloquially term *Măvalivaram*. It is also known to natives as *Măbalipuram*, whence I presume, it became expanded (by Mr. Goldingham if I remember aright) into *Mahábalipuram*. More recently I observe Dr. Babington has made it *Mahámalaipúr*, "the town of the great" (or as Dr. Babington understands it, sacred) "hill." If the said reading be actually borne out by the old Tamil inscription near one of the caves, I must submit; but without copy, or fac-simile, the accuracy of the reading may be open to doubt. There is considerable reason* to believe that the true reading is *Mămallapuram*; and the true reading is of consequence.

Malla is a northern patronymic, or rather titular name of a race, like Cæsar, or the Medicis, or the Bourbons. In local papers of the Mackenzie collections, obscure but numerous indications are given of a race of chieftains bearing that surname; of whom Deva-malla-ráya is most frequently mentioned. This chieftain was a (Peninsular) highlander in origin; not, properly speaking, Hindu, but of an aboriginal race. Now Deva-malla-ráya indicates dignity and lineage: of which title Mă-malla-rája, would be almost an equivalent; indicating indeed a lower rank, but quite suited as a distinctive epithet of a minor offset from the parent stem. Again in the Mackenzie

[* See Appendix.]

* According to legendary tradition, one named Mallásuda ruled in early times. He seems not to have been a Hindu, as he mocked a Brahman, and was metamorphosed into an alligator. An appearance of Vishnu is said to have occurred. Before that appearance the place was called *Mallapuri* and *Mallapuri-kshatram*, from the above Mal-Mandu. Mackenzie MSS., Book No. 33, C. M. 767, Sec. 9. This paper is in the Telugu language.

local papers, there is abundant evidence of a gradual
progress of colonization by Telugu people, from
proximity to the Godavery southwards, at least as
far as Nellore; and various instances[*] occur in
which those who first cleared forest land and began
to build a town, gave their own names to the town
so formed. I would not assert it as a fact, but
I regard it as a probable inference, that the
locality, in immediate question, derived its name
from its founder, an offset, or junior branch, of the
Malla chieftains in the north. I would not leave the
name without noticing that in a modern Tamil poem
written in the south, mention is made of the king of
Máaliwinam: but whether this place be designated
or not, is doubtful; and I do not think such an
authority could be trusted.—Quitting the name of
the place we may further advert to

II. The antiquity, or probable antiquity, of the
sculptures. That the antiquity is not very great may
be concluded by inferential deductions; as 1. The
mythology of the figures is Hindu; the general story,

---

[*] Subsequent to Sal. Sak. 424, or A. D. 502, a person named Mahimalu, or Mavalamu, left his native place owing to oppression; emigrated southerly, and built a village of four or five mud huts. It was
called after the founder Mavamaldr. It increased; and by a separation of brothers at a later date Nandi-varam was founded, ultimately
a town of note. Ibid. Book 49, C. M. 739.

This is merely an illustration. From a yet unpublished abstract of
another paper, I find that two persons named Malla-ráya and Annama-
deva-ráya, emigrated from Vijayanagaram to the district of Arcot,
or neighbourhood of Conjevaram, and obtained some immunities from
the wife, or queen, of Deva-ráyar. These people were of the tribe
of athletæ, proceeding from the original stock of mountaineers. I
cannot identify these persons with Mámalla-puri. At a period later
than Krishna-ráyar, there were four avenues leading from Conjevaram
to distinguished towns, one of which was Mahâbalipuram, then reputed to be of Vaishnava credence.

part of that contained in the Mahábhárata ; the language of the inscriptions, at least in some places, Sanscrit : therefore Brahmans were some way concerned. But there is much concurring evidence to show that the first immigration of Brahmans to the Peninsula was not of remote antiquity. Besides which consideration, 2. It is beyond doubt that before the time of Kulóttunga Cholan, and his illegitimate son Adondai, the whole district bounded on the north by the Pennár, on the south by the Pálâr, on the east by the sea, and on the west by the ghâts, was dwelt in by half-civilized people termed Kurumbar, who had embraced the Jaina religion, brought to them from the north. Adondai chiefly distinguished Káñchí-puram (Conjeveram) and Tripâti, as his places of residence, or capitals. The era of Adondai is not higher up than the seventh century of our reckoning. He is said to have brought the Brahmans from Sri Sailam in Telingána, and certainly attracted a large colony of Sudra Vellâras, or agriculturists, from Tuluva or northern Canara. Soon after him the kingdom, which he acquired by the sword, was broken up into petty principalities, and lapsed into a state of partial anarchy. As we can distinctly trace the founding of Vellore to a period later than Adondai, and to colonization led on by a northern chief, so about the same period, I am inclined to think, the neighbourhood of Múvalivaram was colonized from the north, by one of the Malla family with his clan. Besides, 3. The Inscriptions are in too perfect a state of preservation to be of remote date. As far as my knowledge extends, inscriptions, with a defined year, have not been met with, in a legible state, higher up than the

tenth century.   I am aware of one or two *apparent*
instances of much higher date, but with the absence
of any precise year : hence inconclusive.   Fragments
of inscriptions in the Páṇḍya kingdom, (the oldest
one in the south,) have I believe generally been so
worn as to be incapable of connected transcription.
But the appearance of the chiselling at Mávalivaram, (from the distant recollection of about fifteen
years), is such that it would tax my credulity greatly
to assign them a more distant date than from three
to five hundred years.

If then we inquire into

III.   The origin, or probable origin, of the place
with its sculptures, my own judgment would lead
me to fix the possible origin of the settlement at
Mávalivaram to a colonist family of the Malla tribe ;
subsequent to the rule of Adoṇḍai, and previous to
the ascendancy of the Vijayanagaram ascendancy in
the present Carnatic ; that is, (loosely stated),
between the twelfth and sixteenth centuries of our
reckoning.   In this opinion I am guided by analogy.
The Bhonju family, in that manner, spread itself in
a district ; afterwards subject to the Gajapati princes
of Orissa.   The Malla family, from wild mountaineers, became powerful chieftains in Telingána.
Many families, in that way, made subordinate settlements in different village districts of the same
country ; and, about the period above indicated,
some heads of families emigrated from the Karnátaka-
desa proper, and became local chieftains ; while
many others at a later period, and from different
causes, followed a like course.   But if I am right in
this inference by analogy, it does not follow that a
settlement, made in a before pastoral, or waste,

sedentary, would at once become a place of power or consequence. The same mode of argument would suggest the need of some centuries, in order to produce such a result; and we know that many mutations occur in such kind of states, when near powerful neighbours. Accordingly though the name of the founder may have continued, yet, the conquest of the South, begun by Kriahna-raya of Vijayanagaram, and completed by Achynta-raya, probably* overwhelmed any such principality. Such was the case with the before local powers at Ginjee, and at Tanjore. In those places military commanders became viceroys, and their descendants, kings. And I think it probable that a chief of this latter origin from Karnátaka proper, (borrowing the idea from Ellora), had the excavations and sculptures made and the inscriptions recorded; especially those in the Hala Kannada character and Sanscrit language:

* In my abstract of the Tamil manuscript entitled Karnátaka-rájikal, I do not find definite mention of such a supersession; but I think it probable from the general conquest of the neighbourhood; and suppose the district became subject to the local metropolis of Ginjee. In the paper referred to (note a) it is stated that Sinhama-náyadu of the Vellagativáru race ruled at Márali-varam, and employed many artificers, who resorted thither in a time of famine, in making excavations and sculptures on the hill. Following out this indication, I observe that Tschinna-náyadu and Sinhama-náyadu of that race fought a great battle and gained a victory over opposing chiefs in Sál. Sak. 1523 (A. D. 1601). By that time the power of the Vijaya-nagaram sovereigns was broken; and it said the Mahommedans were concerned in the affair, in connexion with Ginjee and Vellore. The scene of combat was Ootramaloor. This period would mark another change of power superseding the supposed, or rather inferred authority of the viceroys from Vijayanagaram. And if Sinhama-náyadu subsequently employed stone-cutters in the sculptures, then we have the period fixed to the seventeenth century. It is not however absolutely necessary to suppose that all the works were begun by the same chief, or finished (in so far as finished) by the same hands.

of parts of one' of which Dr. Babington has
given a copy and translation. If this inference
approximate to truth, the works alluded to must
have been accomplished in the sixteenth or seventeenth century.

These cursory remarks may be concluded with

IV. Miscellaneous observations; chiefly suggested by Dr. Babington's paper in the 2nd volume of
Transactions of the Royal Asiatic Society; the latest
essay on the subject, of which I have any knowledge.
The value of that paper seems principally to be in
the plates, from drawings and inscriptions, and especially in the deciphering and translation of the latter.
They prove, (as such inscriptions usually prove) very
unsatisfying: for this reason perhaps, that the objects
in the mind of the recorder, and in that of the archæo-
logist, are entirely different.   Of the six inscriptions
at this place, to be found in a volume of the Mackenzie MSS., five are of unimportant donations,
(including, if I mistake not, the Tamil one mentioned by Dr. Babington ;) and one which is of larger
import, has only the name of Deva-ráya' a clue

---

* In that incomplete inscription on the "small monolithic pagoda,"
neither date nor proper name of the king or chief appears. Rája-
rája is a mere epithet, and the other name appears to me strange and
quite unusual if applied to the ruler. I throw out the conjecture that
Jayarasa is a Sanscrit word modified into Tamil. Stambha is pure
Sanscrit for a post, column, or pillar. Jaya-stambha is of frequent
usage for a triumphal column, or pillar of victory. I would render
Jayarana Stambha by "the pillar of the victorious one," without
however insisting on being right, because the construction is a little
forced ; and merely add that possibly Sinhama-náyada may have had
the pillar and the inscription cut to commemorate the victory at
Oetramaloor : still however preferring the opinion before given.

* Connecting this note with note b, I think the same Deva-ráya
may be meant, but am not certain. There was only one (I believe)

to the date.   Now this might be Achyuta-deva-râya,
who was very liberal to Conjeveram : or some one
later, even a local chieftain ; but not, I conceive, any
one of the Vijayanagaram dynasty higher up than
Achyuta-râya.

The paper by Dr. Babington appears to me to
contain some minor inaccuracies,[/] on which it
might be trifling, or invidious, to dwell ; but the
supposition that the place was merely an Agrahâra,
and that Brahmans procured the sculptures to be
made at their own cost,—with the more astounding
denial, that the sea has encroached on the Coast of
Coromandel, are not of trifling import.   As to the
first, it contradicts all known experience, in so far
only as relates to Brahmans laying out funds at their
own entire control, on such sort of works.   The
second is a point of greater magnitude.   I regard the

of the older Vijayanagaram dynasty that bore that name without any
prefix.   He ruled about 841. Sak. 1334, or A. D. 1412.   In these dates
I follow one MS. authority, without deciding that it is the best.   A list
with different dates may be seen in Mr. Campbell's Telugu gram-
mar; in which also instead of simply Deva-râya we read Gauda-
Deva-râya.   But after Krishna-deva-râya all of the second dynasty
bear it with a distinctive prefix.   Probability inclines to the lower
period, between S. S. 1461 and 1588, or A. D. 1539 and 1366.   Nevertheless it must not be forgotten that about A. D. 1400 the power of
the Râyas has been traced at Trichinopoly and Madura, in the person
of a general named Companna-udiyâr, who annihilated the remains
of the first Mahommedan incursion to the southward.   The state of
the modern Carnatic was however too unsettled to permit the supposition of the first Deva-râya making grants or donations within its
boundaries.

[/] It is not my wish to be very particular : however the statement
by Dr. Babington that " the copper and stone inscriptions found..........
in many parts of the country, are all in the Sanscrit language," does
not agree with the mention made by himself of a Tamil inscription
in or near the Varâha-mandapam ; nor with the recent discovery of
some, as is stated, Pâli inscriptions in the north.   But keeping within

few data on which the denial of any encroachment
of the sea is founded, as quite inconclusive ; though
this does not seem to be the place for their discussion, nor yet for the statement of contrary facts and
arguments.   It is a point on which I apprehend
Dr. Babington to be at issue with truth : but beyond
this mere expression of an opinion, it does not
seem important further to pursue the subject, in
these very cursory annotations.

_____

Having had an opportunity of reading over these
remarks after an interval of more than a year and a
half, and having seen, in the interim, copies of two
inscriptions from the neighbourhood of Mâvalivaram, in the Tamil language and old Tamil character,
I find that the spelling therein is _Mâmallaipûr_,
with two _l's._   The language is not the pure old
Tamil ; but the orthography is so generally correct,
that the two _l's_ cannot be an orthographical error ; and
if not, then the word does not mean _hill._   The language is comparatively modern Tamil ; being much
mixed with Sanscrit derivatives, which is not the
case with very old Tamil.   The name of Deva-râya
appears ; and an opinion seems to have been formed

the limits of the peninsula, the interests of truth require me to state
with entire respect, while touching on the subject, that the Mackenzie
papers contain many hundred copies of inscriptions in Canarese,
Telugu, Malayalam, and Tamil ; many of which I have examined, and
can attest that, though copies, they are not translations.   It is not an
unfrequent case to find inscriptions with florid Sanscrit slokas at the
beginning or end, with the real matter of fact in plainer prose of the
vernacular language.   The undeciphered part of the inscription given
by Dr. Babington requires further attention, for its present obscurity
may involve some such humbler termination.*

[* See Appendix.]

that it meant a Chola king. I cannot positively
deny such an inference ; nor yet another inference
that similarity of character in neighbouring inscriptions, must argue identity of origin. The subject is
confessedly open to variation of opinion ; and inquiry
would seem to be requisite before a decision can be
positively made.

_____

Supplement by Walter Elliot, Esq.

Besides the objects of interest usually visited at
the Seven Pagodas, there is a spot about two miles
north of Mahâmallaipûr, the sculptures and inscriptions at which will be found not unworthy of attention.   Proceeding along the sea-shore towards
Madras, at the distance above mentioned, a quadran-
gular space inclosed by mounds of considerable
extent, No. 31 in the map, called by the fishermen
Devanêri, will be observed.   From the appearance
of these mounds, added to the fact that numerous
copper coins, glass-beads, and bits of iron, copper,
&c., are picked up after heavy rain or high winds on
their surface, it might be supposed that they indicated the site of some ancient edifice or fortification :
but an excavation made in 1840, completely through
one side, failed to elicit any discovery in support of
such an opinion.   The section was carried, through
pure sand, to a depth of 20 feet, and the only
extraneous substances met with were some pieces
of charcoal, at different depths.

About quarter of a mile farther, near a collection of
fishermens' huts, called Sâluvan-Kuppam, are some
remarkable rocks, standing a considerable height
above the beach, and known by the name of Idaiyan

Pudal. One of these exhibits a niche or panel, surmounted by an arched border composed of the heads of the Sinha, or fabulous lion of Hindu mythology, carved in relief ; while another has been rough-hewn into the outline of the same animal. Beyond this is a stone Mandapam, or temple, almost entirely buried in the sand. Within is a Lingam. This is the site of the inscriptions referred to by Dr. Babington, in the 2nd Vol. of the Transactions of the Royal Asiatic Society, as having been sent to him by Colonel De Havilland. Of these Nos. 1 and 2 of plate 15, pronounced by Dr. Babington to be identical, are engraved on the end walls of the Mandapam on either hand of the entrance. On the frieze above the entrance likewise, occurs the word, in each of the two characters deciphered by Dr. Babington,

"ATIRANACHANDAPALLAVA"

At a little distance to the north-west of this temple, on a flat stone, (No. 32 in the map), level with the surface, occurs the following in old Tamil characters :—

அழிசி ஸ்ரீ இச்சதவபனஞர்க்கு மந்தவிட்பாரு மாப் பட்டில் திருவமிதிக்கு இருமாலிலபும் திருவிளாக்குக்கு சழஞ்ச பொன்னும் குடித்தது.

"Salutation! two Más[1] of land in Mápalli[2] for a sufficient daily mass offering, and a Karanja[3] of gold for maintaining a lamp, are granted to Ijjagatala[4] Tamkudr."

About 100 yards north of the Mandapam is a mass of natural rock, (No. 33 in the map), one end of

---

[1] A Má is a 20th part, [here of a Véli = 0.6157 acres.]
[2] Mápalli is probably the name of a field.
[3] Karanja, an ancient wright [= about 72 grains.]
[4] Ijjagatala Tamkudr "the Lord of this world." Tamkudr should probably be Tambkudr ; the title refers to Atiranachandavarma.

which is covered with a long inscription in ancient
Tamil. The character, as well as that on the flat
stone just mentioned, is quite different from those
above alluded to; but corresponds with the one first
described in Dr. Babington's paper, as "seen on a
face of rock by the side of the inner entrance to
the Varáhasvámi pagoda"[5] on the south side of the
hill at Mahámallaipúr, and of which an alphabet is
given in plate 13. The greater portion is buried
in the sand; but in 1840 this was cleared away,
and a transcript of the whole carefully made, of which
the following is a translation. The original in
modern characters is given at the end of this article;
(marked A.)

"Salutation!

"In the presence of TIRUVÁYKÁVU.[6]

"In the 37th year (Ándu) of the reign of TRIBHUVANAVIRADEVA,
"Sovereign of the three worlds,[7] who having taken (or holding)
"Madura, Íram (or Ceylon), and Karuvúr, and the crowned head of
"Pándiyan, made the Virábhishekam and Vijayábhishekam, (i.e., the
"lustrations of heroism and victory;............and, by the grace of
"ADIMÁRDÉVARA, in the temple of SUBRAHMANYA DEVAR, in the De-
"vadánam—Brahmadéyam—village[8] of Tiruvirichilúr, in the Amur
"............of the victorious Cholamandalam:

"We Ásálbi Tillai Náyakar, the overseer[9] of (the temple of) Sri
"MAHÉVARA; Chámbiya Múvénda Vélán, the steward[10] of this tem-
"ple; Pan Máhasvara Battan, otherwise called Á.Áronda Villi Bhúp-

---

[5] Page 363, [p. 53, supra.]

[6] This is read in two senses. Some explain Tiruváykávu as Saraswati, the
goddess of learning; while others read the invocation thus, May the
Ágamas and Vedas be pre-eminent.

[7] Tribhuvanachakravartigal, a repetition of the King's titular name.

[8] Granted for the support of the gods and of Brahmans.

[9] Kánigkal, literally a watchman or superintendent.

[10] Srikáryam or chief servant

14

" pirân, a Siva Brahman, having proprietary right[11] in this temple
" and officiating in it[11]; Nârpattonnâyira Battan, also named Âtadaiyân
" Jñânam Paṭṭân, a Siva Brahman, having proprietary right in this
" temple and officiating in it; and Tiruvirichiludaiyân, the accountant
" of this temple; all of us have sold the lands, (herein undermention-
" ed), and executed a deed engraved on stone, in favour of Ânâr Ka-
" ruppûrudaiyân Nambi Aspota Kûttar,[12] performing his adorations
" in this temple. The lands, which we sold to this person because the
" revenue[13] in the treasury[14] of the god has proved deficient, on
" account of the decrease in the collections (or assessment[15]) of Tiruvi-
" richilûr, the property of the sacred name[16] of Pillaiyâr, are as
" follows :

> " In Peri yâri Karani,   Kuri
> " { Adaḷkâdu Tonkhtan.......................180
> " { Attipattan................................990
> " In Ûnal âri Karani,
> " { Âdi Mallai Nâtan
> " { Redtai Chanuru
> " In Tengam Karavu or Aspota Kûttan,
> " { Tâichoruvu [?]
> " { Urâkkuudil
> " { Pâratni   .
> " { In Firâdu Karavu
> " { Cultee Karuvu
> " amounting to Kuri..................2,930

[11] Kâni

[12] Devarkanmi-kshetra.

[13] Kûttan is still a title of the nobler class of Tulavers on the Neil-
gherry Hills.

[14] In the Badsmagaddi, the meaning of this word is given as
Kaḍirkana, the ryot's share.

[15] a sacred treasury. Hence, in the Travancore state, the
terms employed for that Sircar; to intimate that the Government is under
the especial protection of the deity.

[16]

[17] a respectful mode of describing the property of
the god.

In Tulai Sari Pālam,

    " Udaiya Nambi

    " Kottamānu

    " Kulittāgi

    " Sivadāsa

    " Pattavritti

    " amounting to Kuris.................1,440

                          " Total Kuris...4,150

                   " Being Nilams 2, Mā 1¼.[*]

" This extent 2 Nilams, 1½ Mā, and also the building site and
" garden containing 400 Kuris situated to the east of Aapuṭa Kūttan
" and Uvākkuvāḷ, we have sold to this person (aforesaid), to be his
" property, and have received its value, 300 new cash, into the
" Piḷḷaiyār's treasury, and engraved the deed (of sale) on a stone.

" Having consented (to his) irrigating these lands either naturally
" or artificially, and also conveying sufficiency of water to the trees,
" we engraved this on stone in favor of Karuppūrudaiyān Nambi
" Aapuṭa Kūttar.

    " We, the Proprietors of this Temple, have given.

    " Thus (Signed) Tillai Nāyaka.

    " Thus (   ) Pan Mahesvara Battan, or Āḷkoṇḍa Villi
                        Selvappirān, a Siva Brahman, having here-
                        ditary right in this temple and officiating in it.

    " Thus (   ) Āḍuttāyta Jñānam Pettān Nārpattesāyira Bat-
                        tan, a Siva Brahman, having hereditary right
                        in this temple and officiating in it.

    " Thus (   ) Siva [? Sri] Kāryam Uḍaittān Āḷudaiṉa Villan.

    " Thus (   ) Tiruvirichilodaiyān, accountant of this temple.

" I, Nārpattesāyira Pillai, of Tirupperiyūr, know this.

" I, Munichetta Nārāyana Bhattan, of Chisudāvūr, know this.

" I, Vēlān, of Chirodāvūr, Āmūr Nāṭṭu, know this.

" I, Periāndān, for Muran Kali Nesi and Nekkumaravu, [? Kali
Nesi, Manneeri, and Marava] of Māmbākam, know this.

<hr>

" I, Kurári Donaya Battan, of Paiyanár, know this.

" I, Mayindi Kuni [Nárâyana] Battan, [of Paiyanûr) know this.

" I, Vishambûr Kiravan, know this.

" I, Amûr Nâttu Vêlân, of Mâmallapuram, know this.

" I, Kuralaikbannî Maya Kirân Vichau, (? Mâmbâkirân Vichâsiran,]
Warden of the Pillaiyâr temple, know this.

The inscription appears to be an ancient deed of
sale, and its importance in this place depends on the
means it affords of obtaining some clue to the date
at which it was made, and which Dr. Babington
hopes may yet be obtained from the similar Varáhu-
svámi Sásanam.   That however given in the commencement is only the ându, or year of the reign
of one of the Chola Princes, the exact chronology of
which dynasty is yet to be ascertained.   There is,
however, another inscription, of an ascertained date,
at the neighbouring hamlet of Pavarakkâran's
Choultry, engraven on a stone under a large Pîpal
tree, near the steps on the south side of the tank,
the characters of which are precisely the same as
those of the Sáluvan Kuppam rock and the temple
of Varáhasvámi; who appears moreover to have
been the common divinity of all three villages.   It
is as follows: (vide the original, in modern characters, marked B.)

" Prosperity! at the holy time of the Makara Sankrama, on Wed-
" nesday, the 5th in the constellation of Uttirathâdi, in the Brahma
" yoga, in the Bálavâkarana, in the light fortnight of the month of
" Makara, in the cycle year Manmatha, and Saka year 1137, when
" Sríman Mahârâjâdhirâja Parameswara Srí Vîra Pratâpa Vikrama
" Deva Mahârâyar ruled over the earth, (on that occasion,) Tiruven-
" gala Nâyakar gave the piece of land surrounding the Mandapam,
" dedicated by Timmappa, for the halting place at the festivals of
" Pádríwni of Perumâl Âditaráha Jñâna Pirân, the deity of [the three
" villages] of Pûñjéri, Tirupárkadal, and Mahâmallaipuram, extend-

" ing over 1,000 Vélis* of land, in the Vadakankúta,† of the Kóttam of
" Amúr, in the Victorious Cholamandalam.—This piece of land, and
" the salt pan in Kúttapákam, called Vírayn Pámban, have been
" given so long as the moon endures for the Pádivéttai Tiruná̄l of
" this deity. Additions may be made to this donation. May this
" charity be continued so long as the moon endures! Let the
" hidden treasures, waters, minerals, and every thing which the
" land or the salt pan contain within their limits, become the pro-
" perty of this deity. Any person that injures this charity, will incur
" the guilt of having killed a cow on the banks of the Ganges. The
" Kániyálars, (or Proprietors of the land), Sungalaigamúr, Nayina Mu-
" daliyár, and Vayírava Noyinár, have affixed their signatures to this
" gift. Thus also Paiyapáradaiyán Uttamapráyan Annappan, the
" village accountant has signed. May prosperity continue!"

Who Vikrama Deva was, does not appear ; but
he may have been a local officer, perhaps a feudatory
or governor under the Cholas ; which dynasty shortly
afterwards gave way to that of the Ráyas of Vijayanagaram (Bijanagar.) The Sálivâhana year 1157,
corresponding with A. D. 1235, however, gives a
tolerable approximation to the Era of the Tamil
inscriptions ; which, as connected with the worship
of Vishnu under the form of the Boar incarnation,
and the representation of the same subject in one of
the caves, (plate 5 of Dr. Babington), affords also
some clue to the period at which the sculptures were
executed. A further guide to the eras of both the
Tamil and Nágari inscriptions may be obtained by
combining and comparing some scattered notices
obtained in other inscriptions.

An inscription at Dháravaram in Rajahmundry
shews that a Vím Chola Deva‡ was reigning in S. S

[* See note 1, p. 120, supra.]   † Northern District.

‡ He also bore the titles of Kulóttunga, which seems to have been
adopted by several Chola princes : of the 7th Vishnu Varddhana ; and
of Tribhuvana Malla in other inscriptions from the same district.
See MS. Catalogue of the McKenzie inscriptions.

1001 or A. D. 1079. His name too occurs in the
best authenticated lists of the Chola dynasty. I
have no doubt that this is the prince above alluded
to. The grant would, therefore, be in 1038, or about
a century anterior to that of Pavarakkaran's
Choultry.

That these Tamil inscriptions were posterior to the
formation of the Atichandesvara Mandapam, the
Rathas and the temple cut out of a single mass
of rock, (from which Dr. Babington copied the
Kamaraja inscription,) is established by the invocation of Adisandesvar,* the tutelary deity of
Tiravirichilur, in the inscription on the rock.

In a copy of a Grant at Pithapur, in my possession, Vijayaditya, the founder of the Chalukya
dynasty of Kalinga, about the middle of the 6th
century,† is described as " destroying the southern
" King Trilochana Pallava, and, through the decree of
" Fate, losing his life in that country." From the
title Pallava it may be inferred that this chief was
of the same race and probably the same family as
Kamaraja, surnamed Jayaranastambha (the pillar
of successful war), and Atiranachanda Pallava.

Another inscription, engraved on a set of copper
plates, (in the possession of Mahendra Shanta, a Jain
Guru at Hyderabad,) and of an era 60 or 70 years
later, contains the following passage :—

* Adisandesvara must be identical with " Atiranachandesvara," the
Lingam set up by Atiranachanda. See Dr. Babington, Trans. Roy.
As. Soc., Vol. II., p. 267, [p. 59, supra.]

In Tamil, the ச pronounced "ta" at beginning of a word, and "da"
in the middle, is identical with the Grantha and Nagari "ta": and ச
is the only Tamil equivalent for the Nagari "cha," ["sa," and "sa."]

† About S. Y. 474 or A. D. 552.

" Having conquered in battle, the hostile kings in the different
" quarters, &c., he acquired the names of Parameswara and Vikramâ-
" ditya." Moreover, Pallava Mardu was overcome by this Lord Srî
" Vallabha, who annihilated the renown of Narasinha, surpassed the
" valour of Mahendra, and excelled Iswara in affability. He has justly
" assumed the title of Srî Vallabha, being in the unprecedented pos-
" session of Kâñchî, as it were the loosened zone (kâñchî) of the
" Nymph of the south. He is also rightly entitled to the name of Râja-
" malla, having secured his acquisition by his large and strong arms,
" and conquered the chief (Malaka) of the Mahâmalla race."

From these facts it may be inferred, that the
rulers of Mâmallaipura were in a state of independence in the 6th and beginning of the 7th centuries. We know from other sources that the Chola
Kings reduced Tondamandalam about the 7th
century.[†] At that time it was parcelled out among
a number of petty chiefs of the Kurumbar race,[‡]
who with their followers were almost entirely
extirpated by the Cholas. The family that possessed
Mâmallaipura was probably one of the principal of
these. The excavations therefore could not well
have been made later than the 6th century. Neither
could they have been much earlier, for the forms of
the letters both Grantha and Nâgari do not justify
the supposition of a higher antiquity.[§]

Under the Chola dynasty we find Tamil invariably
employed as the character of inscriptions.

* This refers to one of the early Chalukya kings of Kalyân, who is described in the beginning of the copper plates as son of Satya Asya, grandson
of Kîrti Varma and great grandson of Pulikesi. His era was about S. Saka
548, corresponding with A. D. 630. The Kalinga and Kalyân dynasties were
collateral branches of the same race.

† Ellis in Trans. Mad. Lit. Soc. p. 19.

‡ 2nd Report on the McKenzie MSS. by the Rev. W. Taylor, p. 56.
[Madras] Journal VII. p. 311.

§ See Prinsep's comparative table of Hindu alphabets.

Whether all the temples were excavated by the
Pallavas seems questionable. They were evidently
worshippers of Siva. Many of the subjects, particularly those in plates 2, 5, 7, 10 of Dr. Babington's
paper, belong to the Vaishnava creed, which is more
particularly referred to in the inscription at Pavarakkaran's Choultry, and is known to have been of
later origin. It is not improbable, therefore, that
these may have been the work of more recent
devotees, emulous of the fame of Kumaraja and
Atiranachanda Pallava.

In the possession of the Pujari of the modern
temple is a deed in Telugu, engraved on copper
plates connected by a ring, with the figure of a boar
and a sword on the seal, purporting to be a grant of
the village of Nolatur to Kesavarya Sri Rangacharya
by Venkatapati Sridevaraya in the Saka year 1532,
Plava Samvatsara.

A.

ஸ்வஸ்திஸ்ரீ-திருவாய்மொழி முன்பாத திருவாயமா நூதர
வதிச கள் மதுலையும்முறாறும் கருஅரும் பாண்டியன் முடிச்
தலாவும் கொண்ஜி கீரத்லியிடைகாரம் விஜய அல்லிடைகரும்
பண்ணியருளிய திருவைதயிர் தெவற்குவாண்டு - கமிலா-வ
து-ஜுவக்கொண்ட சோழமண்டலத்காமூர்க்கோட்டத்துதெவ
தாளாமுராது தெயம திருவிழிச்சி தாருகடைய வாசகருஜாரு
தெளர்கோலில்அஃலமதெளுமுஉதெவஸருளால் இஃதெவல்வந்த
தெலூர்கங்காளிஅண்டார்இல்லவசயகரும்ஸ்ரீசரிசயதெ
யில மூவெஜதெளாருமிக்கோவில் காணியுடைய தெலூர
ஜாஅம் தெலர்தஜிபிதெயத்தரத்துஅடுகொண்டஞ்சிதெ
வையியரஜூலவயன்மதெலூர்பட்டது மிக்கொவில் காணிடு

டையகிலைமரு ராஜண்தேவர்கண்மிகெஷத்திரத்துஆளுடையா
ன் ராசம்பெற்றருளன காற்பத்தெண்ணூற்படட்டனும் - கோ
யில் கணக்கு திருவிழிச்சிலுடையானும் - இவ்விமோவோருமி
க்கோயிலில் கும்பிட்டிருக்கும் ஆண்டார் கருப்பூருடையா
னம்பி அற்புத கூத்தற்கு நிலவிலே புரா னாம்பண்ணி கல்
வெட்டி குடுத்த பரிசாவது பின்கொயார் திருநாம காணியாக
திருவிழிச்சில் உள்ளூரில் இறை இறப்பு அரிதாய ஸ்ரீபண்
டாரத்தில்தட்டிறை இருக்கையல் காக்கன் இவுக்கு விற்ற
குடுத்த கிலைமாவது - பெரியபெரி கழனிகில் அடைகாடதெண்
கூது - துரஎஅடிம் - அத்திப் பட்டல் து - உளஇடும் - ஊ
ரல் எரிவழிக்கிளைகிமல்கிக ஈாதனும் - செட்டை செறுவும்
தெக்கமகழுவதுமான அற்புதகக்கதலும் - உவாகுண்டிதும்-
பலசாரியும் கீசோபெழுவதும். கீஉஉஉ எழுவலும் - ஆதது -
உடைஅஅடில் - கிகைசரிப்பாலத்தில் உடைய கம்பியும் - கேசற்
நமானும் - குடிதாங்கியுநு - கிவதாசனும் - பட்டிருத்தி
யும் - ஆதது - தசாாசடி - ம் - ஆதது - சதாஇடல் - குன்-
கிலம் - உடன - இங்கிலம் - இரண்டெ தருமாவலையும் - அ
ற்புதகூத்தடுக்கும் - உலாகுண்டிதுக்கும் கேழக்குமிணையும்-
உன்படப்பையும் - துசாஅம்-இவர்க்கு காணியாக பெறும்
கிலக்குவிற்று பின்கொயார் ஸ்ரீபண்டாரத்துக்கு கைக்கொட்
புதக்காக - ஆட - இக்காச முன்னூற்றுக்கும் - கிலக்குறை
விற்று கல்லெட்டக் குடுத்தொமிக்கிலக்களுக்கு கீர்பாயகே
ன்கேதும் - இறுக்கக்கடவதும் - எங்கயிலே கீர்பாய கே
ன்கெம் செருத்த கீர்பாயவும் இப்படிக்குச் சம்மதித்து கருத்த
குடைபானம்பி அற்புதகுத்தக்கு கல்லெட்டி குடித்தொம்
இக்கோயில் ரராதகதேதம் - இப்படிக்கு இவை கிந்கிகாய
கன் எழுத்து - இப்படிக்கு இவை இக்கோயில்காணி உடைய
கிவரராஜண்கெடுத்திரத்து ஆட்கொண்ட கில்லிசெவ்வை
ரானள பண்மாகெலமறப்பட்டள் எழுத்து - இப்படிக்கு இ
கவிகோயில் காணியுடைய கிவரராஜண் கெஷத்திரத்து
ஆளுடையான் ராசம் பெற்றருளுன காற்பத்தெண்ணூர்பட்
டண்ணெழுத்து - இப்படிக்கு இவை கிஎகாரியம் செம்பெறு
வேது வேளான் எழுத்து - இப்படிக்கு இவை கோயில் க

எனக்கு திருவிழிச்சிதுடையான் எழுத்து — இப்படி அறிவேன் எ திருப்பாரிபூர் காரப்பத்தெண்ணுகிர பெங்காபேன் - இப் படி அறிவேன் சிறதாலூர் முடிச்செட்டி காராவணகட்டபேன் — இப்படி அறிவேன் சிறதாலூர் ஆமூர்காட்டி வேளாபேன் ன் - இப்படி அறிவேன் மாம்பாக்பெரான் கஜனெற்க்கு மற வெதிக்குமறவுக்கு பெரியாண்டாபேன் - இப்படி அறிவேன் கைபயூர் குபோல் தொணயபட்டபேன் - இப்படி அதி பேன் கைபயூர்மபிக்கிகுதி காராவண பட்டபேன் - இப்ப டி அறிவேன் விசூர்கிபுஎபேன் - இப்படி அறிவேன் மால்ல ஸ புரத்தோகில் ஆமூர்காட்டிபேளாசேன் - இப்படி அறிவே ன் இப்பிள்கேபார் தேவதருமருகுளேகாக் கண்ணிமாம்பாக்கிமா ன் விசாரிசேன்.

II.

ஸ்ரீமத்ரிமன் மகாராஜாதிராயபரமேஸ்வரிஸ்ரீவீரப்பி சமைய விக்கிரம சேணைகாசாயர் பிருதுனினிசச்சியம் பன்னிய குணாகிற - சகாப்தம் - துளிகே - பேழ்செல்வாகிற்ற ம ஸ்மிதமுகமுதுத்த மகாகாயற்ற பூதபகெத்த பஞ்சமியும் புதாயாகமும் - உக்கிராட்டாதியும் - பிரம்மயோகமும் - பாலவ காணமும் பெற்ற - மகாசங்கரம புண்ணியகாலத்திலே - செ மய்கொண்டசோழமண்டளத்து - ஆமூர் கோட்டத்து - வட காட்டி ஆபிரபேசிப்பற்றுஆண பூஞ்சேரி இருப்பார்க்கெடல் மகாமல்லபுரத்த பெருமாள் - ஆதிநாராகம் - ஞாணப்பிரான் பாடிகேட்ட திருகான் எழுத்துகுளுகிற மண்டபம் சூழ்கார்ப பாற்செல்லையும் பிம்மப்பதுன் சாதனமாகவும் - ஸ்வாமி இற ஸ்குவதற்குதானமாகவும் - இங்கிளகுடத்தபாக்கத்தில் வியபப் பாம்பன் - அரும் - தன்றம் - இக்கப்பெருமாளுக்கு பாடி கேட்ட திருகான் அசக்கிரஹூபேபாக இக்கத்தற்மம் விருத் தியாய் தானமாகத் திருகேங்கெளாகாபக்கன் விட்டதண்மம் - ஆ சக்ரஜூரேபின் கடக்க்கடவுதாகவும் - இக்க காப்பாற்கெள்

சிவிதமும் - இந்த ஒரு அளத்திலும் - உண்டான இந்தக்கிஷி
பஜஊபாஷாணை சஊவழுதாய்ப் பிராப்த்தியும் - இந்த ஞானப்
போதுக்கே செல்லக்கடவதாகவும் - இந்த தன்மத்துக்கு - அ
ச்சிரமம்பண்ணினவன் - செம்மைக்கணையிலே கஷிகையப்பளை
அஷைத்த தோஷத்திலே போகக்கடவராகவும் - இந்த தன்ம
த்துக்கு சாஷியாளர் - செங்கலக்கமர். கயிஷழுதஷ்பார்-வ
பிஊயயிஷர் எழுத்த. இப்படிக்கு ஊர்க்கணக்கு ஊபயஊ
குஊட்யான் உத்தமிபிராயன் அண்ணப்பன் எழுத்து - பஊஊ
ॐ வழு-.

_____

.

V.—*On the Inscription near the Vardhamāni Temple, at Māmallaipuram or the Seven Pagodas, with a transcript and translation.* [By Sir Walter Elliot, k.c.s.i.]

[From the Madras Journal of Literature and Science, Vol. XIII. 1844.]

THE above-mentioned inscription is cut in a niche, on the face of the rock against which the modern pagoda is built. The eastern side of the building abuts on the niche, about one-fourth of which is in consequence covered by the wall, and a considerable portion of the writing is thereby hidden from view. The circumstances under which the transcript was made, will be found in the Proceedings of the Committee of the Literary Society of the 6th July 1844, at the end of this No. [31]. Three copies of the inscription were made by three different parties, which were collated by Tāndavarāya Mudaliyār, the learned Principal Sadr Amīn of Chingleput, who also supplied a Telugu paraphrase of the whole, by the aid of which the present translation has been prepared.

Svasti Sri !

In the 9th *āndu* of Koppara-kesari-varma, also called Udaiyār Sri Rājendra Devar, who having taken the whole Irattaippādi seven lakhs and a half, having intimidated Āhava-Malla in battle amid the *pittu* (koppam) of his army, seized upon his elephants and horses, and performed lustrations of victory, when he deigned to sit upon his throne;—the citizens of Jananāthapura which is Māmallapura the chief city of Âmûrnâd in Âmûrkotta in the prosperous Cholamandalam, (Sôramandalam) and we the inhabitants of Périlam, do remal that the eastern boundary of the land which we have granted for Âlvâr (Ârvûr)[*] in the temple of Paramesvara Mahavaráha Vishnu in our village, inclusive of the land formerly held free of tax, as *Devadánam*, lies west of Sikuttichêri—its southern boundary is the north side of Vayalurân kannâr nilam, belonging to Mahávishnu in this village,—its western boundary is the east (shore of the) backwater (or creek)—and its northern boundary (reaches to the) south side of the temple of Mânnallai Perumâl and to the fresh water well on the south-east of the Kôhêri—we have granted to the Devar as *Devadánam*, free of tax, all the lands within these four limits, over which the goana has run and the tortoise has crawled, inclusive of our *nilams* and *punjay nilams*, setting apart four *tadis* of land with trees and arable fields within this tract, for the expenses of meat-offerings (bali) to the deity, and determining that from the produce of the remaining *nir nilams*, one *padakku* and four *nâris* of paddy, which at the rate of two-fifths are (or yield) one *kuruni* of rice, shall be set apart for the offerings of food to the Devar for the two *sandhis* or stated periods of worship at four *nâris* of rice for a *sandhi*—and also one *kuruni* of paddy for two *sandhis* at four *nâris* for a *sandhi*—for two sorts of *karis* (or meats) for each *sandhi*, two and a half *sevidus* of ghee, one *uri* of curds, *adaikkáya* consisting of two areca nuts and eight beetle leaves for a *sandhi*, in all three *kurunis*

[*] This Âlvâr is still worshipped by the Vaishnava sect under the name of Bhûtam, in the following invocation :

[Telugu/Tamil script line]

[Tamil script line]

"I adore Bhûtam who from a portion of Vishnu's Club, was born in a blue lotus at Mâllipuri on the sea-shore, under the sign of the Balance in the constellation of the Dolphin."

[† *Lit.* "rods." 1 square rod = 1 *kuri*.—See note [*] p. 183, *supra*.]

‡ Two *marcals*, [*marakkâl*.]

§ A *padi* or measure, [= in different localities, from 50 to upwards of 100 cubic inches, the present standard Government measure,] the [fourth, fifth, sixth or] eighth part of a *marcal*.

¶ A *marcal*.

‖ A *sevidu* is the 120th part of a *padi* or measure.

** Half *padi* or measure.

[॥ दूधाबविहाबन्धनं धृतं कल्ठोलमालिनः ।
तीरे कुलोत्सवाकलापुर्यालीरे मद्रिथं ॥]

and four *adris* of paddy for two *muḍhis* should be paid, and that the people who cultivate the lands, and the people in the *Maḍaviḷāgam*[*] of this Devar shall not be subjected to the payment of any tax.—I wrote at the desire of the citizens of Māmallapuram or Jananāthapura and the people of Périlam—signed: Tiruverichiladaiyár Tondas Ádavalān—Karnattán of this village; this is my writing.

This is Ofinágan Mádaiyān Aragiya Chola the Amúr-náḍu Múrēndavēlān's writing.

This is Ofinágan Chandrasekara's signature.

This is Oúnágan Nárāyaṇa's signature.

This is Kalatturán Sūtti Araiaan's signature.

This is Konandai Sirálan Setti's signature.

This is Indipuravan Saṅganágan's signature.

This is Máppūdi Nárāyaṇan Mūlakkuli's signature.

This is Máppūdi Annádi Aráva Murti's signature.

This is Uchchakiravan Mugalinágan's signature.

This is Vandárañchēri Udaiyán Arayan Pichan's signature.

The person who molests this charity will incur the sins of having committed capital crimes on the banks of the Ganges and at Kumari.

Svasti Srî!

In the 9th *áṇḍu* of Koppara-kesari-varmar (or) Udaiyár Srî Rájendra Devar when, having taken Irattaipáḍi of the whole seven lakhs and a half, having intimidated Áhava Malla amidst the pitfal of his troops, having raised upon his elephants and horses, and having performed lustrations of victory,—he deigned to sit on his mighty throne; we the inhabitants of Tiruvorichi, the Devádánam and Brahmadeyam (village?) in Amunádi of Amúrnáḍu in the prosperous Choḷamaṇḍalam, do order—that the eastern boundary of the lands which we are to grant as Devádánam free of rent, for the Álvár in the temple of Srî Parameśvara Maháváráha Vishṇu, in Mámallapuram or Jananáthapura the chief city of this Nád lies west of Kommadikuaḍil in the road to the tank Vanaakkanēri—the southern boundary (of it) is the north of Pallachasuru or the land called Kalatturán paramana mugalt—the western boundary (of it) is east of the field (called) Sáttarán Chandra Sekara kiraṇa vittan—and the northern boundary (of it) south to the field (called) Kariyan manana mottan kunavan. We have granted for this Devar, the three hundred kuris of the land (named) Ennmanna within this boundary as Devádánam free of rent, together with the water to irrigate this land from the tank Vanaakkanēri and also the water channel.—We are to free the cultivators of this land from the payment of the principal

---

[*] The establishment or inmates of the temple.

(*ser=sari* or *oyin*) and sundry (*silavari* or additional) taxes—and also from forced labour, (*vetti*) and the carrying of burdens and pounding of grain for the food of persons of all descriptions. Thus having agreed, we have granted (this) as *Devadanam* free of rent.

I, Bháradvaji Ádavalán, a Siva Brahman of Karpákkam in this Nád, wrote this at the request of the inhabitants of Tiruverichi. This is my writing.

This is the writing of Pádáyakkiram vittan.

This is the writing of Devaganáta pattan of this *kshetram*.

This: Sátandai mallan sannagan.

   *   *   *   *   (effaced.)

   *   *   *   *   Olinágan Náráyanan.

This is my writing.   * * * *

This * * * * of this *kshetram*.

   *   *   *   *   Pattan.

I know, this is the writing of Arumbakirán Kári Iráman, Múvéndadevan of Amáruál in the prosperous Cholamandalam.

This is the writing of Tonda Ádavalán the Karanattán of this village.

In this Nadu, Olinágan Málaiyán, Múvéndadevan of Amáruál, granted 90 goats, for a lamp to be kept always burning.

Kámakódan nolavan, &c.

The remainder is defaced.

Two grants to the same temple are here recorded, both made in the same year but by different parties. The opening sentence of both is word for word the same, and constitutes the most important portion of the deeds; possessing a double value both as affording the means of ascertaining the exact date of the Tamil inscriptions at Mámallaipuram, and as a historical record confirming in a remarkable manner, a fact of some importance ascertained from totally distinct sources. In a paper on the Chalukya Princes of Kalyán in the Dakhan published in the IVth Vol. of the Journal of the Royal Asiatic Society, and republished in Vol. VII. p. 193 of this Journal, it is stated on the authority of an inscription at Anigiri in the Dhárwár district, that Somesvara Deva Chalukya I., surnamed Áhava

Malla had been invaded by the Chola Rájá who had ravaged the southern provinces of Kuntala-desa, and destroyed the city of Pulikara-nagara, the modern Lakshmesvar near Savandr.   The Chalukya inscription asserts that Ahava Malla defeated and slew the invader, and there is no doubt the invasion was ultimately repelled.   But enough is admitted to show that it had been in the first instance eminently successful.   The present inscription evidently refers to the same fact, and there is no doubt that Víra Rájendra Chola, surnamed Koppara-Kesari-Varma is the Chola Rájá above referred to.   This is further confirmed by other inscriptions of this same prince, on the magnificent temple at Gangondaram, on the north bank of the Cavery, of which he appears to have been the founder.   One of these, in the 5th year of his reign, runs thus, "Ko-Virája-Kesari Varma named Rájendra Deva, wielding the sceptre with valour for a companion and munificence for an ornament, freeing himself from the blackest sins, having intimidated Ahava Malla of Kudala Sangama, having vanquished the Vikkilan and Singalan,[*] and taken their queens with their effects and carriages, and having a second time terrified Ahava Malla in battle ; having also recovered Venginádu and fulfilled the vows of his elder brothers, &c." In a subsequent grant in the same temple he is described as "having perpetuated his fame in the northern country which he conquered, &c."

The kingdom of Kalyân had not long before been rescued from foreign enemies by the great grand-

* The Singalan must refer to the King of Ceylon.

father of Someswara Deva I., and may not have been
yet fully re-established, thereby inviting the attacks
of its southern neighbours, who were then in the
height of their power. The inscriptions of the
father of Someswara Deva I. named Jayasinha,
show that he also was at war with the Cholas, but
their differences must have ceased with the content
recorded in the present inscription, for the youngest
son of Someswara Deva,—Vikramáditya II. was the
most powerful sovereign, not only of his race but of
his time, and ruled over an enlarged and extensive
kingdom for 52 years, in the numerous extant inscriptions of which, no mention occurs of a Chola
war. On the other hand, the Cholas had attained
their greatest prosperity at the period of the inscription, in the time of Víra Rájendra Chola, whose
father Rája Rája Narendra, acquired possession of
the whole of Telingána, by intermarriage with the
eastern branch of the Chalukya family, sovereigns
of Vegidesam, and left to his son a kingdom, extending along the coast from the mouth of the
Godávarí to Rámesvaram, and inland probably over
the greatest part of the southern provinces of this
Presidency.

The next point is to identify the era of Vira
Rájendra Chola with that of Someswara Deva I.
surnamed Áhava Malla. The latter has been ascertained with tolerable precision in the paper above
referred to, and is shown from a comparison of several
inscriptions, to be from about S. S. 962 to 991.*
By a valuable inscription recently procured, I find

---

* Madras Journal, Vol. VII, p. 186.

that Râjendra Chola succeeded his father Râja Râja Chola in S. S. 986, and the same authority shows that he still continued reigning in S. S. 1001. It is clear therefore that he was not killed in the action with Somesvara Deva. But besides that the metaphorical language of the inscription does not imperatively require such a rendering, it is very possible that Râjendra Chola may not have commanded in person, but may have intrusted the expedition to one of his generals who, as shewn by numerous inscriptions of that age, were in the habit of assuming the family name of the sovereigns under whom they served. The date of the inscription, the 9th of his reign, would therefore be S. S. 995 or A. D. 1073. The battle of Lakshmesvar must have occurred very shortly after his accession, for the Gangondaram inscription already quoted is dated in the 5th of his reign. The synchronism therefore of the three records is perfect.

The last object of inquiry is the identity of the places referred to as the scene of the war. The term Irattaippâdi used in both the Chola grants, does not occur in any of the Dakhan inscriptions that I recollect. It may, however, have been the familiar term for Kuntala-desa in the south. Instances of such diversity of nomenclature are not uncommon. In the Dakhan, at this day the Tamil country and people are invariably called Konga-des and Kongas. At Malacca and by the Malays generally, the people of Southern India pass under the name of Klings, from the ancient Kalinga. Now we know that a powerful race, the Ratta Kula, originally overcome by the Chalukyas and held in subjection for several centuries, again obtained the ascendancy about the

9th century, and were finally subdued by Tailapa
Deva Chalukya, the great grandfather of Áhava
Malla in S. S. 895 or A. D. 973.   Among the titles
of Áhava Malla himself, we find an indication of
the more recent independence of the Rattas.   In an
inscription at Nilgund in the Dambal Taluk of the
Dhárwár district, he is described as "possessing
the lofty golden parasol and the whole territory that
had belonged to the Rattakula chief, Srí Vira
Mártanda."   A distinguished family of this Rattakula, likewise flourished at Parsghur and Samdatty
in the Dhárwár district under the Chalukya dynasty,
and a considerable town yet exists under the name
of Ratteballi on the Wardah, about 30 or 40 miles
south of Lakshmesvar.

In the Gangondaram inscription, the Chalukya
prince is designated as Áhava Malla of the Kadal
Sangama.   This is the name of the junction of the
Tungá with the Bhadrá river near Huli Honore,
where is situated the Matham of a celebrated Guru
of the Smárta sect, usually called the Kudalgi
Svámí.*

There is good reason to believe, therefore, that
"Irattaippádi" was the name applied by the Tamilians to the southern province, at least of the
Chalukya empire, and even to suppose that it was
used to signify the whole kingdom.   This opinion is
strengthened by the use of the expression "the
whole 7½ lakhs."   In the same inscription that gives

* There are two Mathams of the Sankara Bhárati or Smárta sect
in this neighbourhood—Sringeri and Kadalgi, besides another at
Sankesvar, near Kolapúr.

the history of the union of the eastern Chalukya
and Chola families, it is stated that the first founder
of the former race, descended from the rulers of
Ayodhya, "having conquered Kadamba Ganga and
other earthly rulers, reigned over the southern
country of 7½ lakhs from Narmadá to Setu" and
elsewhere, similar references are made to the 7½
lakhs dominion of the Kalyán kingdom. This
evidently refers to the kingdom of Kuntala-desa
only, of which Kalyán was the capital ; for that of
Kalinga or Vegidesam* was the subsequent acquisition of a collateral branch. What the number 7½
lakhs refers to is not clear. In all the inscriptions
of that era, territorial divisions are designated by a
number unaccompanied by any explanation of the
objects to which it refers. Thus the Kadamba family
which became a feudatory to the Kalyán Chalukyas,
are always described as lords of the Banawassi
12,000. It may refer to the number of villages or
townships, to their revenue, or to the quota of troops
the chief was bound to bring into the field.

The inferences bearing on the local history of the
Seven Pagodas to be drawn from the preceding inscription are the following. The era of the oldest
Tamil inscription is clearly fixed at the latter part of
the 11th century, and that previously assigned to
the rock sásanam of Sáluvan Kuppam is confirmed.
For Vira Chola Deva surnamed Tribhuvana Malla
is shown by the same inscription as that which gives
the date of Vira Rájendra Chola, to have been the
second son of that prince, and to have been

nominated by him viceroy of Telingana in S. S.
1001, (A. D. 1079) which would place the execution
of the rock inscription stated to have been cut in his
36th year, in the beginning of the 12th century or
S. S. 1037, corresponding with A. D. 1115. Further,
it is evident from the facts of the grant to Álvár,
in the temple of Parameswara Mahá-varáha Vishnu,
and the subsequent mention of the temple of Má-
mallai Perumál, that the more modern creed of the
Vaishnava sect had been established, and that of the
Saiva subverted. Lastly, the place appears to have
borne the name of Jananáthapuram in addition to
that of Mámallaipuram, which it is remarkable is
invariably here written Mámallapuram. [மாமல்லபுரம்]

   In the Appendix to Mr. Ellis' treatise on Mirási
rights, a copy and translation of the Sáluvan Kuppam
inscription will be found, which, had it been known
at the time, would have rendered the publication of
that given in a former part of this volume (p. 47)ª
unnecessary.   The two documents agree pretty
nearly, but Mr. Ellis seems to have had a less accurate transcript, than the one prepared for me, which
was obtained from two copies made by different individuals acquainted with the ancient character, and
these were carefully collated by Thodaivaráya
Mudaliyár.   Mr. Ellis has also inserted at the same
place a version of the few initial half-lines of the
Varáhasvámi inscription, but these were evidently
too imperfect to give the true sense. He, however, agrees in referring the local chiefs antecedent
to the Cholas to the Kurumbar race, though he

[ª P. 121. supra ?]

errs in supposing (Álava) Malla to have been one
of them.

The Seven Pagodas have received a greater degree
of attention from their vicinity to Madras, than they
otherwise would have obtained.[*]   The repeated
notice that has in consequence been bestowed on
them, has thus brought together almost everything
of interest connected with them, and the curious
visitor is thus furnished with data, from which to
form his own opinion of their age, origin, and
object.

[*] Heyne's Tracts XXI. p. 333.

முதற்சால்நம்.

ஸ்ரீ இராடையபாடி பெழுன பிலகழுந்தொண்டு
பொரிற்றகையதொடுப்பதாஇயைவைக்க் பருகவிதக்வரு
ஒழுங ருதிகாபுவ காகவொண்டு விஜபால்டியக்ஞசெழுக
ரெவிகராவைதக விற்றிருதருளிய கோவபா வெணினர்
மாளவை.கடபார்ஸ்ரான் யிடிவரகருபணடெணபாவது
இயவெகாவைடசொழுமனடைகக ஞூமகொடடைதஞு
காடே கசமாவையைபுமான ஜிகாதபுரதை காரதாமுமெ
பெகிகானைடபொருமு எழுதை எகைகுரிஜிபாவெமருமைகா
வைரைவிய-வரு வாதகாமுவாகாகு கெவுதாக ஜுகறவிவிர்
கமுவுகைடய கிலறுப்படைவகாடுகக கிவதகருகியுபா

இரண்டாவது சாஸநம்.

ஸ்வஸ்தி ஸ்ரீ இடையபாடி பெழுகாவிலைக்குழைகொண்ட
பொசிற்றை சண்டதொகப்பாததாலைலமலலினி பருகவிததை
ஓகாபுவ ருஜினாபுலைகைகொணடு விஜயால்ஜெகக்குசெது
ஸ்ரீஸ்வஅரஸததிற்றிருகருணிபகொபாரவேஸிவிர்மா
ன உடையாருராஜைபூஜ்ஸ்வாதகுபாணடு உதபதாவது
றுவதொரண்ட சொமுணடலதது துறாகெடடதது த்
மூரட்டு தெவதாரமண்று ஸ்ரீதெயபழிதிருவெழிசதிலொம எழு
ததை இந்நாட்டுக்கொமாமல்லபுரமான ஐஸாதபுரதது ஸ்ரீபா
பெழுன மகலவார்ணதிஷ்டுஷ்டுததாழவாரகூதெவதாச
இதைசிலீபாக எதைலருசில காயகளைகொடுகதிற கிலததைகு
பேபரகெல்ல வணணகைனீயெழிகொமமடிகருணடிதுச
குஅமதகும தெணபரகெல்ல காதததுழுவை பரமணமுகல்
கிலைசன பளாசசெழவுகுருவடகருமமெமபாறகெலல்சாத
துமுன சததிரெசொகதிமளிததன கிலததைகுகழிழுகருமுடை
பாறகெலள் கழிபணசெயமெமெடடடருணவன கிலதது
குததறகும இகைசறபெரெலல் உளைறுமணிடெபடட எத
மெலைதுறுவெணைழுழிமிருகிருதறவு டணடைலைதுறு
தருழியும இதைசதிறின் நிலிழுன இதைசிலைலைருகு வை
னைலைசிலைழிதும கொசிசெதருழுளட இககெவாகு
தெயவதார இதைடிலலைசைசகொகிதொதொம இனைஸிலமுழுகு
டிகொ இனனிலைதான வதகெபெருசியுமகிலைவரியும வெடி
முடைடையாரும எதெசாறைறக கூறறகொகொதும உணைபிடெக
கடிதொணழும காரடடைகடடெயபைல்லைதொமசகறும. இபப
கிஇணசகுதொதெவதாகைஇறைஇழிசசிகெகிதொதொம. திருவெ
ழிதிறொளாருலுவாதனவெணடைல்லழுதிெனன இநாடடெகைறபாக
கததை பிலைபுராழுனை மாராதரஜி கடவைகிரெனை இலை
எைணெழுததை. இலையபாதாவகிசிமலிததெழுதது. இப
படிகுசெததிரததை தெவைகைறைபடடலெழுதது. இபபடிக
ருசசாததைகதைதடலைலனைசைணகதெனை

இவணகைமாடடாலெக்

பழிெனை துளிருகை காரரவண தெனை இலைை எைணெழு

தற இபபடிக்கு   செஷிரந்த

பட்டனே இபபடிக்கு அருமபாகழிச
எகாழி இராமஎன இயஎகெண்ட செஎழஅழூராகாடெ மூ
செஎநதவெஎாஎழுதது. அபிஃஎன இலஆரு காஎஎதாஎ
தெஎண்டஅடலஅலஎஎழுதது. இலஆஎஅட இஎதெஆாகரு
இலஆரு ஒளிஆகஎ மாஎஅயாஎ அழூராஎடெ மூ௸வஎந்தஎ
எஎஎஅவஎத திருஎாஎதாவிஎகரு ஒஅஅகருஅவஎத ஆதி
தொஎஎஅஅஅ. இஎதெஆாகருஇஅடபா

    திருவிஎகருஅஎஎஅஎருஅவிடஅ௸தி   காஅஅ
செஎடஎஎசெஎஎஎஎஅஎஅயூறற   எறுப௸அஅஎது.

VI.—*Notes on the Ruins at Mahábalipuram on the Coromandel Coast.* By C. Grubbs, Esq., B. C. S.

[From the Journal of the Asiatic Society of Bengal. Vol XXII. 1853.]

THE temples of Mahábalipúr or Mávalipuram are situated in Lat. 12° 36′ 57″ North, and Long. 80° 14′ 1″ East; nearly thirty-five miles south of Madras, and about five north of the little town of Sadras.

They are built and excavated from a low rocky ridge that, rising isolated from the plain, runs slant-ing towards the shore for about a mile and a half. The highest part, towards the north, is little more than 120 feet in elevation ; and perhaps a mile from the sea, into which the southern extremity runs. It appears to have some small spurs, which may be seen cropping out at various points on the beach.

It is chiefly* of a binary granite, that conveys to a casual observer the idea of having been recently half-wetted by a driving pelt of rain ; and although extremely hard, splits readily into masses of various but considerable size. I saw a block from forty to fifty feet in length, and twenty-five to thirty feet in width, that had been divided with an apparently† plane surface by a single blast of gunpowder. The hewers of the caves, however, do not seem to have

---

* As far as I could perceive, it was entirely so ; but I had not leisure for an examination sufficiently minute to authorise my speaking positively.

† I say "apparently," because, with reference to the known con-choidal fracture of the rock, it is probable that when closely examined the surface would be found somewhat curved.

enjoyed the assistance of this powerful agent : their method was to trace out on the surface of the rock the line in which they required a separation, along which small holes were made with the chisel and wedges introduced with sufficient force to compel cleavage. It would, however, be difficult at the present day to determine whether these wedges were of wood, well dried before insertion, and subsequently swelled by the application of water; or of metal driven in by repeated blows, as appears to have been the custom in ancient Egypt.*

[* " A series of bare granite rocks, naturally of fantastic contour, nearly a mile long and 120 feet high, has afforded the Hindu artist ample scope for the exercise of his chisel, which must have been wrought of the finest tempered steel, for which India, since the dawn of history, has been justly celebrated. The bronze tools of the Egyptians might answer well enough in the limestone quarries around old Cairo, in working the blocks which constitute the great bulk of the pyramid, but would be of little avail in the quarries of Syene—a type of whose granite we find in the redder felspar Quarternary granites compose the great monolithic *Rathas* of the Seven Pagodas—a mixture of red and white felspar, white quartz, dark mica, and hornblende. It is more than probable that Indian steel found its way into Egypt during the early traffic that is known to have subsisted between India, Judæa, Yemen, and Egypt. It is absurd to suppose that the sharply-cut and deeply-engraven hieroglyphics which cover the granite obelisks of Egypt, were done with chisels of bronze, even armed with corundum dust. Quintus Curtius informs us that Porus presented Alexander with a quantity of steel as one of the most acceptable and valuable gifts India could offer. The granite blocks here, as elsewhere in India, are subject to spontaneous concentric exfoliation and splitting. The globular mass, apparently about sixty feet in circumference, which we see nicely poised on a convex mass of granite—the pat of butter petrified by the god of milkmaids, Krishna—is ascribable to the first process; and the rents in the sculptured rocks—one of which clearing the monolith pagodas, was ascribed by Mr. Chambers to a violent earthquake—have doubtless been caused by the latter process of spontaneous splitting."— Newbold's " Notes on the Coast of Coromandel, from the Pennâr to Pondicherry," in Journal. Asiat. Socy. of Bengal. Vol. xv, p. 216.

† P. 10, supra.]

The rock yields to the weather by conchoidal peelings, which gives to the group the general appearance of a mass of gigantic boulders, or a confused assemblage of ruined domes. Considering its hardness, it seems to be peculiarly affected by the sea air. This was remarked by Mr. Chambers in 1772 and 1776. "All these figures are doubtless much less distinct than they were at first; for on comparing these and the rest of the sculptures that are exposed to the sea air, with others at the same place whose situation has afforded them protection from it, the difference is striking; the former being every where much defaced, while the others are fresh as recently finished;"[*] and it is necessary to bear in mind this characteristic when discussing the antiquity, either positive or comparative, of any portion of these edifices.

The greater part of these temples are excavations after the fashion of Ellora and Elephanta; superior in taste and symmetry, though far inferior in dimensions to the first-named.[†] The most perfect and beautiful is in a narrow ravine, towards the northern part of the range, and facing to the West; whereby it has been well protected from the effects of the sea air. Although small in its dimensions, it is remarkable for its artistic merit: the columns in particular are slender and most graceful; the pedestals couchant tigers facing outwards; the capitals elegant and well proportioned, though fashioned in a style unknown among the orders of Grecian architecture. Mr. Chambers remarks on its sculpture that "the figures of idols in high relief upon its walls are very well finished, and perfectly fresh."* Another appears to have been dedicated to Siva, who is represented, in the middle compartment, of large stature and with four arms. A small figure of Brahmá is on his right ; Siva with his consort Párvatí on the left ; and his left foot rests on a bull couchant. At one end of the temple is a gigantic figure of Vishnu sleeping on a Cobra da capello, with several heads so disposed as to form a canopy above the god. At the opposite end appears Siváni, in the character of Durgá, with eight arms, mounted on a lion ; opposed to her is a gigantic figure with a human body and buffalo's head,† much resembling that which is elsewhere called the Yamarája ; between them is a human figure suspended head downwards, apparently the object of their dispute : and the monster brandishes a club, while the goddess is armed with various weapons and accompanied by some dwarf attendants.

Mr. Goldingham remarks, "The figure and action of the goddess are executed in a masterly and spirited style ;"‡ and Lieutenant Newbold observes that "the best executed figure of the king of the beasts is that on which the goddess Durgá is seen mounted, in the sculptured cave near the summit of the hill."§

<hr>

[* P. 6, supra.]

[† Mahishásura.—Cp. Babington, p. 40, and Braddock, pp. 99 ff., supra.]

[‡ P. 33, supra.]

[§ This passage occurs in a description of the Seven Pagodas quoted, (without Author's name,) at pp. 253 ff. of Pharoah's Gazetteer of Southern India. I have not access to the original paper.—ED.]

Not far off, a large polished slab about ten feet in length, with the figure of a couchant lion at the southern end, is shown as the bed of the Dharma-rája: which may probably be understood as the " Lit de justice," or throne, whence some prince of that name was wont to dispense justice to his people.

Of the other caves some were considerably larger, and had more the appearance of being dedicated to Vishnu : all facing the East.   But the striking point in which the whole series resembles that of Ellora is their unfinished state.   Mr. James Fer-gusson remarks of them in a paper read to the R. A. Society in 1843 :—

"One of the most singular characteristics of this series of caves is that they are all of one age, and probably the work of one prince, who has carried on the works simultaneously, but from some cause or other has been unable to complete even one of them ; had one been finished, or had there been any gradation of style or workmanship, some chro-nological arrangement might easily have been traced ; but nothing of the sort exists."*

Another still more remarkable point of similarity is the repetition of the sculptured group, represent-ing a skeleton figure in a suppliant attitude before a personage appearing to possess authority.   Mr. Goldingham describes the group at Mahábalipúr as follows :

"Near this structure, the surface of the rock, about ninety feet in extent, and thirty in height, is covered with figures in bas-relief.   A gigantic figure

of the god Krishna is the most conspicuous ; with
Arjuna his favourite, in the Hindu attitude of
prayer ; but so void of flesh, as to present more
the appearance of a skeleton than the representation
of a living person.   Below is a venerable figure, said
to be the father of Arjuna ;° both figures proving
the sculptor possessed no inconsiderable skill."†

It does not appear whether Mr. Goldingham had
any authority for this interpretation, beyond that
of the attendant Brahmins, who are always ready to
affix the names of some Hindu god or hero to
every ancient sculpture ; but I could not perceive
in the standing figure the usual attributes of
Krishna ; neither can I recal any tale or legend
that represents Arjuna and his father Pándu as
suppliants to that divinity, in a state of starvation.

When I visited the caves of Ellora in 1841, Lieut.
Howarth, then engaged in making drawings of the
bas-reliefs, informed me that the group was generally
considered to pourtray a miser holding a bag of
money, while his wife and son, reduced to skeletons,
are vainly supplicating for food ; but on minute
inspection I was not satisfied with this interpretation, and find my notes on the subject as follows.

What is assumed to be a purse tied round the
waist of the miser has not the appearance of a sack
containing money ; but might rather represent a
girdle, drawn tight round the body to ease the
sensation of hunger, as is the custom with most
semi-civilized nations : neither can it be a bag of
coins that he holds in his hand, because the thick

_* See note * p. 31, and note || p. 93, supra.]

[† P. 30 f., supra

part is above the hand and terminates in a point at
top; but it *might* be an instrument for cutting the
rock, which he is holding out to the half-starved
figures at his feet. The little fat cherub may as well
be supposed to be bringing him a bag of treasure,
as to be taking it away; and then the entire group
may be imagined to pourtray the cause and mode of
construction of these caves, as a work undertaken
by some prince or wealthy chief during a time of
famine to relieve the wants of his starving people.
Admitting this supposition, we shall have no difficulty
in accounting for a continuation of the bas-relief
which appears appended, not only to this group but
also to a similar one in less perfect preservation in
another cave: and we shall recognize Ganesa, at
the head of a row of females, each carrying a child
in her arms as exhibiting the eventual results of
the judicious disbursement.

This interpretation is merely a conjecture, but it
seems to derive great support from the existence of
the same group on the rocks of Mahabalipuram.[*]
We can hardly imagine sculptors at such very
different parts of India happening to invent precisely the same story : though it might easily occur
that both had to relate to posterity the same events.
It is no very great stretch of credulity to suppose
that in both places the works were undertaken by
some prince to employ his famishing subjects during
a time of great scarcity, and to furnish them with
food without supporting them in slothful idleness.
This is exactly what was done by Sir Charles Met-

[* The identity of the scenes represented in the sculptures at the
two places is not apparent.]

calfs in our Upper Provinces during the famine of
1837-8, and it does not seem impossible that similar
events might suggest similar remedies, to beneficent
and intelligent minds, even at an interval of many
centuries. Nor are we without some indications
that such actually *has* been the case : for Mr. Taylor,
quoting from the Mackenzie papers, says :

" In the Kali-yuga, Singhama Náyadu the Ze-
mindar of the Vellugotiváru race, seems to have
ruled here. In that time, during a famine, many
artificers resorted hither, and wrought on the mountain a variety of works, during two or three years."[*]

This theory will explain how in both cases, (Ellora
and Mahábalipuram,) a number of works were commenced simultaneously, in order to employ at once a
large number of workmen : and how they came to
be left unfinished ; the people naturally returning to
their ordinary occupations, when the pressure of
famine was removed.

I must not omit to mention another tradition
which attributes the construction of these works to
a body of northern artificers, who fled from the
tyranny of their own or some conquering prince, and
were suddenly recalled to their homes, by proffered
favours and concessions on his part ; nor the conjecture of Mr. James Fergusson, who, discrediting
this story, accepts Singhama Náyadu as the prince

[* Madras Journal, Vol. viii. p. 65. Cp. note ɼ, p. 115, *supra*.—
" About 500 years ago a Poligar of the name of Ballonta Ram-
commandu lived here, and began to build a little fort on the top of
the rock, some ruins of which still remain, as bricks, &c. It is also
said that Krishnaraiba, who lived about 250 years ago, employed
some workmen, who had been driven from the north into the
Carnatic in search of bread."—Heyne's Tracts on India. London,
1814, p. 335.]

to whom the excavations are due : and tracing him
to his death in battle, while besieging the fort of
Jalli palli in the thirteenth century, conceives this
event to be a more probable cause of the sudden in-
terruption of the works. " It being entirely a fancy
of his own, and neither indigenous in the country,
nor a part of the religion of the people, it is not
probable that his successor would continue the
follies of his parent."[*]   Either of these suppositions
would certainly account for the non-completion of the
works at Mahābalipûr: but we should then have to
seek out some analogous cause for the same circumstance at Ellora : and the remarkable repetition of
the significant group of sculpture would remain
totally unexplained.

There are a variety of other sculptures both of
beasts and human beings ; and often presenting a
mixture of both.   The most conspicuous is the king
snake, with the head and body of a man, terminating in extensive serpentine convolutions, often
winding round other groups.[†]   They are nearly all
on the eastern face of the rock : and mostly close to
the principal caves, which are in the northern half
of the range.   In the same vicinity is a somewhat
remarkable monolith ; a mass of living rock left
isolated, and artificially fashioned outside, as well as
inside.   It appears to be above twenty-five feet in
height, the same in length, and about half in breadth.
It has a long roof curved like a gothic-pointed arch,
and gabled at each end.

The walls are of great thickness, so that the
interior cell is small : it contains a lingam, and

among the sculptures on its walls, appears the figure
of Ganesa in small dimensions.* Its door faces the
west : and close to it the Brahmans are quarrying
the rock, to repair and beautify the interior of the
brick pagoda ; the only one in which the ceremonials
of worship are performed at the present day.

At the extreme south of the ridge, and separated
from it by a small level space, along which runs the
lower road from Madras to Cuddalore, stand a
group of monoliths, seven† in number, surrounded
by a grove of cocoanut trees.‡ Five of them are
pagodas ; of which the most southern (measured
by Mr. Goldingham forty feet in height) resembles
in general outline a Mussulman mausoleum.
Another twenty-five feet in height, and perhaps
fifty in length, has a long gothic roof as previously
described, and is ornamented on the outside : the
other three are more like modern pagodas. The
two remaining rocks are fashioned to imitate an
elephant and a lion, in colossal proportions. All
these monoliths, though close to the sea-beach, and
perfectly exposed, are comparatively fresh in their
outline, and exhibit very little signs of corrosion.
They are composed of this same binary granite, and
I think we may thence conclude their comparative
antiquity not to be very great.

There still remain two§ temples, differing from

[* The Ganesa temple is more correctly described at page 79, supra.]

[† There are eight, including the figure of the sacred bull (Nandi)
almost buried in the sand.]

‡ () else—palmyras: my recollection on this point is indistinct.‖

§ I have been told of a third farther north, but did not see it. [See
note † p. 105, supra.]

‖ They are palmyras (Borassus flabelliformis) and scrub dates (Phœnix
farinifera) .

the former in being *built*, instead of hewn in the
solid rock. The first, already alluded to, stands
near the village on the level ground not far from
the principal caves, and is of brick, plastered and
coloured in the modern style. It is of considerable
size, and is still used for purposes of worship, and
for the accommodation of Hindu travellers. The
Brahmans enjoy some revenues attached to the
building, and are busily engaged ornamenting and
improving it : all which circumstances,* combined
with its perfectly recent form and appearance, are
conclusive in my mind against any claims to great
antiquity that may be advanced on its behalf.†

The last remaining is that which has attracted
most attention from travellers : it is built of large
masses of hewn granite, on one of the granite rocks
already mentioned, as protruding at intervals along
the sea shore. It is nearly opposite the highest
part of the ridge, and has apparently been built
en rapport with some part of the excavated hill,
from which it is a mile distant in an easterly direction. Its dimensions are small : speaking from
memory, I should say, under thirty feet square :
but its curiously ornamented conical roof rises to an
elevation of nearly fifty feet. It is surrounded on
three sides by a granite screen of ten or twelve feet
high, and about five feet distant from the body of the
temple : on the fourth side (the West,) stands a
miniature of the temple, opening towards the West,

---

* It will generally be found that religious edifices, still possessing
endowments, belong to the later phases of Hinduism : the more
ancient having been lost, in the various political and religious contests.

[† It is called the Sthalasayanasvami (Vishnu) temple, and is said
to be about 100 years old.]

and bearing every appearance of having originally been its principal* entrance. The walls and roof of a connecting passage still exist, but all access by this route is now barred by a slab of black basaltic rock, fixed in the eastern wall of the portico, opposite its entrance. A similar, rather larger slab occupies a corresponding place on the inner surface of the western wall of the temple; and on both are images of *Siva*, *Párvati*, and their child.† I was unable to discover whether the space intervening between these two slabs is vacant, or has been filled up with masonry: but it is my very strong impression, that they and their immediately surrounding blocks of stone are long subsequent in date to the rest of the building, and have been inserted in order to mark the ancient entry. As matters at present stand, it is impossible to assign any reason for the existence of a blind chamber, or other mass of building, between two temples of *Siva* placed *dos à dos*: and there are only two suppositions that will account for the erection of these two buildings, of obviously the same date, with a covered passage of connection. Either the smaller was a sanctuary, to be entered only from the larger; as appears to have been the case in some of the Arian temples still extant in Cashmere: or else it must have been a portico, through which admission

---

* As is constantly seen at present to the rest of Hindu temples.

† The centre is occupied by a large lingam‡ which, from its dark colour, I conclude to be of this basaltic rock, which must have been brought from a considerable distance. The chattyas§ terminating the roofs of both temple and prophyllum are the same. Every other part is granite.

[‡ See note † p. 107, supra.]   [§ See note * p. 172, infra.]

was obtained to the larger or real temple. The
first hypothesis is contradicted by the existence of
the western entry to the smaller edifice, which is
certainly contemporaneous with its construction;
and also by the fact that the stone screen, that so
carefully encircles the larger building, ceases on
arriving opposite the smaller. We are therefore
thrown back upon the second;[*] which is supported
not only by these circumstances, but also by the
extreme simplicity of the present door to the larger
temple; a mere plain opening in the wall. I may
also mention that while the smaller building (and
through it, were the passage still open, the larger
one only) is approached from the west with ease and
on a level; the only access to the simple opening in
the eastern screen now serving as an entry is over
a low but steep and rugged rock washed by the
breakers below. This rock has certainly the appearance, both here and elsewhere, of having been
partly cut into rude steps and partly perforated as
if to receive some superstructure that has since disappeared. One solitary column still raises its head
above the waves, and is commonly considered to have
been a Stambha, to support lamps:[†] it should, however, be remarked that there is no vestige of any mode
of ascent, to place them; neither of niches wherein
they might be placed. The top is formed into a kind
of peg, as if to receive some capping stone, and I

---

[*] The idea of the original entrance having been from the west
will appear less strange if it be remembered that the entrance and
portico of the Kailás at Ellora actually are from that quarter.

[† See note † p. 11, and note ‡ p. 51, supra. The statement that
it is a lamp-post (Dipastambha) appears, from the height and shape of
the pillar, to be correct.]

have myself little doubt that it is the sole relic of some terrace or arcade, once extending in this direction: I also traced out faintly the platforms of two collateral buildings; one on each side of that now standing: and among the débris of the southernmost I discovered several images of the kneeling bull generally placed opposite a lingam, so corroded as to be only recognizable on careful examination. A similar image, in a better state of preservation, is to be seen within the granite screen, on one side of the portico; and on the other, in a closet or small chamber of comparatively recent construction, is a large recumbent statue of Vishnu, with the ordinary Sesh-nâga* below and above him.

On the shore close by are several rudely sculptured rocks: one representing a monster with human arms and the head of an ox or buffalo,† commonly called the Yama-râja. They have suffered greatly from the action of the sea air, as has also every part of the adjacent temple, except its chaityas of basalt. In this respect there is a great difference between its appearance and that of the caves, or even of the group of monoliths placed in a situation no less exposed: and after close examination of all surrounding circumstances, I am unable to resist the conclusion that this temple is by many degrees the most ancient of the remains at Mahábalipûr: in fact, that it is one of the most ancient in India. I am aware that Mr. James Fergusson considers "that its age does not differ materially from that of the rest;"‡ and it is with the greatest diffidence that I venture

[* See note * p. 22, supra.]   [† Mahishásura.]
[‡ Journal R. A. S., Vol viii, p. 87.]

to express an opinion differing from that entertained by so competent an authority : but Mr. Fergusson was specially engaged in the examination of the rock-cut temples ; remarking the similarities and the differences existing between them and similar works in other parts of India ; so that probably he had little leisure for this structure ; to which I, on the contrary, devoted much attention. Besides, if I remember right, he decided these caves to be more modern than those of Ellora : at the same time he considered the celebrated Kailâs of that place to have been copied from some earlier edifice of Southern India : and looking to the very great general similarity of style, I am certainly inclined to refer this shore temple of Mahâbalipûr to the *age* of those earlier structures ; although the precise model of the Kailâs may not be found here, but at Chellambram* or Tanjore. This would give a considerable difference of date ; and the supposition is borne out by the assurances of the Brahmans who attended Mr. Goldingham, that their ancient books "contained no account of any of the structures here described, except *the stone pagodas near the sea* and the pagodas of brick at the village."† The obvious error of the last statement certainly detracts from the value to be assigned to the former ; but it should not be forgotten, that these brick pagodas were in their own possession, and in present use : so that they had a motive for assigning to *them* a fabulous degree of antiquity : while they had no such inducement for making an untrue distinction

between the caves and the other remains, all equally
abandoned and valueless to themselves.

But whatever the age either actual or relative of
the various temples of Mahābalipūr, it seems certain, that at some distant period, the place was one
of no small importance. The ground immediately
inland from the shore temple has obviously been
built over to a considerable extent. The extremely
well-cemented foundations of ancient walls are now
dug out, as required for building materials, by the
inhabitants of the neighbouring village; or for the
improvement of the brick pagoda. I examined a
large mass of concrete, with bricks on the lower
surface, and found it extremely solid and in excellent preservation. It consisted of sharp broken
fragments of the granite of the place, mixed with
unburned shells: the excellent mortar in which
they were embedded being probably these same sea
shells burned. The bricks were of the large size
usual in all old Hindu structures: but not uniform
in their shape. Those I measured varied from
eleven to thirteen inches in length, from seven to
seven and half in breadth, and were pretty regularly
two inches thick;* so well laid in the finest mortar,

---

* I append a memorandum of the dimensions of all bricks I have
collected within the limits of the Mahābhārata, and an average of a
much larger number of specimens from the neighbourhood gives 15¼
by 8½ by 2½.

Panerput Fort ...15 inch. long, 9 inch. wide, 2½ inch. thick.
Barnawa do. ...17   ,,   9   ,,   3¼   ,,
Hustinapoor do...14   ,,   9   ,,   2½   ,,

Average. 15¼   ,,   9   ,,   2½   ,,

It will be observed that here again the most variable dimension is
the length; and the average of these north country bricks will be
found to be exactly of the same proportions as the average of those at

that five of them *in situ* barely measured eleven
inches. Most of the houses in the village are built
of these old bricks; but the ruins are so completely
covered with a deposit of soil, and drift sand, that
numerous excavations would be necessary to afford
even the vaguest idea of their extent. It is however certain that there must have been a wealthy,
and therefore in all probability a numerous popu-
lation, where dwelling-houses were built of burned
bricks, cemented with lime mortar; and where
masons were sufficiently acquainted with the mys-
teries of their art, to use foundations of concrete,
formed of the most durable materials, and on the
most approved principles. It must be remembered
that in classical days the extremity of the peninsula
was the entrepôt of commerce between the east
and the west. Gibbon says, "Every year, about the
summer solstice, a fleet of a hundred and twenty
vessels sailed from Myus Hormas, a port of Egypt
on the Red Sea. The coast of Malabar or the
island of Ceylon was the usual term of their navi-
gation, and it was in those markets that the mer-
chants from the more remote parts of Asia expected
their arrival. This fleet traversed the ocean in
about forty days by the periodical assistance of the
monsoons." Whence we gather that the European
fleets proceeded to India with the commencement
of the S. W. monsoon; and remained there until
the beginning of the N. Easterly; which is conso-
nant with all we know of the habits of the seamen
of antiquity. But, at that time of year, the ports

Mahabalipur, the length 15½ and breadth 9, being pretty nearly to
the length 12 and breadth 7¼ inches as the thickness 2½ is to the
thickness ⅘.

of the Malabar Coast would have been extremely
unsafe; besides that no large city is known to have
flourished at that epoch anywhere near Ceylon,
with access from that quarter.   It is therefore far
more probable that the laden ships, favoured by the
strong southerly current along the shore, passed *by*
the Malabar Coast, and *by* the island of Ceylon, to
find harbour on the Coromandel Coast, and await the
change that would take them on their return voyage.
I have the authority of a commander of approved
skill and well acquainted with these seas for saying
that there are no physical features to prohibit the
idea that Màvalipûr may have been one of these
ports.   He answers my enquiries : "There are no
reefs off the Seven Pagodas; and the only danger
in the vicinity is a small reef nearly abreast of the
Collector's house at Tripalore, hence called the
Tripalore reef, upon which one of the Company's
vessels was wrecked some fifty years ago : but so
near shore (half mile) as not to create any alarm at
the present day," when its situation is perfectly
ascertained.   He adds, that even now ships passing
along this coast generally make Sadras hills, to get
into a good position for reaching more northern parts ;
and that "there is no reason why the anchorage
at the Seven Pagodas should not be as safe as
Madras roads."   Nor are there wanting indications
of the place having formerly possessed far better
anchorage than either Madras or Pondicherry could
ever boast.   Behind and south of the sculptured
ridge for some distance inland, runs a salt-marsh,
bearing every appearance of having once formed
part of the estuary, which debouches about half-way
between Sadras and the shore Pagoda.   The soil is

not at all like once firm ground, overflowed by the ocean, but rather the light pulpy character of silt, deposited by contending currents and streams in some nook, where their forces neutralised one another: an operation well known to be proceeding down to the present day in every quarter of the globe. A corresponding action, minor in degree because only due to rain and atmosphere, has most certainly taken place on the other side of the sculptured ridge; as is shown by the five or six feet of alluvial soil under which the ruins of the city[*] are now buried: and we can with equal confidence assert, that foreigners were in the habit of visiting the place, as among the coins found in the vicinity have been some of Rome, of China, and other distant lands. No very great increase of depth in the estuary would (I *believe*, but I could not obtain accurate soundings) be necessary to admit vessels of the burthen then usual, and to afford them shelter equal to any on the coast. We have, therefore, I think, good reason to conclude that in the olden days of which so few records have reached us, when the Chinese, the Phœnicians and the men of Tarsis united, as in the present day, the extreme east and west in bonds of amity by the mutual interchange of commodities, Mávalipúr or Mahábalipuram was a place of considerable commercial resort; and perhaps one of the chief ports of Southern India: very probably the Maleurpha of Ptolemy.[†] I am far from considering it equally certain that this was the capital city of the mythological hero Bali. We

[* The writer here begs the question.]

[† Heeren's theory.—See his Historical Researches, Asiatic Nations, Vol. ii, pp. 83, 295.]

all know the tendency of the Brahmans to appropriate to their own sect every relic of antiquity
they found in the countries over which they extended their influence : and beyond their own assertions
I do not know that we have the least evidence to
the fact. "The name still surviving" will seem to
many a strong argument : only it will not prove a
sound one.   The name of Mahábalipuram, "the city
of the great Bali," is only known at the present day
to the Brahmans, and to Europeans who derived all
their information either directly or indirectly from
the Brahmans : and as there is no reason to believe
that Sanscrit or Hindi was at any epoch the
vernacular of that part of the country, we can
hardly suppose that such a purely Sanscrit name
ever was in common use thereabouts.   Had the
current name among the people been one that might
possibly be considered a Tamil version of this
significant epithet, we might certainly give some
weight to the fact of such a name lingering about
these remarkable antiquities : but on the contrary,
the common names* of Mallapúr or Mávalipúram
are said to have no such meaning ;† and the similarity of sound would rather favour the idea that
the Brahmans, finding these remains with a name
firmly annexed, adapted both to their own purposes ;
by fixing upon that one of their fabulous heroes,
to whose title the foreign word could most easily
be converted.   Their own books do not afford much

[* The common name is Mávalivaram, apparently a corruption of
Mahábalipuram. The old name given in the Sthalapuran (see
Appendix) is Mallápuri, but it is now entirely in disuse.]

† I cannot speak positively nor of my own knowledge, not being
sufficient of a Tamil scholar

support to their present claims.   The Mahábhárata describes the city as being

मनुजाः दक्षिणे भागे योजनानां शतद्वयं ।
पञ्चयोजनमात्रेण पूर्वाब्धेरेव पश्चिमे ॥*

"South of the Ganges 200 Yojanas, 5 Yojanas westward from the Eastern sea." It must be admitted that we do not know the exact equivalent of the Indian Yojana :† but it has generally been considered between nine and twelve miles, either of which would carry us far south of Ceylon! If therefore this quotation refers to any city on the present continent of India, we must greatly reduce the length of the Yojana : say to five or even four miles, which would about bring us to the latitude of Mávalipuram.   But we must suppose that the proportion of two hundred to five was somewhat near the truth : and this would oblige us to look for Bali's capital not on the sea shore but twenty miles inland, where to the best of my information no vestige of a city remains. If we assume the Yojana five miles instead of four, we shall certainly be able to satisfy both conditions pretty well in Combaconum, the Benares of the south, or in the ancient capital‡ of the Pándya kingdom, but either explanation is equally fatal to the claims of Mávalipuram.

It is true that it has been generally believed that

[* See Appendix.]

† A Pandit in this neighbourhood (Rohilcund) called it "four kos :" which would be from five to six English miles; as the local kos is seldom as much as 1½ miles: and from a note to Chap. xxb § of Fa Hian's pilgrimage it would seem that farther south the Yojana was only four miles.

[‡ Madura.]

[§ See also Note 1, Chap. xiii]

the sea had encroached on this shore, and that many
pagodas and buildings of this ancient city had been
submerged even since the English settlements took
place ; and it may therefore be said that in all probability the site of this city was actually twenty
miles from the sea in the days when the Mahábhárata was written. This idea is founded partly on
the mariner's name of the Seven Pagodas, said to
indicate the existence (in the early days of English
intercourse with India) of seven Pagodas on the
shore where now only one remains. But personal
inspection at once shows the fallacy of this derivation of the name : the shore temples being far too
low to be perceived at the distance that ships usually
pass : more especially as they are backed by the
cave-hewn ridge ; and it is infinitely more probable
that Mr. Chambers was correct in referring the
appellation to the peculiar appearance presented by
the rounded peaks of this ridge itself, especially
as temples were vaguely known to exist in that
neighbourhood without their situation being very
accurately settled. He says, "The rock, or rather
hill of stone, on which great part of these works
are executed, is one of the principal marks for mariners as they approach the coast, and to them this
place is known by the name of the Seven Pagodas ;
possibly because the summits of the rock have
presented them with that idea as they passed."*

A far stronger evidence however, in the general
opinion, was the tradition imparted by the Brahmans,
and perhaps other inhabitants, to the earlier European visitors of the place. Mr. Chambers relates :

[* P. 2, supra.]

"The natives of the place declared to the writer of this account, that the more aged people among them remembered to have seen the tops of several Pagodas far out in the sea; which being covered with copper (probably gilt) were particularly visible at sunrise, as their shining surface used *then* to reflect the sun's rays, but that now that effect was no longer produced, as the copper had become encrusted with mould and verdigris."* Passing over as a minor objection that "at sunrise" the dark sides of the pagoda tops would alone be visible from the shore, and that they would be best seen when illuminated by the *setting sun*, I would enquire how is it possible that these slender ornaments should shine "far out" in the surf of the Coromandel Coast, where not years or months, but a few hours of the stiff gales, with which it is so constantly visited, would be all-sufficient not only to destroy the lustre of gilt copper, but to dislodge every stone between high and low water mark? It cannot be supposed that any sudden convulsion lowered the whole coast, so that all at once the waves should roll within a few feet of the top instead of below the foundations of the pagodas; for such a convulsion must infallibly have shaken them to pieces, as well as levelled the existing temple, whose still uninjured pinnacles clearly disprove the hypothesis: therefore the subsidence, if ever it took place, must have been extremely gradual, like those of the Swedish and parts of the Italian coast: and recollecting the numerous years, (not to say centuries) that would be required to sink the forty or fifty feet which may

[* P. 11, *supra*.]

reasonably be assumed to have been the height of the vanished structures, I only ask is it credible that the waves should have spared them until only their tops (still bright and glittering notwithstanding the dashing spray ! ! !) remained above the surface.

I am sorry to be obliged thus to demolish the beautiful romance of the "Wave-covered metropolis of Bali ;" but it is not the first of the aerial castles of Indian tradition that has faded before the fuller light of modern European investigation. Like Bishop Heber I find it difficult to understand how this particular spot should have sunk so much, if (as other writers aver) the rest of the Coromandel Coast, both north and south, has rather risen within historical times. I have already mentioned the local features leading me to conclude that this immediate vicinity has not suffered any encroachment from the ocean, but has rather gained from, and increased in elevation above it by alluvial deposits from the higher lands :* and if a Brahman legend is required, there happens to exist one in the Mackenzie papers (vide Mr. Taylor's 3rd report, section 2, page 63,†) that comes as near to my view of the formation of the salt-marsh, as those tales generally do to the natural truths they often dimly chronicle.

---

* The brick foundations I have mentioned as being five or six feet below the present surface of the land, are very considerably more than that amount above high-water mark. I have not noticed Captain Newbold's argument in favour of the submersion of the city, viz., that Chinese and other coins are often washed ashore in storms; because the fact is equally explicable by the supposition that this was a port frequented by foreign ships, of which some must necessarily, in the course of years, have been wrecked and sunk in the vicinity.

[† Madras Journal, Vol. viii.]

[‡ Notes on the Coast of Coromandel, in Journ. Asiat. Socy. of Bengal. Vol. xv, p. 210.]

n

In early times one Mallesudu ruled here prosperously ; but having refused charity to a Brahman, he was changed into an alligator. A *Rishi* named Pundarika, going to pluck a lotus flower in the tank where the alligator lay, was seized by it, but had power to drag it out. The king thus obtained release and went to Svarga. The *Rishi* wished to present the lotus flower to Vishnu, but the sea barred his way, and would not retreat ; so he sat down to bale the sea out ! While thus occupied, an ancient Brahman came and asked for boiled rice, offering to do the *Rishi's* work, while the latter should go and cook it. By taking up a single handful of water the sea retreated a whole coss, and when the *Rishi* returned he found the Brahman reposing in the manner in which statues of Vishnu are sometimes represented. He now recognised the god, and a fane was built by him over the spot. If this tale have any real foundation, it probably indicates that after a period of abandonment this site was re-occupied, and great increase of land discovered to have taken place about the time when the worship of Vishnu was introduced into the southern peninsula ; which being a date tolerably ascertained, may possibly guide some future visitor in fixing the age of the various structures ; especially if assisted by some translation of the inscriptions which were unfortunately quite unintelligible to me.

It will be observed that I have made the freest use of the accounts of other travellers : partly, in order to present in a general view the remarks now scattered in half a dozen volumes, and partly in order to support by the authority of others the conclusions drawn in my own confessedly hasty visit. Had I only been as well acquainted at that time as I am now with the writings of my predecessors, I should have investigated far more closely several points that I now perceive with regret I almost overlooked. The shore temple alone can be said to have been thoroughly examined: and I suppose it must have been deemed less worthy of notice by former travellers: else I do not understand how it could escape remark that the original entry of the building must have been through the portion, which is in rear at present.[*] I trust what I have said may draw the attention of men better versed in Indian antiquities to the subject of the direction in which the entrance is placed in Hindu temples: as it may possibly prove characteristic of some particular sect or epoch. At the present day, all temples in these Upper Provinces (and as far as my observation goes, in the other Presidencies also) are turned towards the east: and a Brahman at Huridwar gave me as a reason the rising of the sun in that quarter. I remember to have seen one exception (besides the Kailâs at Ellora already mentioned;) which is on the grand trunk-road on the banks of the Burseher near Taldanga.[†] In a group of four temples, not differing essentially in style or architecture, and all apparently quite modern, one is turned to the west, while all the others are to the east. I could not discover that

---

[*] I have not been able to procure the papers of Mr. Babington or of Mr. Walter Elliot on the subject: but of the four or five I have perused, no one touches this point.

[†] And I think that among the Âryan temples of Cashmere, is said to be a group of four facing to all four cardinal points.

they belonged to different divinities, but there was no person near from whom I could positively ascertain that such was not the case.

Another point that strikes me as deserving attention, more particularly from Engineers and persons engaged on public works, is the very great durability of the basaltic rock as compared with the granite of the Coromandel Coast. We have no reason to believe that the umbrella-shaped summits of the temples, which for want of a better term I have called *chaityas*,* are otherwise than contemporaneous with the rest of the temple ; and they are, of course, equally exposed to the spray and saline atmosphere : yet they appear perfectly fresh and uninjured, while the granite has lost the whole of its outer surface by gradual disintegration and exfoliation.

I append two sketch plans to elucidate the above descriptions of locality : but they have no pretensions to strict accuracy, being done entirely from memory, months after I visited the place.

[* Kalsas is the proper name of these pinnacles.]

of the country around
MÁVALÍPÚR.

*Sketch Plan of the Temple
on the Shore*

APPENDIX.

[By the Editor.]

The Sthalapurâna.

The Sthalapurâna or Local legend of Mallâpurî has been examined. It professes to be contained in Adhyâyas 93—100 of the Kshetrakhanda of the Brahmândapurâna, and is styled Mallâpurîmâhâtmya.

The opening lines are as follows :—

एकदा नारदो योगी माक्कती वाजिबो बबा ।
संचुब्धरदयोमीक्षं नाह्रब्धिन्ने समाधित: ॥१॥
बच बुभाप्रवी योगी विचिन्वन् तस्स कारणं ।
न किंश्चिम्राप मतिमान् बङ्कधापि विचारयन् ॥२॥
बच चेतस्समाधानं तपष्षेति विचिंतयन् ।
मतिमांसख्ख परष्षे स्खानवर्षमचिंतयत् ॥३॥
दिचु षर्वासु ते मेरौ निवषं मे अपीजुषा ।
संतुष्टया षया तस्स आभतो मुनिरैधत ॥४॥*
ततस्स नारदो योगी जमाम षयषमर: ।

* Three MSS. examined, read as above; the following reading of the 4th sloka has been suggested by a Pandit :—

दिचु षर्वासु तं मेरौ षिषघं समुपेषिवान् ।
संतुष्टा च बया तस्सा आमतो मुनिरैधत ॥

वल्लकीकान्तदेकाकी अटामंडलमंडित: ॥५॥

य मुक्तेन मतिमान् मुमेरं रब्पमेस्वरं ।

चक्रेन तु तटे रम्ये प्राप श्रीचं सुनोश्वर: ॥६॥

य गत्वा तच अटिच्चान् मुनीश्चिरक्रतायनान् ।

भाद्यायन्यस्तनयनान् भाभवार्पितच्लेव: ॥७॥

वषमानाच दर्भाच्चैनिव्वलान् निव्यनिर्मदान् ।

ददर्य नारदो दृष्टस्तानन्तनाम सहस्रम: ॥८॥

भैत्यं कुयमं दृष्टो बङ्कधा परिभाचित: ।

इट्चागमनार्चे च वश्राचे वचनं मुनि: ॥८॥

लुनचो योगबंविद्गा: संतुष्टं मानचं मम ।

दर्यनाद्भवतां मद्घ: भूयतां वचनं मम ॥९॥

भवतां सन्निधाद्यच तपच्चरणनिच्चात् ।

चागतोद्यं मनस्तोवाद्यच्चोकाम्मुनीश्वरा: ॥११॥

वांक्रते पुनरप्यच मनोनुमतिमच व: ।

तस्माच्चि क्षपावज्ञा दिचाम्य: क्षुच चोनिनि: ॥१२॥

एतच्कृम्वा वचो रच्वं चीर्क्मिनो चोचिनस्तत: ।

संतुह्राच्लुचुरुच्चानं ब्रह्माचममुदाहृतं ॥१३॥

पुरा किल मुने तातस्तव लोकपितामह: ।

चचिमचापाभिभ्रतस्वन् संचुचचदचस्तथा ॥१४॥

माधवेन मचवेन निचुक्तस्तचमे क्षचं ।

अगम्वृचचमी श्रह्मा तपच्चेपैतिदुचरं ॥१५॥

चचाष्ट्यचतमच्व्राच तम्राच्चुर्यं परं तप: ।

अष: प्रापातिविमलं मनोचिचचमात्मन: ॥१६॥

तान्स्थानं परमं दिव्यं तव तातच्च नारद।

अचस्सिद्विक्वरं पूर्णां तदेव तच च रच्चं ॥१७॥

वर्षेवामसवर्षे तु परमं तप आचर ।

इति तयायगुष्टानतपपद्वरचक्राक्षम्: ॥१८॥

भावर्तघन् मधातंचमतिइझ्खुचिरं मुनि: ।

यतं तु देक्तर्षीणां च चरणं दुखरं तप: ॥१८॥

"Once upon a time, Nârada Yogi became, like
one of the vulgar and ignorant, much disturbed in
mind, and meditation no longer occupied his thoughts.
2. Then the Yogi with mind thus agitated sought
for the cause thereof, but the wise man found none,
though he searched in many ways. 3. Afterwards,
thinking that by penance peace would be restored to
his mind, the wise man bethought him of an excellent place for its performance. 4. Out of all places
he fixed on Meru, and the Muni greatly rejoiced at
the prospect. 5. Then Nârada Yogi, adorned with
braided hair, departed speedily and alone from
Satyaloka. 6. The sage reached in a Muhúrta the
gem-tipped Sumeru ; quickly, in a moment, did the
great Muni reach the lovely height. 7, 8. He,
having gone there, saw the Munis with braided hair,
in long continued postures, with eyes fixed on the
root of the nose, with minds devoted to Mâdhava,
clothed in *dorbha*, &c., motionless, ever humble.
Nârada rejoiced and saluted them thousands of
times. 9. He was enquired of them regarding his
health, and conversed with on many matters ; asked
the reason of his coming, the Muni said—10. 'O perfect Munis! by seeing you my mind is instantly
rejoiced, listen ye to my speech : 11. With the
resolution of performing penance here, in your
presence, O great Munis, have I come with joyful

mind from Satyaloka. 12. Now my mind desires
to obtain your consent here, and therefore favor must
be shown towards me. What place will the Yogis
appoint me?' 13. Then the Yogis, having heard
the sweet speech of [Nárada] Yogi, rejoiced ; and
praised the place called Brahmásrama. 14. 'O
Muni, was not thy father, the grandfather of the
world, formerly humbled in like manner by Atri's
curse, and disturbed in his mind? 15. Brahmâ,
powerless in creating the world and commanded to
do penance by Mádhava, performed penance the most
difficult. 16. Here for eight hundred years having
performed penance meritorious and most severe, he
obtained again his own very pure and settled mind.
17. O Nárada, that, thy father's excellent and heavenly place which instantly perfects a man, that is
thy place also. 18. Here, in the excellent Ásrama,
perform the highest penance.' There, thus permit-
ted, he was eagerly desirous of performing penance.
19. That Rishi remained for long repeating the
Mahâmantra,* and for a hundred divine years performing severe penance."

Nárada however does not experience any benefit
from this protracted austerity, and finds his mind
remain as disturbed as before. He then goes sor-
rowing to his father Brahmâ in Brahmaloka, and tells
him of his state. Brahmâ bids him recall any probable cause for it, when he recollects having denied
Vishnu's accessibility *(saulabhya,)* and maintained
his inaccessibility *(parates).* (xciii, 20—41.) Brahmâ
then relates to him the discussion between Agastya
and Súta on this topic, which again involves Siva's

* The Ashtâksharî.

answers to Púrvati's questions regarding Vishnu's attributes. (xciii. 42—95). In reply to Párvatí's question as to how Vishnu became accessible, Siva related the story of Pundarika Rishi who went to Yadugiri,* to worship Vishnu, meeting with sundry adventures on the way. The Rishi afterwards visited the sacred places on the East Coast, coming to the Varáhakshetra. From thence, going South, he came to a beautiful garden where he saw a *Yogi*, named Vishnusarma, and near that garden he perceived a pond *(pushkarini)* in which were wonderful lotuses. While plucking these, Pundarika heard a voice from heaven, saying, 'Lo! here are large and priceless lotuses of the colour of gold, of delightful perfume, having a thousand petals—these are fit for the worship of the god who dwells on the Sea of milk, but not for that of other deities.' Greatly rejoicing, the Rishi proceeded to pluck the whole of the flowers, when a crocodile came to attack him, but mistook a lotus stalk for the holy man's leg, was pierced in the tongue by the thorns, and from loss of blood lay as dead on the water. (xciv. 1—86.) The Rishi went near, and the crocodile addressed him in a soft voice and told its story, commencing :—

पुरा जन्मान्तरं ब्रह्मन् राजा सर्वमहीपतिः ।
राजा च सर्वकामानां मल्लापुर्वीं वसाम्यहं ॥

'In a former birth, O Brahman, I was king of the whole earth, and dwelt at Mallápuri, granting to all their wishes.' Then the crocodile gave the Rishi

---

* A sacred hill at Mélkóta in Mysore.

N

an elaborate and extravagant description of Mallápuri, adding :—

मन्नेयर दति ख्यात: भुवनचयविभुन: ।
विष्णुमन्नष्यतानंद: पुत्रो मम महानुति: ॥

'My son Satánanda, a votary of Vishnu, of ex-
alted mien, and famed in the three worlds, is celebrated as Mallesvara.'

After this follows a description of Satánanda's
Court, &c. The crocodile then told the Rishi how
Varáhasvámi came to Mallápuri, according to the
tradition he had received from his forefathers. Formerly there was a king called Harisekara, endowed
with all good qualities. He was in the habit of going
daily with his aged and pious mother to worship
Vishnu at Varáhakshetra,* a *yojana* distant from
Mallápuri, to the North, and feeding Brahmans after
coming back to his city. One day, Hari came to
Mallápuri disguised as an old decrepit Brahman,
accompanied by his daughter, and asked for food.
The king requested him to wait a little until he returned from Varáhakshetra. The old man begged
for immediate relief as he was greatly fatigued and
his daughter was hungry. The king then suspected
that he had been visited by Vishnu in disguise, worshipped the old man and gave him food. He then
saw Varáhasvámi in his proper form, with the goddess Earth on his right hip.

The Brahmans who had come as usual for food
were suddenly and miraculously filled up to the neck
(*ákanthapúrnáh*) and afterwards besought Varáhasvámi to remain always at Mallápuri. The god

* ? The village of Tiruradandai, near Covelong (Kórlam.)

consented, and being asked why he looked towards the West replied that he did so because the Punya-kotivimânu* was to come in the East at a distance of five *yojanas.*

The crocodile added that his father Harinandana abdicated the throne in his favor and became an anchorite. His own name he stated to be Haripriya. (xciv. 87—180.)

The crocodile than told the story of his being cursed. One day a Brahman came and asked for food. The king in his pride treated him with contempt. The Brahman enraged cursed him saying "Become thou a crocodile, O king." The people afterwards interceded with the Brahman for their king, and were told that when he met a votary of Vishnu, the curse would be removed. (xcv. 1—30.) The crocodile then was transformed into a youth of 16 years and went to heaven. Pundarîka Rishi taking with him the lotuses strung in garlands, set out to worship Vishnu on the Sea of Milk and arrived at the shore of the Salt Sea. (xcv. 21—55.) The Rishi attempted to bale out the ocean in order to proceed on his journey! This he continued for a year, when he desisted being wearied. At this time an old Brahman approached and questioned him.

The Rishi told the Brahman his story and of his wish to visit Vishnu, and the latter recommended him to abandon his attempt to get over the Sea ; this enraged Pundarîka who requested the Brahman either to help him or to go about his business. The old man then asked for food, girded his loins and commenced to bale. At the first handful thrown out by

---

* The name of the large Vishnu temple at Cunjeveram.

him, the Sea receded a *lôs.* Pundarika went for
food and on returning perceived that his Brahman
friend was no other than Vishnu, whom he found
reclining on the shore, with the lotus garlands round
his neck, facing to the East. The *Rishi* then
worshipped the god, as Sthalasayana, with praises and
offerings of lotuses. (xcv. 56—75. xcvi. 1—10.)
Vishnu then told Pundarika to ask a boon. The
Rishi replied that having obtained Vishnu he sought
for nothing else. " Will he who has reached the
boundless Sea of nectar care for the water of a small
muddy pond ?" He begged that the god would
always remain in that place, saying he required no
other boon. Vishnu consented and praised Pundarika for making this request. Then came Brahmá
to the Sea shore with *Yakshas,* * *Gandharwas* † and
Apsarases. ‡ The drums of the gods sounded, flowers
rained from heaven, and the sound of "JAYA !"
(Victory) was heard like the roaring of the Sea.
All worshipped the god and godlings that praised
Vishnu for his sensibility *(sadáshya).* Afterwards the Brahmans, and the king Mallâdhipa or
Satânanda, with the people of the city, came to the
Sea shore. All were intoxicated with joy at Vishnu's
appearance among them, and worshipped him. On
being asked under what name he would dwell
among them he replied " Know me as Sthalasáyî,
who here recline on the ground." The King and
people worshipped Vishnu and praised Pundarika.
Mallesvara then heard the *Rishi's* history and was
rejoiced to learn that his father had been released

* Demi-gods attendant on Kuvera, the god of wealth.
† See note § p. 204. *infra.*   ‡ Nymphs of Swarga, Indra's heaven

from the Brahman's curse and had gone to heaven. The Brahmans then bathed in the Pundarikasarasu and made offerings. The King, following the counsel of Pundarika, bestowed gifts and lands upon the Brahmans. Afterwards a *Vimána,* called Ánanda-nilayam, having 7 pinnacles and containing a shining image, descended from Vaikuntha,* round which the king built a wall with a *Gopura.* Siva concluded with praises of Mallápuri, (xcvi. 11—73, xcvii. 1—78, xcviii. 1—115).

Agastya accepted the arguments of Súta, (which embodied the story of Pundarika *Rishi* given above), took leave of him and set out for Mallápuri. He met with favourable omens on his way and came to a great mountain called Samvartana. Hearing a confused noise above him he looked up and perceived some of Yama's† soldiers dragging away a Brahman. He then saw Vishnu's soldiers release the prisoner and heard the dispute between them and the servants of the god of death. The latter described all the great sins which the Brahman had been guilty of, the like of which had never been seen or heard, while the former maintained that having gone to Mallápuri, and stayed one day at that holy place, all his sins had been washed away and that they who laid hands on him themselves committed sin and rendered themselves liable to be reduced to ashes. (xcix. 1—77).

Agastya was astonished and pressed on towards

---

* Vishnu's heaven.

† "The Deity of hell; he corresponds with the Grecian god Pluto, and the judge of hell Minos, and in Hindu mythology is often identified with Death and Time."—Wilson.

Mallâpuri. Passing through a dense forest, he saw six virgin devotees performing penance. He approached them, told them he was Agastya and saluted them. They received him with great respect, and told him they were Gangâ, transformed by a curse into the form of six bodies.

The virgins added that formerly when they were performing penance in the forest called Tilavanam all the Rishis assembled on the Himavat mountains and discussed the relative merits of the holy waters (*tîrthas*). They praised the Gangâ and Kâverî, but agreed that the Pundarîka pond was the most excellent of all, and that Gangâ and the other rivers should be its slaves!

The Munis having thus decided, went to their respective homes. Gangâ, wandering sorrowfully, met Shanmukha,* while he was performing penance in a certain place, and told him the cause of her grief. He in reply said that she had no ground for complaint, as, great though she was, the Pundarîka pond was yet far superior. Shanmukha then told Gangâ how, after incurring the sin of killing a Brahmin in his fight with the Dânava named Târaka,† he had been cleansed from all guilt by bathing in the Pundarîka pond at Mallâpuri. He then told Gangâ that all would approve of her putting aside her jealousy and self-love, and that she would be freed from slavery by bathing in those waters. Shanmukha

---

* Kartikeya, as the "Six-faced."

† Kartikeya (Skanda) was born to lead the armies of the gods, and to destroy Târaka.—See Coleman's Mythology of the Hindus, p. 74 ff, Wilson's note on v. 207 of the *Meghadûta*, and Muir's Sanscrit Texts, Part IV., pp. 392 ff. 308.

then taught Gangá the Rámatáraka,* and told her to perform penance, repeating with six faces this mantra. This she was doing in the Tila forest. Agastya, leaving the virgins, again hastened on to Mallápurí. (xcix. 78—134.)

Agastya reached Mallápurí and met there a crowd of Munis round the temple of Sthalasayanasvámí, called Ánandanilayam. Some lived on water, some lived on air, some on roots, fruits, and leaves. Emaciated in body, they retained life solely by the power derived from penance. They assumed the *Garuda*-posture, lay like snakes, or sat like fowls. Some stood on the point of the toe, others with upraised arms; some sat self-supported in the air, others between five fires.† They were Brahmins and Kshatriyas. Agastya saluted them and told them his name. They received him with different marks of respect, and he begged to be allowed to live with them without performing penance or repeating prayers, on the ground that Hari would be satisfied with simple worship. To this the Munis agreed, and told him to bathe in the Pundarika pond with a prayerful mind. Agastya did so and then visited the temple. There he saw Sthalasayana, who had graciously descended at the prayer of his worshipper Pundaríka, reclining with his head resting on his right hand and with his left inviting his worshippers to approach him.

Agastya was submerged in the ocean of delight, and offered worship and praise to the god. Vishnu received him graciously, commanded the Muni to

* A formula addressed to Ráma, as *Bándya maneá.*—Wilson.

† *Pańchágni.*—four fires and the sun overhead.—See plate 13 in, Mrs. Belnos' *Suadhya.*

worship him daily and to perform the five *Dikshas*,[*]
and appointed him an *Asrama* named Aṣvatha on the
North side of the Pundarika pond.   Vishnu then.
at Agastya's desire. condescended to narrate to him
how Tārksha lost and recovered his wings.   On one
occasion when Vishnu called Garuda to carry him
on a visit to Svarga, the bird came so fast that the
dust he raised fell on a pious worshipper of Vishnu
who was engaged in his devotions.   Vishnu then in
anger caused Tārksha's wings to drop off, and the
bird fell into a forest on the shore of the Western
Sea.   After bathing in vain in many holy waters he
at last came to Mallāpuri where his wings began to
grow.   Vishnu then instructed Agastya in the mode
of worship and declared that those were dear to him
who loved those that loved him (*matpriyā matpriye
priyāh.*)   Agastya took up his abode accordingly at
Mallāpuri.   (c. 1—113.)

Then Brahmā concludes :—

तस्माकारद् जानीहि विष्णुं जीवस्ततंत्रं ।
तेन निर्वंद चित्तं मवेन्तव न वैशः ॥ ११४ ॥
यो जानाहीष तस्तीर्य मस्वद्दोजभवागरं ।
न तत्र सुभसे सुद्धि: यथा न सक्तचेषि च ॥ ११५ ॥
तस्माच्चं तत्र गत्वा तु देविता स्वतमाधिनं ।
स्नात्वा मरति पुण्ये च चित्तनैर्मल्यमन्वषि ॥ ११६ ॥

114.   Therefore, O Nārada, know thou Vishnu to
be an ocean of accessibility ; by him, without doubt,
thy mind will become clear.   115. His understanding

---

[*] *Diksha* is the ceremony of initiation. the essential part of which is
the *Tapta Mudrā* or branding the novice with the conch and discus.—
Wilson's *Essays*, Vol. I., p. 56.

will not be confused who in this world knows Lakshmísa,* an ocean of accessibility to his votaries; even at the destruction of the world, [he will suffer] no pain. 116. Therefore having gone there, and bathed in the holy pond and worshipped Sthalasayi, thou shalt obtain purity of mind.

Nárada then goes to Mallápuri and staying there for "many days," obtains all his desire. (c. 117, 118.)

Note.

It will be observed from the foregoing analysis of the Sthalapurána that (1) it contains no mention of any of the old rock cut temples or of the shore temple. The Varáhasvami temple is not an exception, inasmuch as the formation of this temple by enclosing the sculptured representation of the Boar Incarnation on the West face of the hill is of modern date.† And (2) no allusion whatever is made herein to the story of Bali or the submersion of his city.

This legend appears to have been composed for the purpose of attracting pilgrims to the place after the construction of the modern Vishnu temples. The Vaishnava author ingeniously makes Brahmá, Siva, Kártikeya and all the Saints extol the sin-destroying virtue of Mallápuri.

The names of kings mentioned in the Mallápuri Máhátmya appear to be fictitious.

---

* Vishnu, as "Lakshmi's lord."   † See p. 55, *supra.*

Description of the Pagodas, &c., at Māvalivaram,
written in the Telugu language by Kavali Laksh-
matya *in* 1803. [*With a translation.*]

[From the Mackenzie MSS., No. 23. C. M. 757.]

౧. సర్వకాలి శ్వరరఖాగము యాగ్యమవిరోకల. ఇందుకా యాగ్య
పడు శ్వాదు. ఈ కొంబలయంతరబందిన రాష్ట్ర శ్రేత్ర యొత్తుగాని
శొయూగాదు.

౨. దీనిమీంచెర రెండు కొత్తలు శెయమాయకొంటూ త్రన్నవి.

3. ఆపడమటివక్కుమ కొండవులధర్థపత్ని అయిన శ్రావది శిరుసురిత
ఆశొక్ష వగలి మంతూగా త్రన్నది. మూడెయంతరులు యెక్షలమ సవ్య
మూగా కొంచిమరి త్రన్నది. పాటుకము ౧ ఆస్త దిశ్రాల అస్వరవాం
తాం ౨, పాటుల మద్ద చింతులూవాలోశి ఆస్త. తానాకొండ్యక్సాం
ష ఆస్త. ష్ష్ష రెండు అనెక ఇశి శ్రావరమగా త్రన్నది. ఈ
తుల దక్షీంత్రీరువు ఇబివితిముఖముచేముగాని వగ దుష్ట ఆష్టతువాం
కొత్తి మహిషాపురునిరెక్షప్రుమిద కసహదముని శ్రాక్ష్య త్రన్నది.

౪. ఇంచుక సహిపవముగా దక్షిణఖాగమంచు భాటక దపమటిపైత్ర
ధిమపాదు పాకముచేసిన చాయ త్రన్నది. కావిమీది మొక్ష టంచుక
కాటికాలు త్రన్నది.

౫. ఆంచుక సహిపరమాగా దక్షిణఖాగమంచు టంచమీదను శ్రావది
చేసపొన్నముక్త వగ సొప్పసుంచుగా త్రన్నది. ఆంచురో చగతం పిల్లి ఇపిత్
చాశది ఆది మొర్రిగా ఆసుపతుతూ త్రన్నది. ఆ పిల్లి ఆశుపచు కుట
శృచేమకొంటూ త్రన్న సర్వరాపక కట్టిచేపష్టుగా ఉంచరికొశ్శ పైక
చొత్తునాని త్రన్నది.

౹. ఇందుకు దక్షిణపు వైపు మొకలంలోనే ఆళాసువిరళము ఉన్నది. ఈకల రోలిని ఇంద మంటపములోనిది రెండు స్తంభాలతో అందులో నున్న గర్భనుడి యొర్నది కవప్రతిష్ట చేసినది. ఆ లింగాన్ని చూ•• యొస్తురుపోతే యీ స్థలములోహాయి దగ్గర పత విజయుకుకు ఉండిగా తిముకపోయి అందులో ఉండిరి. ఈ గర్భనుడి దక్షిణపు గోప మాచక కాసనమేమేహు ప్రాసినాయు. ఆది యే రిధి ఆయినది రొరిచి కాదు.

౨. ఇందుక పమిరతము గా దక్షిణభాగమందు తరాశాస్యిమి ఉండే యో కలామంటపముకు ఉన్నది. ఇందులో స్తంభాలు ౨, గర్భనుడి గాయూ గర్భ నడిలో యొరూ ప్రతికలు లేవు. ద్వారపాలకులు యున్దరు. ఈ గర్భన కీ వ్రతపభాగమందు గోవమోదకు పరాహాస్యిమి సామపాదము భూమి యందు ఉండుకొని, దక్షిణహురము ఆరోకుమిళకళున్సూర రెట్టి, దక్షిణో నవ్రమోర లక్ష్మిఅమ్మకారినా ఆభిముఖముగా ఉండుకొని, దక్షిణోన్రతము అత్త వారి పియమలమీద ఉండుకొని, హాపశాస్యమచేత దక్షిణోహురము భకించి రొత కప్పికుభముకుపై అమ్పహాయు పూర్యాధిముఖముతో ఉండుగా, పరా హాస్యిమివాయు కదమ రెంపుకాహింలందుకు కంభన్క్రాలు భరించి తత రువ్యయంపుపై ఆసౌష్యవ్యముకాపరాపికప చెర్తూ శ్రీదాదింలాహార్జకము అత్త కారి దక్షోస్తపను కపపరాహామఖముతో చుంలపమచేర్తూ ఉన్నాడు. ఇక రెరుకర పూర్యాభాగము పకుర్పుపాయొర్కముగా పత పురుపప్రతిక ఉన్నది. ఈ ప్రపికత ఆభిముభముగా పక శ్రీ ప్రతిప ఉన్నది. ఈ యిర్ధు పాద పక భర్తకు కృపాంబిలిపపుక్షైపై పుపోర్పూ తన్నారు. నిర్ప శాస్యమిలి యుస్తుయు రప్తిలు కుళర్తూ తన్నారు. అంత ప్రపర్ర్పపూరిం ఉండే ప్రతికము గా. పూర్యభాగము గోదిమోదకు పకృపుపసంఘముగా పత్తి పపముమీద గణింప ఉన్నది. ఈమొకళున్సూర గళపుఖాల రెండు ఉన్నది. ఈ లక్షీ థలయుపాస్యోమలయందు యుద్ధరయ యుద్ధరయ శ్రీ ఆభిప్కార్యము పూర్ణకంభాలు గపరొంచిపత అందిస్తూ ఉన్నాడు. ఇద్ప గరాలకుడు పకడు ఉన్నాడు. అంతు శ్రీ ల శ, ప్రయవప్రతిప గ, గవ ముభాల ౨ ఉన్నది. దక్షిగహాగమందు రొపెర్పత్రము భరించి పకుర్పుపా యాస్తురాలైప పత దుర్గ ఉన్నది. ఈమొక దక్షిగహాగమందు ముస్తయ భటుప

రఘునాథునై పర్వపవాళిపట్టై పున్నాడు. ఈ కృష్ణుని నామభాగ
మందు పర్యకము చగిలినది గమక హారాళోకముఖంచి శాఖశన్యలు
లల్లిపచ్చిసన్తుగానె పంచకన్యలలోకూడా ఆలాఞని ఉఞ్కేంచి శాఖ
కన్యక పచ్చినది. ఇయుక పుత్రకభాగమందు ఎరాపకమనె గలచుడిడ
ఇందుక సౌర్యాయుఞ్తముగా కపర్దళావాపక పద్మినాను అన్నట్టుగానె
పున్నాడు. ఈ ఎరాపరావక వెమక వశ దేవసు పున్న. ఎరావశము
కింద దేవసుపిల్లలు మాడు పున్నవి. పల్లి శన ప్లలంలోకూడా పూర్వక
రాచుత్రులతో పూర్వ్యాధిముఖముగా పున్నది. ఈ దేశంద్రుని పలయు
కృశగా గవడుక అద్రౌశిళ్ళి రంత్రకుపపిత్రవిద్యాధరుల తెంపడైవామ గాం
డు కార్యపిఞళ్తి కాండయ భార్యాఒహితుఞ్తి కదళూర్యానై కవ
దళెనాశక పచ్చిస్తునానె ప్రతిమలు చెప్పినావు. ఇక్కడ ప్రతిమలు
3చ పున్నవి. ఈ దేవళలమధ్యమందు ౭౦చ్ 3 పున్నవి. ఒటెనెఎళ్
పుత్రకభాగమున మధ్యముందు హింహాల 8 పున్నవి. గొఱ్ఱె ౧ పున్నవి.
ఇత్యాదయ దఞిగభాగమందు హాపిశ్తుక భర్ఱరాం ధిముద కవపృచె
ష్ట్రా కూర్చుస్నారు. ఒక దఞిమందు కంది వ్యాప్రిమ పున్నవి.
ఇత్యలదరి దఞిగభాగకాండ ప్రమధగకాం ఉయుపల కపదళెవాశక
పచ్చిస్తునానె చెప్పిపున్న ప్రతిమలు ఎరపున్నవి. హింహాము ౧౦పంది
౧ంచంలు కె-వ్యాప్రుమ ౧-కొకెలు ౩-ఈప్రపకాముగ భార్యా హాత్త
ముగా చిత్రవిచిత్రముగా పున్నారు. అంతప్రతిమలు స్త్రీ పుంహుమ పహ
లా పున్నవి.

౧౦. ఇంచక దక్గిణా దేవలాంఉంరంఉం ఏంతకఉఎండుకం మఉ
కఇంచుక పున్నవి. ఇందుక పంద్రాం గానెఎ ఇళసెళోఉంచ ౧ నాళె
కఇర్పు ౧ చ పంద్రాలు. కఇర్పు ౧ చ పంద్రాలలోఒక కాంఇరుకాఞ్ఱ ఎరుస
చూడెపచ. లోకఞ్మ్యపి రాగ పున్నవి. మంచెఇ పంద్రాంచ హింహముం
చూడఉం పున్నవి. ఇెరల హింఝలుఇ ఈ మంటపముఇపఞ్యపి ఆరఉళెఇ
పున్నది. ఇందులో కుదేమి కెదు. ఈ అరక ఉయ్రెఉర్యాఇళా ఆరలు
కృఇపఇదెపి తెందపఇళ్త్తీయహునాని పూరాకాఇెదు. అఇళ ఉయఇలు
మఉయఇ అపకెలపంఉఇక్తి హపఇహను ఇఇ శాకంఉా ఇండుపెముఇళఇ
పున్నది. కుదేమి చెఞ్లక ఇఞ్రాళెఞ్క, పాఇఇ.

౧౧. ఈ మంటపానకు దక్షిణము నాయలగోపురమునొక్క ఆదిన నాయలనుగోపురము మంటపాత్రముచేత నాలుగువముపులా నాలుగు ఖండాలయమార్క్రము నాతివాడు. ఇట్టా రాతితోన్న దేశనాయకాని గోపురము నాకేదు.

౧౨. ఇంచుక తూప్పవయిత్ర ప్లే శేషశ్వామివరడి.

౧౩. పర్వతానికి ఊర్వ్వదాగమందు కృష్ణను గోవర్ధనగిరి యెత్తిన మంటవము ౧. ఇంచుక ఖండాలయ ౧౨. ఈ మంటవము పర్వతముకు అంటా కొంచి ఊర్వ్వాధిశుఖముగా వున్నది. ఈ మంటవములో ఊండే ప్రతిమలు కృష్ణను కామరూస్తముతో గోవర్ధనగిరి గొడుగుగా యెత్తివారు. దక్షిణ ఉత్తరముచేత గోపికాలనాలక అడ్డరము యింద్రూత్రున్నారు. ఈ హవ్వమి నాతుభాగమందు 3 శ్రీ ప్రతిమలు తున్నది. ఇండిలో యిద్దరు శ్రీలు నిలుయగాని వున్నారు. వారికి తలయివాడ వెయసకంద ఊందురగాని నిర్మ వాన్ని మందర పెట్టువాని వున్నది. దీనివెనుక వకగొల్లవాడు యెత్తిమొద వకపిల్ల చేత వకగడుపను ఊందురగానివ్వువున్నారు. ఈ నలుగురుమొద గోముభాలు ఉ. వున్నది. దీనివెనుక వృవకేశ్వముకు శ యింపించినారు. ఇదనివెంత వింహాలు ౪ తున్నది. ఈ కృష్ణని దక్షిణభాగమందు బల రాముడు తున్నాడు. ఇదికు తన నాతుత్రూమ మగ్గొల్లరయివారు వకు గొల్లప్రత్తిపిల్లు యెత్తున్నారు. ఈ గొల్లరతో నాతుభాగకు వక శ్రీ తల్లది యిదవారు గోపురముల X వున్నది. ఈ బలరాముని దక్షిణ మంది ఆవుల కాలు దికుదురగా యెక గొల్లవాడు వున్నారు. ఈ ఆవు మందర దీనివల్రుము యెకటి తున్నది. ఇందుకుమొదము ఆవుల చేనదాని ౹ఉ వక గొల్లవాడు పిల్లంగ్రోవి ఊదుకూ వున్నాడు. ఇదనియంతువ వక శ్రీ పిల్లకు ఖండురగాని తున్నది. ఈ ఆవు మందరి కోలు మొదళగాని ౹ఉ శ్రీ యెయసకందలవున్తి చేశవట్టురగాని తున్నది. దీని దక్షిణగాడ వృవ కేశ్వడు నిలుయగాని వున్నారు. ఈ వృవధము వెక వక గొల్లగాడు గొల్లది నిలుయగాని వున్నారు. ఈ వృవధము వెక వక గొల్లగాడు శ్రీ తలుగున్నముము తన నాతుత్రూమచేత చ్చుర్లురగాని వున్నారు. ఈ వృవధము మొద గోముభాలు ౧౨, మందరభాగమందు దూన ౧, వకినగ్రగోవు వింహముభాలు ఉ. తున్నది. అంద యా మంటవములో ఊండిది తున్రది

[Telugu text — largely illegible due to faded print]

గా. పచ్చకలివ-ీగాభాగమండు కండమాడ యోగేశ్వరామంటపమయు
వున్నది. ఇందు గ్రామనామము యథప్రకరింతుపమని అంటూగ. ఇందు
కు్తంభాలు ఒ, శిలలేమైన ్రంధ్తు గ నాలు శతి్మ ౪ ్రంభాలు రాగా
వున్నది.   నర్పశుక్లు 3-౹ మస్తంత్రస్న గర్భగుడి ౹ైలానముశే శారము
కెలిగినది.   ఇందులో చతుర్భుజాకృతిలో వాముహుసము కృనధముహిర
్తండుగాని వరమేశ్వరుడు వున్నాడు.   కుడి వాముభాగమండు కువ్వతి
తురురుశ్వామిని ్రాయ్రదయికి మోడ ్రండుకొని వున్నది.   ఈ కువ్వతి వరభి
కృ్తలమధ్యమండు కంభుత్కృగకారధురుడై చతుర్భజాకృతిలో విష్ణుతు్న్నా
డు. వరమేశ్వరకదీనాభాగము ప్రహ్మ చతుర్ముఖాలలో్ వున్నాడు. కువ్వతి
౹ంత వేవకలనము శ్రీ గ వున్నది.   ఈ కువ్వతివవకేర్శ్వరయము ౌండు
ౌంశ-ేలుతోశే కాగ్రకా కలిగిత మండుచుమాడ కూచ్చుండి యున్నారు. ఈ
మంటుమకింద ధ్వడభము గ ౹ధ్వనివామతూచము హాముగాని వున్నది. శ్వారః
చాంశేలు ౾ వున్నారు.   ఇదుకు భుధదయశాన్వే్మలయంగునున్న వున్న
నర్పశుక్లలో ్రతిమలు లేత్ర.   మంటువముచో౹ దశ్చిగావురుగోడమ కేవకల్పమ
హిర రంగనాతుకుల ఫూర్ణేకరస్పుతో్ కయవించినారు, వవ్వమహిగమంG
డు కాలాలనన్నిక యర్దరు భటుల.   ఇద్తులో్ రంగనాతుకుల్కాలినిభటులు గ,
మహితాఝిముద భటుల గ. ఈ భటులం యర్ద్గని కావోకావాం బుర్ద్కత ఫు్ప్తి
ముతునాతం మ్పుఫుప కేరిఢుకంలో్ ఇదమ రెతుఝుగా ఫుల్నాLు.
బ్వుత్వి చుఇ్తికి్రిఝ్రుబ్వ ఝ్ఝ్త ఫుల్నాLు. ఎఝిఝ శారణా జనలం మ్నస
రత ఫుల్నాLు.   ఈ భట్తేప్లు్ ఋవ మఝిత-పురమర్దని అమ్తవాతు అస్తకు
వాంలో్   భ్వగ్ధూర్తప్రై ్రమథగశాలు ఆయిన భటులు ౾ా మంది, శ్రీ
్రతిమ గ, వెళి ౾ ్రతిమలచేతేను యఝ్క్తమైనవర్ప వింహసాహావమహిర
కూచ్చుంది ఫూర్వా్భిముఖముగా ధమస్ను కన శామహస్తముచేత నరింది
దశ్ఝీఝు-్రతుఝిలో్ కాగనంధానముచే౹ యఝ్ధావతి అఝిముభ౹దైన మహి
హాతుఝమహిర వెఝ్ఝ-కరెరఝి ఆక్ఝ్ఝాంతము యాద్ఝ్యఝి.   కదమ కాశంల
యండు భ్వగశదాఝూఝుంటూ-లంఝుకరఝులో్ శురంతులంౌకోడఝ్దైన ఆయఝూఝంయల
ధరిఝింది న్ఝ్త్రచాశురంతులఝుకన్తూఝ్ఝ్గా-ని కేవగ౹కవఝు నఝిశేఝ్వింఝియంఝ్నదిగా
కా్శ్మీ్త్తిఝ్తురఝె మహిహితుఝుని పంహరకమచేయఝివఝని కావాశఝా
ఝు దేవఝి.   కూఝ్ౖ౹ యెఝుఝు గా మహివవమఝుము కఞి వవ్గిమూ్ఝ
ముఝుౖ అఝ్తఝా! ఆఝిమఝుముగా కన ధ్వకాఝంలంఝుందు గవచగఝి

ఇంది తిరుస్థై అమ్మవారితో యాఖ్ఖముచెయ్యవలెనని మహిషాసురుతు ఉన్నారు. ఇదీవిఖ చర్చ్రాచమకాలఖరిండి ఆయాఖఖఖహీతఖరై ఛటులఖ యాఖ్ఖముచేశఖాటకరౌనే ఉన్నారు. ప్రతిఖలు ఇ ఉన్నవి. ఈఖంట ఖాఖఖచుఖదఖాగా ఖూర్ఖరాగఖఖందు ఖందు ఖకటి విఖూఖముచేయఖలెఖని ఆరంఢముచేఖాఖ. ఆది ఖూరా ఖా కఖదు. ఈ ఖుఖటి తిర్తఖర్ఖగఖందఖ ఖహిఖాఖుఖఖఖరలఖగఖ ఖఖుఖ ఖకటి రాఖతో ఉన్నవి.

౧౯. ఈ ఖంటఖఖుఖఖఖ తిఖ్ఖఖ్న్మైఖ్ఖఖఖఖ్ఖఖఖఖగుఖడి. ఈఖఖదీలో ఖఖఖఖ్ఖఖఖఖారఖ ఖఖారఖ్ఖఖ ఖఖాఖా ఖఖ్ఖదఖఖ్ఖు ఖంగఖఖ ఖదఖ్ఖఖారఖ ఖాఖఖ్ఖ ఖాఖఖఖఖఖ్ఖఖఖ ఖఖ్ఖఖ. ఖఖఖ ఖఖటఖలో ఖాఖఖఖఖఖఖా ఖాఖ ఖ్ఖ, ఖంటఖఖ. ఖఖఖఖఖఖ కఖ్ఖఖదఖ అఖి ఖంటఖఖ. ఖఖ్ఖఖదు ఖాఖ్ఖఖ ఖాఖ ఖిఖ్ఖ ఖఖఖ రాఖిఖఖఖఖాఖ. ఆఖఖ ఖాఖఖఖ్ఖ ఖఖఖఖ్ఖ ఆఖఖ ఖఖ అఖఖఖఖఖుఖఖఖ అఖ్ఖాఖ.

౨౦. ఈ ఖఖ్ఖఖాఖఖ ఖఖ్ఖఖఖఖఖఖఖాఖు ఖఖరాఖఖ్ఖ్ఖఖఖాఖఖఖడి ఖఖ్ఖఖ. ఇంఖఖఖ్ఖంఖ్ఖాఖ ఖ, ఖఖ్ఖఖఖడి ఖ. ఖఖటఖ ఖఖా ఆఖఖ ఖఖ్ఖ. ఆఖ ఖఖ్ఖఖఖాఖఖఖ్ఖోఖఖఖిఖాఖ. ఖఖఖఖఖంఖఖ ఖఖఖా ఖఖ్ఖాఖఖ ఖ. ఖ్ఖంఖఖాఖ్ఖో ఖఖటఖఖుఖఖ్టఖఖఖిఖాఖ. ఖఖటి ప్రాఖారఖు ఉన్నది. ప్రాఖారఖఖ్ఖ ఖఖదఖ ఖఖరాఖఖ్ఖఖ ఖంఖాఖఖఖ్ఖఖఖ్ఖ్ఖఖ్న ఉన్నది. ఈఖఖదఖ్ఖఖఖ ఖఖ్ఖఖఖఖి ఖుఖఖఖఖా ఉన్నది. ఖఖ్ఖఖఖడిఖో ఖఖాఖాఖ్ఖఖి ఉన్నాఖ. ఈ ఖఖా ఖాఖ్ఖఖఖి ఖాఖఖఖదఖు ఖూఖఖఖఖదు ఖుంఖఖోఖి ఖఖ్ఖఖఖాఖఖఖఖఖ్ఖిఖ ఖోఖ్ఖఖ్ఖఖ్ఖఖ్ఖఖఖ్ఖఖ్ఖ ఆఖిఖేఖఖఖిఖఖఖోఖ ఖుంఖఖోఖి ఖఖ్ఖోఖ్ఖఖ ఖఖ ఖఖ్ఖఖఖఖ్ఖఖి ఖఖ్ఖఖఖఖఖఖ్ఖాఖఖఖోఖ ఖఖఖఖఖఖఖఖ ఖఖఖఖఖంఖ ఖఖ్ఖఖఖఖ ఖఖఖఖఖ ఖఖఖఖ్ఖఖఖఖ్ఖ ఖఖఖఖఖఖఖఖఖఖ ఖఖ్ఖఖఖఖఖఖఖ్ఖై అఖ్ఖఖాఖ ప్రాఖ్ఖాఖఖ్ఖఖుఖఖఖ్ఖో ఖంఖఖా ఖఖఖఖఖ్ఖఖ్ఖఖ ఖాఖ ఖఖఖ ఖంఖుఖఖాఖాంఖఖఖఖఖు ఖంఖఖఖ్ఖ్ఖఖఖఖఖఖఖఖ దఖఖ్ఖఖా ఖాఖఖ్ఖై అఖ్ఖఖఖఖ్ఖఖఖఖాఖఖోఖఖఖేఖ్ఖ ఖ్రిఖాఖిఖఖ్ఖాఖఖ అఖ్ఖఖాఖ ఖఖీఖఖ్ఖఖ ఖూఖఖఖాఖఖఖఖఖఖో ఖంఖఖఖఖఖేఖ్ఖ ఉన్నాఖ. ఈ ఖ్ఖాఖఖాఖఖ ఖంఖేఖఖఖాఖఖ ప్రఖ్ఖఖ్ఖఖఖఖాఖ ఖఖఖ అఖ్ఖఖ ఖఖఖాఖఖ్ఖఖఖాఖఖి ఖఖ్ఖఖఖఖిఖఖఖఖఖా ఖఖ్ఖఖిఖ్ఖఖఖ ఖంఖఖఖ ఖా అఖఖిఖేఖ ఆంఖఖ ఖ్ఖాఖఖఖాఖ ఖూఖఖ ఖంఖిఖో ఖ్ఖఖ్ఖఖోఖిఖఖ ఖఖఖఖో ఖఖఖఖాఖ్ఖఖ్ఖఖఖాఖ అఖఖఖఖఖఖఖ్ఖఖ ఖఖఖ ఈఖఖఖఖఖా

ఈ పర్వతాపు పశ్చిమభాగమందు గోపురపు దోవకులోమంటప ముల ౨-౩ గ్రంథేమ కఠ ఉన్నది. ఇందుకు మంటపము దక్షిణభాగ మందుప్రస్నదాని గ్రంథాలు గ౨. ఇందులో గర్భగుళ్ళు ౪. ఈ గర్భగుళ్ళ లోనా దేవుళ్ళు ప్రతిమలు లేవు. ఇందుకు గర్భగుడి గ-౨ ద్వారపాల కులు ౨ చొప్పి గగ మంది ద్వారపాలకులు ఉన్నారు. ఉత్తరపుగోడకు కంభము ఉన్నది. ఇందులో లింగాలను తీసివేసిన సంక పగా ఉన్నది. ఈ గుడిమందిర విశ్వనిలిచేమంకు గ ఉన్నది. అక్కడ చేమహాదేవం ఉన్నది. ఉత్తరభాగమందుప్రస్న మంటపము గ్రంథాలు ౪, గర్భగుళ్ళు లేవు. ప్రతిమలు వాళ్ళు. ఈ మంటపము ౫౬ పూరా కా లేవు. ఈ మంటపాపశక గోడల-టపము గ-౧ గ్రంథాలు ౨. మఱియొక్కు-డాను లేవు. ద్వారపాలకులు ౨ ఉన్నారు. అర వగటి ఉన్నది.

౨౫. తక్కింపు స్తంభాల మంటపము వగటి.

౨౬. కాణప స్తంభాల మంటపము ౪౦టి.

౨౭. రెండు స్తంభాల మంటపము వగటి.

౨౮. ఈ కాణపకు వడవటిహార్వ్యము ఉన్నప్పకయ్య ఉన్నది.

౨౯. ఈ ఉప్పకయ్య పశ్చరము సందు మూము రఖాంతఉన్నవి. రెండు రఖా-ట్ర-ము రోవల చెలవోవిచి ఆరు చేశాను. మఱిపక రఖానె గా అర ఇందు పెట్టికారుగాని పూరా కా లేదు. ఉఇదప్ష లింగము కాంత రఖా ఉవిదిన్నెఉక్షకాంతక రఖాతక్ష పఉవహ్త కృప్రా-ట్ర-కం కా చేస్తా ఉన్నది.

౩౦. పర్వతాని డవీనభాగకు ఆరగణియదూరము ౪౫ రఉమ్నహాయ కం కంమగా ఉన్నది. రఉనపూ-ట్ర-మందు దర్భము కరించెన. ౫లును కటలు అఆర్థదాయనె ఇర్దయహార్వ్యమందులంత ఆరుఇ-క-పఫ-య-న డి. ఈమె పర్వ-మ-రివముఖముకాత ఉన్నది. గుఇదురనా పఫ-య-పఫ-య-ను పర్వరాఅవిముఖముగా ఉన్నది. ఈఉ౩విభానను రోదకలో ఉన్నది. ద్వార కాలకు శ్రీ లు ఉయ్టుము ఉన్నారు. రఉఉన్హ కాయర్ఈముగా శ్రీ ప౬

మలు దక్షిణభాగమందు ౧, పూర్వమందు ౧, చుత్తరమందు ౧, యీశనలో ఇంకెళ్ళికను తెలియశెలు. అందు శ్రీ ప్రతిమలు ౧౨.

౩౧. ఈ విమానముకైవెళ పశ్చిమమశయము సా చెద్ద వృషభేశ్వరప్రతిమ చున్నది. అది భూమిలో ధ్రాడి చున్నది. అది శూచవలెని కొంత యిముక శివాయగళక సగము అగవడుతూ చున్నది.

౩౨. ఈ విమానపు దక్షిణభాగమందు శకలంవివిమానము యేకలలోశి చున్నది. కానికి అనుసున కొంత మంటపము చున్నది. అందులో ప్రతిమలు లేవు. ఈ విమానపు చుత్తరభాగము ప్రతిమలు ౨, పూర్వభాగము ప్రతిమలు ౫, దక్షిణము ౬ చున్నది.

౩౩. ఈ విమానపు పశ్చిమభాగమందు సమాశేషవివిమానము యేకలలోశి చున్నది. మంటపమును చున్నది రెండుస్తంభాలలో దక్షిణముభమసా చున్నది. యిందులో ప్రతిమలు లేవు. ఈ విమానమురుట్టు చిత్రయన చున్నది. ఓ ఆందువనే పూర్వభాగమందు యేకలలో శయేషశక దక్షిణాభిముఖ ముగా చున్నది.

౩౪. ఈ విమానపు పూర్వభాగమందు భీమవివిమానము చున్నది. యేకలలో మంటసమురెంక చర్దిపరభణనసా చున్నది. చూందిక స్తం — కర్దిమసందు ౨, దక్షిమసం ౨ — ర ౪, — ౧౨ — — — — — — — — — — — — — — చిరిమోర విడుగ పడి సరిమిక విడిగు.

౩౫. ఈ విమానాని దక్షిణము ధర్మరాలివిమానము చున్నది. ఇందుక ప్రాంగాలు పశ్చిమమందు ౪. ఈ విమానముత్తట్టు ప్రతిమలు ౭ చున్నది. ఈ విమానముమీద ప్రదక్షిణము చెయ్యడానకి రెండు ప్రాకారములు చున్నది. ఈ ప్రాకారములలో చిత్రయప్రప్రతిమలు ౨౧. ప్రాకారములో రెండులరెంక, ప్రంభాలు ౨ చున్నది. ఈ పయిల్రాకన ౭ ప్రశిలలో దక్షిణపుష్పే శ్రరమాచున్న ౫ ప్రతిమల ౮రసుమీద ఆత్తరాలప్రాశివాయ. అది తెలియ లెదు.

౩౬. గ్రామములో క్షలరయవస్వామిసుడితూపూర్వల్రరముగో పూరమ వాల్లెక్కి ౫ చున్నది. దక్షిణముపయిపున ప్రాకారాశలోలు గళ్ళానిడి

లో స్థలయసస్వామివారు దక్షిణకరముపెట్టుకొని శయనించియారు. హాహా అదిశిల ఫుండరీకమహామునిని రామరయాన్ను స్థనని. ఈ మహాముని ఇక్కడనే మృక్తికాటికడి. ఇందుక దక్షిణపువయిపు యలమంగళాంరా యురడి, పుత్తరపుఫైపున మాడికమతఆమ్మవారిడిది, చుట్టూ ఆగ్నేయ్లపక్ష — , తిమపడనర్ణిగ, ధృవక్షంతముగి, కర్ణాక సామ్మగ్రీపుండే పృ్రాయములొట్టు చకటి. గోఫురమనాఖలే యిరుబార్స్యాములలో జొప్పలు గౌడుఉకఖ౬ఇచత్తరుప్కువ్రా౪ స్థనని. గోఫురము వాఖకించరల పృత్తర ఖగమంచక ముప్మ్రెఆరుకార్జమంచరమ, స్వామినారు పృక్నిచవిచిపాలలో అందరలొదప్తుంచేని. ఈఅఖౖ ్రా౫గము చకటి, చుట్టునప్నస్తం కొబ్బ ిగ౨.

౩౨. గోఫురమనాఖఖే తిన్నగా కూర్ఫ్వర్ధాగన రాయలసగో పురము అంతొ చిచ్రమైపోయిపడి. ఇంచువేతేమ చతుప్నముమ కఖ అరు గూఅ కంచిమ్ప్తు యింకెల కఖ అరలానస ఫుంటుంది. అందులో ౖహరేమ యొక్ఖక ఫింకలు కేత్ఫ. ఇంగుక కూర్ఫున కృష్ణస్వామివారి ఇజ్ఖ్త మహావాయ పుక్ఖనొయెక్ఖ్ఖమంటవము. అంకుక స్తంభౖలు ఖ, రఖన గో్ఫురము.

౩౩. ఇంచుకకూర్ఫున స్థలయసస్వామివారిఫుఫ్వలొట. అంచు లో స్రిపాఖకూస్లగుడిమంటవమ. ఆగొఖల సధఖగడిలో స్వామి. ఆ ఖజ్ఖౖఖఖ అందిఖిమ మొక్జుకొంఫొతెుత.

౩ా. ఈ ఖహఖస్ఖ్ఖఖౖఖ ప్రుఖ్ఖజఖ ఫుఖఖ్జ్ఖ్ఖ్ఖఖ అఖఖంఫఖ్ఖజౖఖ పమ. అఎ ౪ఖలమంచంఖొయిపఖ. ఇఖ్ఖ్ఖ గఖ స్ఖఖౖఖు ఖ్ఖ్ఖ దప్నని. ఈఅఖంటపుఖమముంచరఖ పఖ ఖుఖపఖ ఫిచ్రఖఖంఖొయిపఖ.

౪౦. ఈఖుఖంటపుఖపఖ దఖిగఖౖష్యేఖమ ప్రాఖౖ ప్రౖస్ఖ్ఖ్ఖ్ఖఖ ప్రఖత ఖఖ్ఖప్ఖ్ఖ్ఖ ఖిఖి. ఈఖ్ఖౖఖ్ఖ్ఖఖిఖెఖమధ్యమంచు ఖాఖగుస్ఖ్తంఖౌఖంఖంఖ్ఖఖ. ఖిఖీ పుక్తరప్ఖఖౖప్ఖఖౖప్థిఖక ఖఖ్ఖ ఖాఖయగుఖాఖ్ఖమంచఖఖమ. ఈ అఖ్ఖ్ఖౖఖఖిఖ యాఖు స్థలయసస్వామివారిఖే దా౪ ఖంటపఖముచన్ఖిర పఖిఖ్ఖ్తఖి౪ అఖిఖ కొ్ఖస్ఖఖపఖుచేఖ్ఖారు. ఇంఖుఖ ఖొఖాఖాఖ అఖుఖుఖ్జ్తు అంఖుఖపుఖ్ఖ పొఖ్తు గఖ. ఇంఖుఖ ఖుఖ అఖుగుఖ ౩00, అఖౖగ అఖుఖగుఖ ౩00.

౪౧. శూర్ప్పణఖిదికి వుత్తరవువయవు యిప్పు8్ోట. శూర్ప్పణఖిది డిశీనాపుసయుత్ర ఈశివుామిడిశెల్లు.

౪౨. గ్రామిణి శూర్ప్పసముద్రతీరమందు చప్పల్రా కాలములున్న కాలయామేసు. శూర్ప్పమిశేష ష్లలపురాగామితోౌటి పోయినవి. ఈ కర్యాత మొనవిన్ని తెలియ లేదు. సప్పల్రా కాలములతో యిప్పుడు రెండుప్రారా రమందుమార్క్రము అగువదుశూవువున్ని. శూరుప్రారా కారములలకు అడియిాగ మం వున్నరి. కరిష్పప్రారాకారములకు అడియిాగకము వుస్తరిలిగిని ఆగవిడి కుండా సమ్రువుమురాౌ మునిగిపోయను. సప్పపుష్టు ౨, అంయులౌ కర గర్వుసర్లౌ కలింగయు వున్నరి. దావిపుష్పతేము రాెమ్చురెాిమగువువున్నరి. శివువర్తువు కవుశవ లేదు. ఆ లింగము కింద యెంచెరివువత్తో తెలియ లేదు. ఈ గర్వుశతిది ఈ వృష్కాతిలింద పాస్తేయి వాదమంచి ఆవ సంధర్పవుములు గి రగ్తినావి. అందులో రెండుమునులు మెుసౌి శివసర్పులు శికుర చాయినావి. ఇప్పుడు నాబుగుశెక్కులు వున్సిరి. చవముటిగిొదవు శూర్పరివెపమేశ్వరష్ల యిద్దరయు బాలమబ్రష్పాశావ్సామిని ఇద్దరియందున్న కూయ్యండిశెట్టుకాొని వున్ణ్నాు. యిమహాశాౌరాలలో బ్రష్తా విష్టువు యిద్దరు ఉష్నారి. ష్యామిి కలమిాద రెబ్చ కఖిశెరి. శాౌనెమిి రీఖ్షముగా తష్సేి. ఇమహాశాౌరాా ఆశ్వరలంఅశలంి రెంద ప్ర౨శెలిష్టష్యి ఇంకు రౌోలఅం తునరి. ఇందకిరుదుకూవులఅత ప్రిశిలెలఅుద్రఅుప్రిష యిఅంలరాౌశి అాునెరఅేఅ అి. గర్వుతి తువుత్ెళోౌి వేచ్చ శివయొామెశివదలఅయినవి కతి పవిరూత్ష్నరి. ప్రి కారములతయిందువున్నకంయులు కిందుది మూరరిల వసికెఅది. కాౌన్నటిక కాళ్లుపోౌయినవి. ఇందో్ప్రారాకావురౌ ప్రిమహా విష్టువు దక్షినాము శలవెట్టుకాొని పవుఱాౌావారు. స్వామిసుఖిశి రౌడుటుష్తవు ఢమవాడిశివారు. ఆఫ్తబందఢము యిప్పుడు సమ్రువుమురౌావున్నరి. అక్కడ వుేశారలిఒంటిఅిళ్లు.

౪౩. పవముటిశక్క_తు ఇన్నశౌొ్ఘురము. కర్వ్వఆదివున్నరి. అంయలౌ శూర్ప్పశీ శరవేశ్వరయేలు ఇద్దరు బాలమబ్రష్తాశ్తేశ్వకనాౌసామిని దెుష్తరౌ శ్నాేరి. యిమహాశ్ఞారాలము బ్రష్తా విష్టువు యిద్దమాఖువున్ణరి. ఆ్ష్రారా ఖ్ఉిదరి విశాయకిలము శెక్క_సారి. నాౌనసవెయిఖ్తురౌ కాౌయబిఖింర్ఊౌ అవిా ఢికరమురాౌ వున్నరి. కరిష్పు ఇ్ఖ్సషాలు ఇ్బ్రిమువయిరౌఊవి

౨౩. ఈగర్భగుడిమీదను గోపురముగాత్రున్నది. ఈరెండుగుళ్లకునైన గలం
కారుచెక్టిత్రున్నవి.

౨౪. ఈదేవస్థానికి ప్రస్తలవు వయిత్ర యోకచింతో కదుగాదేవువిఱిఱి
కొలిపించిరినారు. అందులో రాజప్రతిమ చెక్కిసారు. ఆకలలో ప్రస్తరరత్న
వయిత్ర మాహిషాసురను కదుకొనివున్నారు. ఈకలకు సముద్రములో
ఆలలలరేగులురయా వున్నవి. చంద్రోదయము ఆయినప్పుడు లేరంగాలు
కొట్టినే డుట్టూ గీరు వస్తుంది.

౨౫. ఈఆలయానికి నిఱ్ఱ పరివారరాు మూర్త్రము సముద్రురు వుంది
ఱ్ఱఱఱఱఱఱఱఱ ఎర రారరు పదవుటకి రోదుకదర్చినారు.

౨౬. ఈ ఈఆలయానికి దక్షిణభాగము మాదులిలలు త్రున్నవి. అందు
లో వకలమీదను మూర్ద్వయిత్రున దిన్నఆరలోొలిచి ప్రతిమను వుంది
సారు. ఆరకు ప్రస్తిరవయిత్రి దేనుగుమూర్తి నత్రిగము ఇక గుత్రరం వున్నది.
ప్రస్తరపంచాత్రన రేడుగుసుకూదము కనవడంకూలున్నది. పదమటు ఇక ఆర
రోొొలిరినారు. అందులో ఇక స్త్రీ ప్రతిమవ్రాత్రనారు. ఆ కింద రిన్న
ప్రతిములు మూడు త్రున్నవి.

౨౭. రెండౌకలను సింహాయుధమూగా కవడంతుంది. ఇదిఇకకో. ఇం
దుకు యింక చిత్రముగాని మరియేమి రెుక్కువ రేదు.

ఇక్కో ఇ మూర్దౌకలమీదను చెడ్డకరలానున్న కదుత్రు చిన్నఆరాముత్ను
ఱఱఱ దిఱ్ఱరోఱరాఱఱకఱా ఱ్ఱఱ.

Translation.

1. On the North side of the hill, is an Ísvara temple. In this is Ísvara. Lord Clive took away the Nandi in front of this temple.

2. In front of this are two monkeys, freeing themselves from vermin.

3. On the West side of these figures is a round churn used by Draupadí, the lawful wife of the Pándavas. There are three *Mantapas*,* hollowed slenderly out of the solid rock. The sculptures in the first Mantapa are two Doorkeepers, a four-armed Durgá inside, and four figures of attendants. The other two excavations have the same figures. On the South side of this rock, and facing to the West, is an eight-armed Durgá, treading with her foot the head of Mahishásura.

4. Near this, to the South, on the West side of the road, is the fireplace in which Bhímasena† cook-ed. There are steps to get up to the top of this.

5. Not far from this, to the South, on the face of the rock, is a large round butter ball made by Draupadí. Half of this is said to have been eaten by a cat, which gives the ball a chipped appearance. The cat is seen, with its fore paws upraised, tied to the hill on which Arjuna is performing penance.

6. On the South side of this is Arjuna's *Ratha*,‡ cut out of a single stone. The stone has been cut

---

* An open temple building. Also written Mandapm.

† The third of the five Pándu princes, commonly called Bhíma.

‡ See note * p. 213, infra.

into the shape of a *Mantapa*, with two pillars and a *Garbhagriha*,* in which was placed *Siva*. When that *Linga* was carried off by Bu * * [*sic*], the people of this place took an image of Vináyaka† which was near and put it in the *Garbhagriha*. On the wall to the South of the *Garbhagriha*, is some inscription written, the character of which is unknown.

7. Near to this, on the South, is hollowed out of the solid rock, a *Mantapa* containing Varáhasvámi. In this are two pillars and a *Garbhagriha*. In the *Garbhagriha* are no figures. There are two Door-keepers. On the wall to the North of the *Garbha-griha* is Varáhasvámi ; his left foot is placed on the ground ; his right foot rests on the head of Ádisesha;‡ on his right thigh is seated, facing him, Lakshmí ; his right hand is on her hinder parts, his left hand holds her right leg ; he faces to the West, and the goddess to the East. The four-armed Varáhasvámi's two other hands hold the *Sankha* and the *Chakra*.§ The god and goddess are regarding each other, and he with his boar-mouth is, in playful dalliance, kissing her right breast. Behind him, to the East, is a four-armed male figure. Facing this figure, is that of a woman. Above these two is a votary with joined hands, uttering praises. Three votaries are praising Varáhasvámi. Altogether, there are nine figures at the

---

* The sanctuary or adytum of a Hindu temple.
† Ganesa. ‡ The thousand headed serpent.
§ See note † p. 202, *infra*.

North end. On the East wall and facing to the
West is Gaja Lakshmî, on her lotus throne. Above
her head are the heads of two Elephants. On either
side of Lakshmî, stand two women reaching pots
full of water to the Elephants' trunks, for bathing
the goddess. There is one Doorkeeper. Altogether,
there are figures of five women, one man, and two
elephants' heads. On the South side [of the *Garbhagriha*] is a four-armed Durgâ, holding an umbrella.
To the South side of the goddess are three attendants, carrying swords. There is also a deer. On the
North side, are three more armed attendants, and a
lion. There is one Doorkeeper. Altogether eight
[human] figures, a lion, and a deer.

Facing Varâhasvâmî, on the South wall, is eight-
armed Trivikrama* holding the *Sankha*, *Chakra*,
Gadâ,† &c. Bali Chakravartî had given him three
paces of land, whereupon the god usurping the whole
earth by placing on it his right foot, stretched his left
foot to the sky for the purpose of seizing the upper
world. Brahmâ is bathing this foot with water from
his sacred water pot and worshipping it. In front
of Vishnu is Jâmbavat.‡

Bali Chakravartî, thinking it wrong to withdraw
a gift, is praying to the god, near his [right] foot,
wishing to give him ground for his third pace.§

---

* Vishnu, as the "Three-Stepper."
† Vishnu's conch, discus, and mace.   ‡ King of the bears.
§ Bali when reproached by Vishnu for failing to give him all he
had promised, besought the god to place his third step on his head.—
See Muir's *Sanscrit Texts*, Part IV., p. 127 f.

Behind him is Sukrácharya.* Two of Bali Chakravarti's soldiers are on the East side, and four on the
West side [of Trivikrama]. Altogether, there are
11 male figures. This *Mantapa* faces to the West.

8. On the East side of the hill, on a rock at the
foot, are 11 steps on which Krishnasvámi used to
play at Mounting the Throne. There is also a slide
on which he used to amuse himself.

9. On the East side of the hill, the rock has been
fashioned into figures representing Arjuna's Penance,
as [in the story of] Kiráta and Arjuna.† Here is
Arjuna, his two arms extended over his head,
performing penance; and here is four-armed Ísvara,
as he appeared [to Arjuna,] holding the *Páaupa-
tástra*,‡ *Damaruka*,§ *Trisúla*,¶ &c. Between Ísvara
and Arjuna stands Visvakarma,‖ with an adze on his
right shoulder, the handle of which he holds in his
right hand. Above Ísvara's head are Súrya,
Chandra, &c. Below Arjuna, is Krishnasvámi in a
fane, four-armed and holding the *Sankhu*, *Chakra*,
Gadá, &c. To his right, is Dronáchárya,** seated in
the lotus-posture,†† with emaciated body, performing

* See note * p. 63, supra.   † See p. 80 ff., supra.
‡ A fabulous weapon.   § A sort of small drum.
¶ Siva's trident.
‖ The son of Brahmá and architect of the gods.—Wilson.
** See note * p. 31, supra.

†† "The thighs crossed, one hand resting on the left thigh, the
other held up with the thumb upon the heart; the eyes directed to
the tip of the nose."—Wilson.

penance. On Krishna's left, the rock is fissured, so Nâga-maids* appear issuing from Pâtâloka, and with the five virgins comes a Nâga-maid for Arjuna. On the North side of these appears Indra, accompanied by his wife, mounted on the elephant called Airâvata, coming to visit Siva. Behind Airâvata is another elephant. Below Airâvata are three elephant cubs. And there is a cat, with her kittens, facing to the East, with upstretched paws.†

Round the god Indra, in the form of a ring, are figures of Garudas,‡ Gandharvas,§ Kinnaras,¶ Kimpurushas,¶ Siddhas,‖ Vidyâdharas,‖ &c., some with wives, some without wives, coming, as ascetics, to visit Siva. There are here 36 figures. Amongst these demi-gods are three deer. Behind them, to the North, in the middle [of the rock] are seven lions and one sheep. To Isvara's right, and above, are Dharmarâja and Bhîma sitting, performing penance. On their right are a hog and a tiger. On Isvara's right are 24 figures of troops of Pramathas,** and Rishis,†† coming to visit Siva. Also a lion, a hog, three deers, a tiger, and two monkeys. They are thus represented accompanied by their wives [?]. Altogether there are 80 male and female figures.

---

* See note ‡ p. 58, supra. † Cp. note § p. 58, supra.
‡ The bird and vehicle of Vishnu. § Celestial musicians. ¶ Demigods or musicians in the service of Kuvera. ‖ Demigods of undefined attributes, inhabiting the middle air.—Wilson.
** Attendants upon Siva.
†† Saints or mortified sages, of whom there are seven orders.

10. To the right of the above is a *Mantapa* [excavated out] of the solid rock. It is called "The five Pándavas." It has 18 pillars, of which one is broken, leaving 17 pillars. The shafts of four of the 17 pillars are broken; the rest are perfect. The front pillars rest on lions' heads. The total number of lions is eight. In the middle of this *Mantapa* there is a chamber, which contains nothing. On either side of this chamber, the commencement of other chambers, which have not been completed, is visible. There is nothing but a sort of cave on each side of the chamber, with no sculptures; all is plain.

11. To the right of this *Mantapa* you ascend to the *Ráyala Gopura*,[*] the foundation only of which has been built, and four pillars set up on the four sides. Round this the rock has been shaped into a seat but the *Gopura* has not been constructed.

12. On the East side of this is the Sthalasekharasvámí temple.

13. On the East side of the hill is a *Mantapa* containing Krishna lifting the mountain Govarddhana.[†] In this are 12 pillars. The *Mantapa* joins the hill and faces to the East. The figures in this *Mantapa* are as follows: Krishna holds up the

---

[*] I. e. the *Gopura* of the *Ráyalu*, the title of the princes of Vijayanagara. A *Gopura* is the pyramidical tower over the gate-way of a Hindu temple.

[†] See p. 92 l., supra.

mountain Govarddhana with his left hand like an
umbrella; with his right hand he is giving the sign
*Abhaya** to the Gopikás. On the left of the god,
are three female figures. Of these, two are in a
standing posture. One has a pot of curds on her
head, and a little boy before her. Behind her is a
cowherd with a child on his head and an infant in
his arms. Above these four are the heads of six
cows. Behind them lies Vrishabhesvara.† Beneath
him are four lions. On Krishna's right, is Balaráma.‡ His left hand is on a cowherd, and he is
standing with one foot advanced. On the left of
the cowherd is a woman. Above them are the heads
of five cows. To the right of Balaráma is a cowherd milking a cow. In front of this cow is her
calf. Above this, is a cowherd playing on a fife to
collect the cows. Near him is a woman with a
child. In front of the cow is a woman carrying a
??? and holding in her hand a net containing pots
of curds. On her right stands Vrishabhesvara.
Behind the bull stand a cowherd and cowherdess.
Behind [? on the right of] the bull is a cowherd,
holding with his left hand the right hand of a
woman. Above the bull are the heads of 16 cows;
in the front there is a calf. On the South wall there

---

* Holding up the right hand, with the palm to the front, as an
assurance of safety. This however is not the attitude of the god,
whose right hand points to the ground, a sign, probably, to the people
that they should take refuge at his feet. See plate II., supra.

† Nandí, the sacred bull of Siva.   ‡ The half brother of Krishna.

are 6 lions' heads. Altogether, in this *Mantapa*, there are 10 lions (on the North and South walls,) 16 figures of men and women, 5 children, 2 bulls, 1 cow, 2 calves, and 27 cows' heads.

14. To the South of this *Mantapa* is the Râmânuja *Mantapa*. This is excavated out of the hill. In the middle are two pillars. East and West [it measures] 20 feet, North and South 26 feet. There are no figures in it. [At the bases] of the pillars in this solid rock *Mantapa* are 4 lions' heads. Inside, the North and South walls are formed like small *Gopuras*, with niches. In those niches there are figures. In the front of this *Mantapa* are 6 stone pillars. On the South side of it are 13 steps cut out of the rocky hill. Above this *Mantapa* is the *Mantapa* of Velugôti Singama Náyadu. This has 4 pillars.' It is not built with stones brought by workmen, nor is it built artistically. It is now all in ruins.

15. On the South side of this, two pillars have been made and the rock a little hollowed out, with the intention of forming a large boulder into a monolithic *Mantapa*. The work is unfinished and serves only as a mark for the boulder.

16. To the South of this *Mantapa* is another, cut out of the solid rock, called Dharmarâja's *Mantapa*. It has 4 pillars and 3 *Garbhagrihas*. There are no figures in it. The centre *Garbhagriha* has 2 half finished figures of door-keepers. This *Mantapa* is in as good preservation as if just made.

17. To the East of this *Mantapa*, at the foot of the East side of the hill, are two large boulders on which is figured the Penance of Arjuna. There is Îsvara, in his four-armed form, holding in his left hand the *Pâsupata*.* Arjuna, with upraised arms *(Ûrdhvabâhu)* is performing penance. On the North side of these are figures of *Garudas*, *Gandharvas*, *Kinnaras*, *Vidyâdharas*, *Siddhas*, *Châranas*,† *Rishis*, &c., and of women; also of elephants and lions. This is partly finished, partly unfinished.

18. On the South end of the hill, on an elevation, is a solid rock *Mantapa*. The name given to this in the village is Yamapuri‡ *Mantapa*. This has 6 pillars of which one is broken, and the remaining five are in good order. Of the 3 *Garbhagrihas*, the centre one is called Kailâsa. In this, in his four-armed form, with his left foot on a bull, is Paramesvara.§ On his left is Pârvatî, with Kumârasvâmi¶ on her thigh. Between Pârvatî and Paramesvara is Vishnu in his four-armed form holding the *Sankha*, *Chakra*, and *Gadâ*. On the right side of Paramesvara is Brahmâ with four faces. Below Pârvatî is a female attendant. Pârvatî and Paramesvara are sitting on a couch, the legs of which are lions' heads. Below this couch is a bull, bearing Siva's left foot. There are 3 Doorkeepers. In the *Garbhagrihas* on

---

* See p. 89, supra.　　† Bards, panegyrists of the gods.

‡ "City of Yama," the god of death. The confusion between Yama and Mahishâsura is probably the origin of this name.

§ Siva.　¶ The son of Siva and Pârvatî.—Cp. note ‡ p. 107, supra.

either side of the centre one there are no figures.
On the South wall of the *Mantapa* is Ranganáyaka,* reclining, with his head towards the East,
on his *Sesha* bed.† At the West end [of this figure],
near the feet, are 2 soldiers. Of these two, one is
the soldier of Ranganáyaka, and one of Mahishásura. These two soldiers appear fighting, arm to arm,
fist to fist, tooth to tooth, nail to nail, hair to hair.
Above Vishnu are 2 *Gandharvas.* Below are 3
attendants. On the North wall is the goddess
Mahishamardini‡ with eight arms, surrounded by
8 soldiers armed with swords, representing troops of
Pramathás, and 1 female figure—altogether 9 figures
—mounted on a lion, facing the East, holding a bow
in her left hand, an arrow strung with her right hand
and stretched back to her ear against Mahishásura,
who is confronting her for the battle. In her other
hands she holds a *Khadga,*§ *Gada, Ghanta,*¶ *Sankha,*
Parasu,‖ *Tomara,*** and other weapons, also a
Chhatra,†† and *Chámara,*‡‡ and surrounded by attendants, she, inflamed with anger, has strung an
arrow to slay Mahishásura. In front of the *Sakti*§§
and facing the goddess, is the buffalo-headed Mahishásura, holding a club in his two hands and
furiously intent on doing battle with the goddess.¶¶

---

* Vishnu, as the 'Lord of Ranga' (Srírangam, near Trichinopoly.)
† See note * p. 33, *supra.*   ‡ Párvatí, as "Slayer of Mahisha."
§ A sword. ¶ A gong. ‖ An axe. ** An iron club. †† An umbrella. ‡‡ See note * p. 100, *supra.* §§ The energy or active power
of a deity, personified as his wife.—Wilson. ¶¶ See p. 99 ff., *supra.*

Soldiers, equipped for war, appear also as engaged in the battle, and holding over Mahishásura the *Chhatra* and *Chámara*. There are 7 figures. In front of this *Mantapa*, to the East, the commencement of forming a boulder into a *Vimána** has been made, but the work is unfinished. On the North side of this temple is the stone bed and pillow of Mahishásura.

19. Above this *Mantapa*, is the temple of **Olakkanneuvarnsvámi**. When this city flourished, a small fanam used to be collected from each shop, making a quarter measureful *(kálapadi)* of fanams, for the god in this temple. In the Tamil language they call a quarter measure *olakku*.† In Telugu it is called *tavvedu*. The god has rolled away somewhere. They say that if all the jungle is cut down, that *Linga* will be found.

20. At the South-west corner of the hill is the *Rudrastotti temple*. In this are 4 pillars and 1 *Garbhagriha*. It is called "The Cave." This is excavated out of the hill itself. Exactly in front of it, the votaries and others have erected a *Mantapa* having 6 pillars. There is a wall round this. In the middle of the walled enclosure are a well and cocoanut trees. This temple faces to the West. In the *Garbhagriha* is Varáhasvámi. This Varáhasvámi has his left foot on the ground ; his right foot is placed on

---

* A pyramidical temple in the form of a god's chariot.
† Prop. Urakku (உறக்கு.)

the head of Ádisesha, who is near him with his wife; on his right thigh, and facing him, is the goddess Lakshmi; his left hand holds her right foot, and his right hand is on her hinder parts; he faces to the West, the goddess to the East. The other two hands of the four-armed Varáhasvámí hold the *Sankha, Chakra,* &c. The two are looking into each other's face, and Varáhasvámí in playful dalliance is, with his boar-mouth, kissing the right breast of the goddess.

This very god appeared to King Harisekhara, and when asked by him the reason of his facing to the West, the god replied that Varadarájasvámí[*] would thereafter appear as an incarnation in the Punyakotivimána at Kanchi[†] and that therefore he faced in that direction. This is celebrated in the Puråna.[‡] The worship of this god continues to this day. The god has been painted in colours, as in pictures. On the South side of the *Garbhagriha* is a *Sakti* with four arms. To the South of the *Sakti* is Harisekhara and his two wives. On his left is a four-armed male figure. On the North side of the *Garbhagriha* is Gaja Lakshmí. On the wall at the North end is a figure of Srí Ráma. Áñjaneya[§] is praising Srí Ráma. There are also some other figures there, the names of which are unknown. On the North side of this temple,

* Vishnu, as "The boon-conferring god."
† *Prop.* Kåñchí (Conjeveram). ‡ See p. 178 f., *supra.*
§ Hanumán, the monkey chief; so called from his mother Añjaná.

within the enclosure, is an inscription. This god is celebrated in the Purâna.

21. To the North of this temple, on the middle of the hill is a *Mantapa*. It is in the jungle, on the West side of the *Olakkannesvarasvâmi* temple. It is cut out of the solid rock. In it are no particular figures. Four niches have been commenced, but are unfinished. There are 4 pillars. Besides this, there are 24 steps on the hill, on the North side.

22. In the middle of the hill is Draupadi's turmeric vat.* Near this, is the place where the palace was recently built. There are signs of this, viz., bricks, &c.

23. To the North of this vat is the lion-pillowed couch called Dharmarâja's throne *(sinhâsana)*. To the North of this are 5 pits used by the Pândavas for burnt offerings.

24. On the East side of this throne is a channel which carried away the water used by the Pândavas for washing rice. On the edge of that channel is [a stone] in the form of a bag, just like a treasure pack. To hold the water there is a reservoir. On the East side of the reservoir there are steps to descend into it. When the foundation of what is called the *Râyala Gopura*, was laid in a line with the Palace, holes were made in the large rocks on the hill near the *Gopura*, with the intention of splitting the stone.

*1. a bath. Turmeric (Curcuma longa) is smeared over the body by .... after bathing.

That work is unfinished. The rocks are called the "Monkeys' Rocks." There is a story connected with the two solid rock *Mantapas* adjoining each other, on the West side of the hill. Of these, the *Mantapa* on the South side has 12 pillars, and 5 *Garbhagrihas*. There are no gods or figures inside these *Garbhagrihas*. To each *Garbhagriha* there are two Doorkeepers, making 10 Doorkeepers in all. On the North wall there is a *Sankha*. In these [*Garbhagrihas*] there are holes from which *Lingas* have been taken out. In front of this temple the water collects and forms a pond. In this are reeds. The *Mantapa* on the North side has 4 pillars—no *Garbhagrihas*. Figures *nil*. The work is unfinished. To the North of this *Mantapa* is a solid rock *Mantapa*, having 2 pillars. There is nothing else particular about it. There are 2 Doorkeepers and one chamber.

[The above 3 *Mantapas* may be enumerated as:—]

25.   A twelve pillared *Mantapa*.

26.   A four pillared *Mantapa*.

27.   A two pillared *Mantapa*.

28.   On the West side of the hill is a salt-marsh.

29.   Between this salt-marsh and the hill are three *Rathas*.[*] In two only of these is the rock hollowed out and formed into chambers. In the third the commencement of a chamber has been

---

[*] Chariots, or chariot-shaped temples, otherwise called *Timdaus*.

made on the North side, but it is unfinished. Near this are a *Linga* and *Yoni*[*] and a temple with a four-armed village goddess. Stones are being cut from the hill near this and sent to Tiruvalikkéni†† to build a [temple] kitchen.

30. At a half *gadiya's*‡ distance from the hill to the South is a *Sakti* with four arms. In her right hand she holds a *Chakra*. In attendance on the goddess, on both sides of her, are 6 soldiers armed with swords. The Sakti faces to the West. In front is a large lion facing to the North. The *Vimana* of this Sakti is monolithic. There are 2 female Doorkeepers. There are figures of four-armed females—1 on the South, 1 on the East, and

---

* The *Linga* is the phallic emblem of Siva, symbolic of the attributes ascribed to him by his worshippers, as the supreme lord, the beginning of all existence, the cause of causes. The *Linga* word (Sanscrit) about translated, " *Yoni*" properly signifies the pedestal on which the *Linga* stands. The *Yoni* (*vulva*), an emblem of Parvati [...] For a discussion of the question as to whether the phallic emblem was derived from the religion of the aboriginal or non-Arian Indians, see Muir's *Sanscrit Texts*, part IV., p. 344 ff. For Mythological accounts of the origin of Linga-worship, see the same work, p. 325 ff. Also Vans Kennedy's *Researches*, p. 296 ff.—Twelve great Lingas were set up in different parts of India, several of which were destroyed by the early Mahomedan conquerors. See H. H. Wilson's *Essays*, Vol. I., p. 171 ff. where the names and localities are given.—A miniature Linga is worn on the person by every Lingayet, generally round the neck in a silver casket.

† Triplicane, the Mussulman quarter of the town of Madras.

‡ The Indian hour of 24 [...] minutes, [...] into [...] of which the Hindus divide the day. An [...] [...]

I on the North side. The name of the Sakti in this temple is unknown. Altogether there are 12 female figures.

31. Behind this *Vimána* is the figure of a large sacred bull facing to the West. It is buried in the ground. Some of the sand has been removed for the purpose of seeing this figure, so half of it is visible.

32. To the South of this *Vimána* is Nakula's[*] *Vimána* formed of a single stone. At the bottom of this is something of a *Mantapa*. There are no figures in it. On the North side of this *Vimána* are 6 figures, on the East side 5 figures, and on the South side 7.

33. On the West side of this *Vimána* is Sahadeva's *Vimána* formed out of a single stone. The *Mantapa* has 2 slender pillars and faces to the South. There are no figures in it. This *Vimána* is carved all round. Near it, on the East side, is a monolithic elephant facing to the South.

34. To the East of this *Vimána* is Bhíma's *Vimána*. It is of one stone, like a *Mantapa*, and faces to the West. It has 6 pillars on the West side, 2 on the South, and 4 on the East—with 12 pillars in all. This *Vimána* is a very large one. It has been struck by a thunder bolt and split in the middle.

35. To the South of this *Vimána* is Dharma-

* Cp. note † p. 103, supra.

râja's *Vimâna*.   It has 4 pillars on the West side.
Round this *Vimâna* are 8 figures.   On this *Vimâna*
are 2 parapets for the performance of *Pradakshina*.*
On the parapet walls are 21 carved figures.   There
are 2 chambers on the parapets, with 2 pillars.   Of
the above mentioned 8 figures, there are letters engraven over the heads of 5 facing to the South,
East, and North.   These are not understood.

36.   In the village is the Sthalasayanasvâmi
temple with the entrance to the East, a *Gopura*,
and 5 doorways.   At the South end, within the
enclosure, in the *Garbhagriha* reclines Sthalasayanasvâmi with his head to the South—near his feet are
Pundarika Mahâmuni and a lotus.   This *Mahâmuni*
here obtained final emancipation (*mukti*).   On the
South side of this is Yalamanganânchâru's† temple.
On the North side is the goddess Cûdikodula's‡
temple ; around are 8 Ârvârs' temples, 1 sacred kitchen, 1 flagstaff, and 1 store room containing utensils.

In the doorway of the *Gopura*, on either side,
are paintings of groups of figures and monkeys.

---

* " Reverential salutation by circumambulating a person or object,
keeping the right side towards them."—Wilson.

† *Prop.* Nilamangainâchiyâr, the goddess Earth, Bhûdevi.

‡ So called because she, when a girl, took the flowers kept for
offerings to the deity, and wore them in her hair. She is said to
have sprung from the earth, and to have been found by Peria Ârvâr
in his *Tulasi* (Ocymum sacrum) garden. The Ârvâr called her
Kôdai, brought her up as his own daughter, and offered her, at her
own desire, in marriage to Vishnu, at Srîrangam.—See *Guruparam-
parâprabhâvam*, p. 17 ff.

On this side of the doorway at the North end is a *Mantapa* of 36 pillars. The god comes into this on festival days. This temple is enclosed by a wall and round it are 123 pillars.

37. Straight in a line with the *Gopura* doorway, to the East, is the *Ráyala Gopura*, all in ruins. The foundation is 44 feet square and on this side there is a sort of chamber. In that there is nothing very extraordinary. To the East of this is the *Mantapa* in which Krishnasvámi is swung the day after his birth-day. This has 4 pillars and a *Gopura* (?) on the top.*

38. To the East of this is Sthalasayana's flower garden. In that is a temple of Sri Hanumán. The god was inside, in the *Garbhagriha*. He was taken away by Andilin (?).

39. To the East of this Hanumán temple is the *Mantapa* into which Púdattálvúr† descended. It is in ruins. Now only 16 pillars remain. In front of this is a ruined *Mantapa*.

40. On the South side of this *Mantapa*, to the East of the village, is the *Pundarikapushkariní*. In the middle of this tank is a four pillared *Mantapa*. On the North bank of it is a small *Mantapa* with 4 pillars. On festival days, they say, sheds are erected near this *Mantapa* for Sthalasayanasvámí, and the anointing-feast *(abhishekotsava)* is celebrated. This tank has 16 steps to the bottom of it. It is 300 feet square.

41. On the North side of the Pushkariní is a date garden. On the South side are cashew nut trees.‡

* See note * p. 34, supra, and plate XI., No. 1.

† The third of the 12 Árvár or apostles of Vishnu.—See Ziegenbalg's *South-Indian gods*, p. 71 f. Also note * p. 133, supra.

‡ Anacardium occidentale.

28

42. On the Sea shore to the East of the village is the seven-walled *Siva* temple. The [local] name of the god went with the Sthalapurâṇa, and has since become known to none. Of the seven walls *(prâkâra)* only two now appear. There are signs of three [more] walls ; whether traces remain of the other walls cannot be ascertained as [their supposed site] is buried in the sea. There are two *Garbhagrihas*, in one of which is the *Linga* of *Siva*. Its height is that of a man's chest. The *Yoni* is not visible. How deep the *Linga* is below is not known. This *Garbhagriha* had been built with six sandal wood beams above the god. Of these, some sinners have taken away two. Four beams now remain. On the western wall are Pârvati and Parameswara with the young Subrahmanyasvâmi seated between them. On the two sides are Brahmâ and Vishnu. The god has had a blow on his head, and is somewhat cracked. On the two sides are figures of two Doorkeepers and two monkeys. The figures of lions, &c., only have become effaced by the action of the waves. The figures of twenty or thirty lions, &c., are now visible. The *Nandis* which were on the walls have fallen down and had their faces broken—some have lost their legs. Within the second wall lies *Sri Mahâ Vishnu* with his head to the South. In front of the temple is placed a pillar. That pillar is now in the Sea. The water there is knee deep.

43. On the West side is a small *Gopura*. There is a *Garbhagriha*. In that are Pârvati and Paramesvara carrying the young Subrahmanyasvâmi. On the two sides are Brahmâ and Vishnu. In front of the doorways Vinâyakas have been carved. On the four sides are four lions, very terrible. The

rest of the idols are defaced. There is [as before stated] a *Gopura* over this *Garbhagriha*. *Kalasas*[*] have been placed on both these temples.

44. On the North side of this temple, a temple of the god Varuna[†] has been cut out of a single stone. In that is sculptured a figure of a King. On the North side of that rock lies Mahishásura. The waves of the sea reach this rock. At moonrise[‡] when the waves beat, it is surrounded by water.

45. The sea has kept himself only 10 fathoms away from the mound on which is the Siva temple. On the North and South sides of it, he has receded 24 fathoms to the West.

46. To the South of this Siva temple are three rocks. On the East side of one of those rocks a small chamber has been hollowed out and a figure placed in it. On the North side of the chamber is an elephant's head; and on the South, a horse. On the North side [of the rock] appears an elephant's foot. On the West side, a chamber has been hollowed out. In that is sculptured a female figure. Below that are three small figures.

47. On the second rock appears a lion's face. This is one stone. On it there is only this carving, nothing more.

48. On the third rock are a large head, a belly, and a small chamber, of very misshapen form.

---

* See note * p. 172, supra.

† The deity of the waters and regent of the West.—Wilson.

‡ The popular notion is that the Sea boils with delight at the sight of his offspring Chandra, who was produced at the Churning of the Ocean. The phenomenon of the moon's influence on the tides doubtless underlies this fiction.

Sanscrit sloka—pp. 13, 166.

The statement that this couplet is a quotation from the Mahábhárata appears to be inaccurate. It would seem to have been borrowed from Conjeveram (Káñchípura) whose Máhátmya contains the following lines[*] :—(Seshadharma xlix, 10, 11.)

गंगाधा दषिणे भागे योजनानां शतद्वये ।
पंचयोजनमावेष पूर्वाब्धेस्तु पश्चिमे ॥
वेगवत्युत्तरे तीरे पुखकोषां हरि: खयं ।
वरदस्सर्वभूतानामवापि परिदृश्यते ॥

South of the Ganges two hundred *yojanas*, five *yojanas* westward from the Eastern sea; on the north bank of the Vegavati,[†] in the Punyakoti[-*vimána*], Hari himself, the giver of boons to all living beings, is even at this day present.

---

[*] Affixed to in Heyne's Tracts on India, p. 384 n.

[†] The stream here called Vegavati is not to be confounded with the river in Madura which formerly bore that name and is now called the Vaigai. The Nipavana Máhátmya tells us of a great *linga* situated on the North bank of this river, and half a yojana west of the "famous city" (? Kalyánapura.—Cp. Nelson's *The Madura Country*, part iii, pp. 6 f., 44.)

मपबुषाद् परमं शतसंघकरावधि ।
वेगवत्युत्तरे तीरे मराधिंजच योत्तरे ॥
पश्चिमे श्रीपुरखाषि योजनार्धे तपस्वचं ।
तव लिंगं प्रतिष्ठाय मज्ञेचरखमाङ्गं ॥
सर्वजवामवायवेहितवां समर्चयुमे: ।
स्रत्र श्रीखुर्जतीख ब्रह्मदीवांके च ॥

The Inscriptions—p. 53 ff.

Mr. Arthur Burnell of the Madras Civil Service has been good enough to place at the Editor's disposal copies of the inscriptions on the Ganesa temple and Ratha at Mâvalivaram, and the buried Siva temple at Sâlavan Kuppam, made (so far as the inscriptions were legible,) by that gentleman in 1867. They are here given in the modern Devanâgari character :—

Inscription on the Ganesa temple—p. 57 and plate XIV.

वश्वश्विनिश्चरत्वारचं रौणारुः प्रभारद्यमभावाद अलां बाभमदुचैः ॥।

घनतासिवनाचौसाम्रुबो चुमाना चा — [ओचात्]

एताहुरुम्रद्वात्रा: कैलाच; घद्दारुण; घातानामिद्यमरूद • श्रीविविश्वता —

प्रविमादे समवा अभ्रुच्यवीषया दौच्वा च वो म • भारत्बीयात् म श्रीमरविदं ॥।

वञ्चलावी घूनिनिर्बिनारद्यमिव्यद्रुध: आलो रचत्रव; मधोरनेबं बक्ष कार्तिनं ॥।

• • • • • विजयती घद्दर काम • घ: ॥।

• निक्र; चोम; •

एकत्रबी • एतत्कमविश्चमार्धिन: नारबायियनि: आलो घघानागराब्दुर: ॥।

श्रीगनेौरीणायनस चिचुर्पायोद्याति: श्रीनिधो: कामराक्ल भरावाम बंधिलन ॥।

घविद्यकालार्थी चिनरमानुप्रमार घातौ विचार्ये घ्रम्बु: चिरतनादि भद्दर: ॥।

वेंकटहरिणि षोडा   .   .   भक्तिरं रत्नमं प्रभालिङ्गिविष्णुं —

यदि   .   .   .   विष्णुं • वेराश्वतिनरदे सुखलति चित्रां †

घां दह्यः ||| बलनबलमपनवार श्री —

† This line and the next down to ||| occur on the floor of the Rāmānuja Mandapa—pp. 45, 267. The words after ||| occur also on the East face of the 3rd storey of the Sonbhormost (Dharmarāja's) Ratha, but the ending is घा र चालव :

Inscription on the Unrided Siva temple—plate XV.

श्रीमतोद्यमनाम्नञ विवर

चीषयहरिष्व: कृतिनिषे: काम

राजव स्ररारुम धचिज्ञम: |||

चविनेकव्रत्तपुर्णे चिंदराष्वानुकार

घास्ते विञारवे युवु: चिरस्वरति महर: |||

नैस्तरितिरति पक्रेविक्ने ग्रतवे मुद्र: के

घाघमविरतिनम श्रमलाव् मग्रि लिडाल ||| भक्तिमरिडे

व मनया मनं शबघलीबच देविता न घो शूल भग्ने

कैलाश की अदिंतं ॥। पंसित्रुषक: पंसित्रविनु
वा पंसित्रक्षेत्रहरतेति । निर्मिस्ति ल
तर गुरुषकेलिकी निम्नत्तमन्तिनिन्देद्व पठ
पति: ॥। तुर्नितमाद्यमनिम्, यौलनिम्रायणौ तुर्नवदम भारतुकौ
तिद्धमात्रायुगां पटवे पंसित्रयुद्धायया
स्वर्ने निर्भेषिणेन्निनिन्निता   पत्ता दैन्ताले अप्सौ च्रद्रात्रता
नाम्मा तुर्निनित्रविद्रमण्यौते पाठ जिद्रा   [गिप्पु: ॥

•
•
•
•
•

क्रदाष ॥ क्त्रद्रप्राप्तच्य: संभवमौंद्रे: ॥

Note.

It will be observed that in the Gaeca temple inscription Mr. Durand reads Rauijaya instead of Jayarana. This agrees with Dr. Babington's own manuscript (plate XIV.) though in the translation the name has been changed to Jayarana.

The following is a revised translation of Slokas 1, 2, and 5 of the Ganesa temple inscription :—

1. May Kâmamardana,[*] the cause of existence, continuance, and destruction, [himself] uncaused, be [propitious] to the boundless desires of the world.

2. May he, [himself] without illusion, [yet] of multiform illusion—without attribute, [and yet] the divider of attributes * * * be triumphant.

5. The king of fully satisfied desires and crowds of conquered enemies, known as Ramjaya—by him was this house of Sambhu[†] built.

Inscriptions on Dharmarâja's Ratha—p. 57 ff. and plate XVII.

Northern face—base.

श्रीमर्विंद: *(left hand.)*

Eastern face—base.

? सुखसागर: *(right hand.)*

शिशिविवार: [? रशिबीवार:] श्रीबर: *(left hand.)*

Southern face—base.

पादमकाम: धनेवोभाय: *(right hand.)*

? धनेब: पैत्रीकानहृंन: विधि: *(left hand.)*

Northern face—second storey.

स्थिरबनिग्धि: मदगाभिराम: *(left hand.)*

विधि: (1)

* Siva, as "Slayer of Kâma," the god of love.—See Coleman's *Mythology of the Hindus*, p. 75 and Vans Kennedy's *Researches*, p. 297 ff.
† A name of Siva.

ओनरर्मिंद्र: भुवनभाजन: श्रीमञ्च:

चमसिंहनयाजन: (2)

कामजक्मित: चमेघमाघ:

चकचकज्ञाच: (3)

नयनमनोचरवान: (*right hand.*)

चतिमान: (4)

Eastern face—second storey.

चनुपम: (*right hand.*)   चान: (*left hand.*)

? भचोंतर: (*right hand.*)   परावर: (*left hand.*)

Western face—second storey.

चत्रयपराक्रम: (*right hand*)

परावर: (1)

Southern face—second storey.

चक्मित (1—*unfinished—left hand.*)

नचनमनोचर:

चर्वंतीमद्र: (4)

चीनिधि:

निवसर: (3)

विधि: (*right hand.*)

विभान: (1)

Eastern face—third storey.

• चम्मनकामपच्चवेचर श्री द्रा (*middle*)

रचजच: (1)

Annexed (plate XXIV.) is a sketch taken by
Mr. Burnell of the buried *Siva* temple (Atiranachanda Mandapa) at *Sáluvan Kuppam*, after it had
been excavated for the purpose.

Arjuna's penance—p. 90 and plate I.

The following description is contained in slokas 1537—1542 of the Vanaparva of the Mahábhárata (Calcutta edition, Vol. I., p. 468) :—

रमणीये वनोद्देशे रमनाणोऽर्जुनसहा ।
तपस्युपे वर्तमान उप्रतेजा महाबला: ॥
दर्भचीरं निवस्वाच दछ्राजिनविभूषित: ।
त्रीर्येष पतितं भूलौ पर्णं वमुपयुक्तवान् ॥
पूर्णे पूर्णे चिरात्रे तु मासमेवं फलाश्रय: ।
त्रिगुणेन दि कालेन द्वितीयं मासमत्ययात् ॥
त्रतीयमपि मासं च पञ्चवासादमाचरत् ।
चतुर्वत्वच संप्राप्ते मासे भरतसत्तम: ॥
वायुभचो महाबाहुरभवत्पाकुन्दन: ।
जर्ध्वबाहुर्निरालम्ब: पादाङ्गुष्ठाधिधिष्ठित: ।
स्नीपल्लवांशाच बस्तुरजितौल्यः: ।
विद्युदजीहरविणा चटालस्य महात्मन: ॥

Then Arjuna delighting himself in the pleasant forest, awful in his brightness, magnanimous, clothed in a *darbha** garment, adorned with a staff and deer-skin, performed severe penance and fed on the withered leaves which fell on the ground. He spent one month feeding on fruit once in three days; a second month eating at intervals of double the length; a third month also eating food once a

* Poa cynosuroides, a species of grass used in many solemn and religious observances (Wilson)—also called Kusa.

fortnight ; when the fourth month arrived, the most excellent of the Bháratas* feeding on air, having long arms, the son of Pándu,† with upraised arms, unsupported, stood on the point of his great toe. By constant ablutions, the matted locks of this man, of boundless brilliancy, lofty minded, were like lightning and the lotus.

Death of Mahishásura—p. 101 and plate IV.
Extract from the Márkandeyapurána—(Ed. Banerjea, p. 441 f.)—Devímáhátmya.

इति क्रोधसमाक्रान्तमापतन्तं महासुरं ।
दृष्ट्वा सा चण्डिका कोपं तद्वधाय तदाकरोत् ॥
सा क्षिप्त्वा तस्य वै पाशं तं बबन्ध महासुरं ।
तत्याज माहिषं रूपं सोऽपि बद्धो महामृधे ॥
ततः सिंहोऽभवत्सद्यो यावत्तस्याम्बिका शिरः ।
छिनत्ति तावत्पुरुषः खड्गपाणिरदृश्यत ॥
तत एवाशु पुरुषं देवी चिच्छेद सायकैः ।
तं खड्गचर्मणा सार्धं ततः सोऽभूद्महागजः ॥
करेण च महासिंहं तद्व्यकर्ष जगर्ज च ।
कर्षतस्तु करं देवी खड्गेन निरकृन्तत ॥

---

* Descendants of Bharata, from the extent of whose authority over the greater part of India, the country was called Bháratavarsha.—Wilson.

† So styled by courtesy only, Arjuna being in truth the progeny of Indra, the god of the firmament.—See Wilson's preface to Johnson's *Selections from the Mahábhárata*, and his note at p. 7, ibid.

ततो महासुरो भूयो माहिषं वपुराश्थितः ।
तथैव क्षोभयामास त्रैलोक्यं सचराचरम् ॥
ततः क्रुद्धा जगन्माता चण्डिका पानमुत्तमम् ।
पपौ पुनः पुनश्चैव जहासारुणलोचना ॥
ननर्द चासुरः सोऽपि बलवीर्यमदोद्धतः ।
विषाणाभ्याश्च चिक्षेप चण्डिकां प्रति भूधरान् ॥
सा च तान् प्रहितांस्तेन चूर्णयन्ती शरोत्करैः ।
उवाच तं मदोद्धूतमुखरागाकुलाक्षरम् ॥

रेवुवाच ॥

गर्ज गर्ज क्षणं मूढ मधु यावत् पिवाम्यहम् ।
मया त्वयि हतेऽत्रैव गर्जिष्यन्त्याशु देवताः ॥
एवमुक्त्वा समुत्पत्य आरूढा तं महासुरम् ।
पादेनाक्रम्य कण्ठे च शूलेनैनमताडयत् ॥
ततः सोऽपि पदाक्रान्तस्तया निजमुखात्ततः ।
अर्धनिष्क्रान्त एवासीद् देव्या वीर्येण संवृतः ॥
अर्धनिष्क्रान्त एवासौ युध्यमानो महासुरः ।
तया महासिना देव्या शिरश्छित्त्वा निपातितः ॥
ततो हाहाकृतं सर्वं दैत्यसैन्यं ननाश तत् ।
प्रहर्षं च परं जग्मुः सकला देवतागणाः ॥
तुष्टुवुस्तां सुरा देवीं सह दिव्यैर्महर्षिभिः ।
जगुर्गन्धर्वपतयो ननृतुश्चाप्सरोगणाः ॥

Then Chandikâ seeing the great Asura thus coming, filled with anger, to fall upon her, became wrathful for his destruction. Throwing over him the noose, she bound that great Asura. Bound in the great battle, he relinquished the form of a buffalo and immediately became a lion. No sooner did Ambikâ cut off his head, than he appeared as a man, sword in hand. Then Devî quickly with arrows destroyed the man together with his sword and shield. He then became a great elephant. With his trunk he dragged the great lion and roared. Devî with her sword cut off the trunk of that dragging one. Then the great Asura again assumed the form of a buffalo, and as before agitated all things animate and inanimate in the three worlds. Then Chaṇḍikâ, the mother of the world, having become wroth, drank good wine again and again, laughed with her red eyes, and roared. That Asura also, filled with strength, valour, and pride, hurled mountains at Chaṇḍikâ. She crumbling his missiles with a cloud of arrows, her countenance inflamed with wine, spoke to him in confused accents thus : " Roar, roar, O fool, for a moment while I drink wine. The gods will soon roar when thou art slain here by me." Having thus spoken, she sprang upon the buffalo. Placing her foot on his neck, she struck him with her trident. Then trodden under foot by her he came half out of his own mouth,* and was overcome by the great valour of Devî. The great Asura doing battle was slain by Devî, who with a great sword cut off his head. Then with lamentations perished the whole army of Daityas,† and all the troops of Devatâs exceedingly rejoiced. The Suras‡ with the heavenly Maharshis§ praised Devî, the chief Gandharvas sang, and the troops of Apsarases danced.

* I. e. He came in his proper form out of the buffalo's mouth.
† Demons, Asuras, children of Diti, the mother of the Titan or giant race of Hindu mythology, by Kasyapa, grandson of Brahmâ
‡ Deities, Devatâs.   § The fourth of the seven orders of Rishis.

Notices of the SEVEN PAGODAS *will be found in the following works :—*

GENTIL, Voyage dans les mers de l'Inde, Vol. I. (Paris, 1779.)

Asiatic Researches, CHAMBERS (William) in Vol. I. (Calcutta, 1788); and GOLDINGHAM (J.) in Vol. V. (1795).

SONNERAT (M.), Voyage aux Indes orientales et à la Chine. (Paris, 1782). English translation, Voyage to the East Indies and China. (Calcutta, 1788-89.)

CRAWFURD's (Quintin) Sketches of the Hindoos. Vol. I. (London 1792.)

HAAFNER, Reise längst der Küste von Coromandel, Vol. II.

BARTOLOMEO (Fra Paolino da San), Viaggio alle Indie orientali. (Roma, 1796). English translation, Voyage to the East Indies. (London, 1800.)

DANIELL's (T. and W.) Oriental Scenery, (London, 1795—1808.)

VALENTIA'S (Lord) Voyages and Travels to India, &c., Vol. I. (London, 1809.)

Allgemeine Geographische Ephemeriden, EHRMAN in—1800, and DALBERG (Baron), 1810.

SOUTHEY's (Robert) Curse of Kehama. (London, 1810.)

GRAHAM's (Maria) Journal of a residence in India. (London, 1812.

GRAHAM's (Maria) Letters on India. (London, 1814.)

HEYNE's (Benjamin, M.D.) Tracts on India. (London, 1814.)

Oriental Magazine, Antiquarian (? Lieutenant John BRADDOCK) in Vols. I, II. (Madras, 1819—20.)

HAMILTON's (Walter) East India Gazetteer. (London, 1815.)

.... (London, 1819.)

HAMILTON's (Walter) Description of Hindostan. (London, 1820.)

LANGLES (L.) Monuments Anciens et Modernes de l'Hindoustan. (Paris, 1821.)

HEEREN (A. H. L.), Historische Werke. (Göttingen, 1821—26). English translation, Historical Researches, Asiatic Nations, Vol. II. (London, 1846.)

FULLARTON (John) " Manuscript notes extracted from the Journal of his travels through Hindostan, during the years 1817, 1818, 1819, and 1820." (List of authorities in Hamilton's Gazetteer, edn. 1820.)

WILSON's (Horace Hayman) Descriptive Catalogue of Mackenzie's Collection of Oriental Manuscripts. (Calcutta, 1828.)

HEBER's (Bishop) Narrative of a Journey through the Upper Provinces of India; with an account of a Journey to Madras and the Southern Provinces. (London, 1828.)

CONDER (Josiah) Modern Traveller, Vol. X. (London, ...)

Transactions of the Royal Asiatic Society of Great Britain and Ireland, BABINGTON (Benjamin Guy, M.D., F.R.S.) in Vol. II. (London, 1830.)

BOHLEN (P. von), Das alte Indien mit besonderer Rücksicht auf Ægypten, Vol. II. (Königsberg, 1830.)

Calcutta Christian Observer, PERCIVAL (Rev. Peter) in—(Calcutta 1832.)

RITTER (Carl), Erdkunde, Vol. 6, Ost-Asien. (Berlin, 1836.)

Madras Journal of Literature and Science, TAYLOR (Rev. William) in Vol. VIII. (Madras, 1838); and MALON (Rev. George William A.M.), BRADDOCK (Lieutenant John), TAYLOR (Rev. William), and ELLIOT (Walter) in Vol. XIII. (Madras, 1844.)

FERGUSSON's (James) Rock-cut temples of India. (London, 1845.)

Journal of the Royal Asiatic Society of Great Britain and Ireland, FERGUSSON (James) and NEWBOLD (Captain T. J., F.R.S.) in Vol. VIII. (London, 1846.)

Journal of the Asiatic Society of Bengal, NEWBOLD (Captain T. J.) in Vol. XV. (Calcutta, 1846); and GUBBINS (Charles) in Vol. XXII. (Calcutta, 1853.)

LASSEN (Christian), Indische Alterthumskunde, Vol. I. (Bonn, 1847.)

FERGUSSON (James) Illustrations of Ancient Architecture in Hindostan. (London, 1847.)

PERCIVAL's (Rev. Peter) Land of the Veda. (London, 1854.)

PHARAOH's Gazetteer of Southern India. (Madras, 1854.)

GRAUL (Karl, D. Th.), Reise nach Ostindien, Vol. III. (Leipzig, 1855.)

BRUCE's (James) Scenes and Sights in the East. (London, 1856.)

Murray's Hand-book of India, by EASTWICK (Edward B.) Part I.—Madras. (London, 1859.)

FERGUSSON's (James) Rock-cut temples of India. (London, 1864.)

FERGUSSON's (James, F.R.S., M.R.A.S.) History of Architecture, Vol. II. (London, 1867.)

ZIEGENBALG (Bartholomaeus), Genealogie der Malabarischen Götter, erster, ungeänderter, vollständiger Abdruck, besorgt durch Dr. Wilhelm Germann. (Madras, 1867.)

INDEX.

A

Abhaya 206*
Achyuta-rāya 115, 117
Adam's Peak 20
Allimaniasvēra 194
Amaravati 207, 211
Admarus 5
Adoulai 69, 113 f.
Agastya 176, 181 ff.
Agrahāra 47, 117
Āhava Malla 132, 134 ff., 139, 142
Airāvata 104*, 204
Ajanta (Ajyanti) 57*
Alphabets, Andian 56‡
Amara 77 f.
Amara 188
Amarāvati 188 f.
Āmaravati 138 f.
Ānandanilayam 181, 183
Anigiri 135
Aniruddha 13
Añjana 211§
Añjaneya 211
Armama-deva-rāya 112b
Anurādhapura 24
Apollo 5
Apsarases 180, 229
Ardhanārīsa 37‡
Argha 214*
Arlna temples 157, 171*
Arjuna 30, 151, 226 f.

Arjuna's penance 4, 87, 59 ff., 200,
  203 f., 208, 226 f.
Arjuna's Ratha 79*, 105*, 200
Armenia 71
Artaxata 70
Avvār 153, 216
Āryan 51†
Āryan temples 171†
Ashtākshari 176*
Āsrama 176, 181
Asuras 47, 83, 99*, 101*, 229†
Asvatha 184
Atiranachanda 53
Atiranachanda Mandapa 120
Atiranachanda Pallava 120, 126, 128
Atiranachanda Svara 50, 125*
Atri 175
Australia 71
Ayodhyā 140

B

Bagistan 76
Bālakrishna 94
Balarāma 206
Balbārn 96
Bali 3, 13, 47, 165, 169, 185
Bali, submersion of his city (?) 11,
  15, 34, 46, 169, 185
Bali Chakravarti 202
Balloota Simroumaidn 165*
Bamoon 71
Bāṇāsura 12, 14

Banawassi (Banavāsi) 140
Behar 21, 96†
Beirout 73
Bulnos' (Mrs.), Sandhya, referred
  to 183†
Belzoni's Egypt and Nubia, re-
  ferred to 71
Be-Sitoon 73 f.
Bhadrakālī 50‡
Bhadrā river 139
Bhāgavatapurāna, referred to 93
Bharata 227°
Bhārata 227
Bhāravi 91‡
Bhava 102°
Bhavānī 101, 103°
Bhīma 200†, 204
Bhimasena 200†
Bijena's Hatha 10, 103†, 147°, 215
Bhonju family 114
Bhūdevi 210†
Bhūta 183
Bigandet's Life of Gautama, re-
  ferred to 20°
Bodhi tree 20°
Bogahah 20
Bonomi's Egyptian Antiquities,
  referred to 48
Bo tree 20†
Braddock (Lieutenant J.) 68 ff.
Brahmā 33, 84, 97, 149, 176, 180
  184 f., 202, 208, 213, 229†
Brahmaloka 176
Brahmāndapurāna 173
Brahmārama 176
Bricks 161
Bruce's Scenes and Sights in the
  East, referred to 11†, 77°;
  quoted 77†
Buddha 17°† 20‡, 31†, 52°
Buddha, worship of 24
Budha 21†

Durachar 171
Burckhardt's Travels, referred
  to 73
Burnell (Arthur) 221, 223, 224
Burnes (Sir Alexander) referred
  to 71
Burton's Excerpta Hieroglyphica,
  referred to 72
Buto 71

C

Canara 113
Carnatic 114, 117°
Cashmere (Kasmīr) 157, 171
Cat's penance 55§, 204
Cavery (Kāverī) river 136, 132
Ceylon 102 f., 160
Chakra 85°, 109, 201 ff., 208, 211,
  214
Chalukya dynasty 139
Chalukya dynasty of Kalinga 135
Chalukya inscription 135
Chalukya Princes of Kalyān 127°,
  135
Chalukyas 137, 138, 140
Chāmara (chanrī) 100°, 208 f.
Chhud 19†
Chandī 101°
Chandālā 225 f.
Chandragiri 99°†, 161°
Chandra 199, 208, 219‡
Chārana 208
Chhetra 209 f.
Chellambram (Chitambaram) 160
Cholas 127, 137, 140 f.
Churning of the Ocean 219‡
City of Bali, submerged (?) 11, 15,
  34, 44, 159, 185
Clemens Alexandrinus 27
Clive (Lord) 200
Coins found at Māvalivaram 16,
  104, 160°

Coleman's Mythology of the Hindus, referred to 182†, 215°, 224°
Combaconum (Kumbhakonam) 166
Companra-udiyàr 117†
Conjeveram (Kâñchipura) 80, 112°, 113, 117, 127, 176°, 211, 220
Coromandel Coast 162, 169 ; encroachment of the Sea on 46, 52, 117 f.
Covelong (Kôvalam) 2, 179°
Ctesias 74
Cûdikodum 216

D

Daitya 84, 229
Damaruka 203
Dênara 91†, 183
Dancing women 23
D'Anville, Antiquité géographique de l' Inde, quoted 26†
Durbha 173, 225
Date trees 180[†]
De Havilland (Colonel) 53, 69, 130
Dance, Egyptian referred to 73
Depedled 61
Deva Malla-rája 113
Devanâgarî alphabet 9
Devanêri 110
Dera-râya 112°, 115, 117°, 115
Devatás 23, 99°, 220
Devi 50§, 85, 101°, 220
Devîmâhâtmya 101°, 227 ff.
Dhâravarsm 125
Dharmarâja 6, 36, 104, 204
Dharmarâja's Mantapa 207
Dharmarâja's Ratha 106°, 216, 222, 224
Dharmarâja's throne 6, 7, 32, 56, 150, 212
Dharwar (Dhârwâd) 133, 159

Dîksha 183°
Diodorus Siculus 74
Dîpasambha 51†, 155†
Diti 230†
Dolotsava Mandapa 34, 50, 217
Doorkoepere 50°, 200, et al.
Dow's History of Hindostan, referred to 3
Draupadî 7, 104, 200
Draupadî's bath 7, 32, 86, 212°
Draupadî's Ratha 104†
Dronâchârya 31°, 89[], 203
Durgâ 33, 49, 77, 87, 99 ff., 140, 200, 202
Durgâpûjâ 99°, 101°
Duryodhana 89
Dvajastambha 114
Dvârakâ 13
Dwârapâlas 50

E

Earth, the goddess 175
Fenwick's From Sligar, quoted 93†; referred to 99°
Eclesiuns 76
Edén 95
Egypt 71, 73
Egyptian Architecture 8
Egyptian quarries 167°
Egyptian Ruins 70
Egyptians 71
Ehud 73
Elephanta 31, 37, 40, 45, 71, 118
Elephants 8, 33, 77, 57, 104, 202
Elliot's (Sir H. M.) History of India, referred to 26°
Ellis (Francis W.) 46, 60, 127†
Ellis' (Francis W.) Mirasi Right, referred to 141
Ellora (Elûra) 37°, 52°, 99†, 115, 118, 150, 151, 171

F

Fa Hian's pilgrimage, referred to 166†

Fergusson (James), quoted 37*, 139; referred to 153

Fergusson's Ancient Architecture of Hindostan, quoted 108*

Fergusson's Rock-cut Temples of India (1840), quoted 150

Fergusson's Rock-cut Temples of India (1864) referred to 45

Farishta, referred to 21

G

Gadâ 202 f., 208 f.

Gadiya 214

Gaja Lakshmi 50§, 207, 211

Gajapati princes 214

Ganda Deva-râya 11†*

Gandharvas 180, 204, 208 f., 229

Ganesa 35*, 72, 79, ff., 152

Ganesa temple 4, 38, 39, 67*, 69, 70, 154 f., 200, 221 ff.

Gangâ 182 f.

Ganges 13, 52, 93†, 106, 230

Gangadharan inscription 150, 165 f.

Garbhagriha 201, et al.

Garuda 184

Garuda-posture 188

Garudas 204, 208

Gautama 20*†

Gentil, Voyage dans les Mers de l'Inde, referred to 11*; quoted 37 ff.

Ghantā 208

Ghasikâ 214†

Gibbon, quoted 162

Ginjee 115

Godâvarî 137

Goddiladomni 24

Goldstücker's Sanscrit Dictionary, referred to 47†

Gopâla 5

Gopâlas 42, 58

Gopikâs 208

Gṛida 31

Gopîs' churn 77*

Gopura 181, 205*, 210, 213

Gothic Architecture 5

Govardhana 91 ff., 205 f.

Graham (Mrs.), referred to 45 ff., 52, 56*, 60

Granite at Mâvalivaram, Description of 146, 147*

Grantha alphabet 54*, 56‡

Gray (Captain), referred to 71

Guruparamparaprabhâvam, referred to 216§

Guseras 25

H

Haimavatî 102†

Hala Kannada alphabet 115

Harndall 20

Hanumân 211§

Hanuman temple 217

Hari 99†, 173, 183, 220

Harimedhasa 173

Hariqulya 173

Hariskidra 173, 271

Heber's (Bishop) Narrative, referred to 11†, 45, 53, 169

Heeren's Historical Researches, referred to 164†

Herodotus, referred to 71 f.

Heyne's Tracts on India, referred to 145*, 230*; quoted 148*

Himâlaya 69, 108

Himavat 102†, 182

Hiranyakasipu 12, 84*

Hiranyâksha 12, 84

Hobart (Lord) 505
Howorth (Lieutenant), 151
Hadleston (Andrew), 15, 44 f.
Hali Haruru 139

I

Ilaiyan Pudai 119 f.
Indra 14 f., 89§, 92, 104*, 204, 237†
Indra Sabhā, at Ellora 93*
Indra's heaven 190‡
Inscriptions 9, 32, 35, 37, 58 ff., 60,
  98‡, 103, 113 f., 116, 120 ff.,
  129 ff., 135 f., 141, 221 ff.
Irattaipādi 132, 134, 136 f.
Isvaram K., 200, 202 f., 208
Isvara temple 200

J

Jallipalli 154
Jain temple 106†
Jaina religion 113
Jāchavai 209
Janachhampūra 132, 134, 141
Jayamma (?) 136
Jayatunga, Sangha (?) K. C.
  Jayatilaka (?) 137
Jehangiri 96†
Job, Book of 73
Jones (Sir William), quoted 93,
  101 f.
Journal of Royal Asiatic Society,
  referred to 135
Judges, Book of 73

K

Kadal Sangama 136, 139
Kadamba family 140
Kadamba Gangn 140
Kailāsa 69, 99*, 208
Kailāsa, at Ellora 169, 171

Kalasa 172*, 210
Kali 101*
Kalinga 126, 140
Kalinga dynasty 127*
Kalpa 204
Kalyān 127*, 136 f., 140
Kalyāṇapura 220†
Kāma 224*
Kāmamardana 224
Kāmarūpa 55, 175*, 126, 128
Kanchi 211
Kāñchi 127, 211†
Kāñchipura Mahātmya 220
Kandy 24
Kapilavastu 174†
Karṇāṭakadeśa 114 f.
Karṇāṭaka-rājākal 115*
Kārtikēya 69, 107, 167*, 166 ; ori-
  gin of name 107‡
Kasyapa 213†
Kauravas 31*
Kāvari 132
Kamarah (Kāmbaei) 68
Kotmody's (Papa) Perumudan, re-
  ferred to 98*, 104*, 216*
Korudu 170
Kurumadesh 78
Kesavārya Srī Rangāchārya 136
Khadga 209
Kimpurushas 204
Kinnaras 204, 208
Kinnar (Macdonald), quoted 74
Kirāta 95*, 208
Kirātārjuniya 91‡
Kirti Varma 127*
Klinga 138
Knox's History of Ceylon, refer-
  red to 19 ; quoted 20
Kōdai 216‡
Kolapūr 139*
Kongadeśa 134
Kongas 158

Kuppara-Kesari Varma 136
Kávil 23
Ko-Viraja-Kesari Varma 136
Krishna ... 13 f., 30 f., 88, 92 ff., 151, 205 f.
Krishna Mantapa 5, 48 f., 53, 56, 92 ff., 203 f.
Krishna-ráya 112*, 115, 117*, 16?*
Krishna's butter ball 7?, 77*, 147*, 200
Krishnasvámi 203, 217
Krittikás 107?
Kadalgi Svámi 139
Kulóttunga 133?
Kulóttunga Chola 113
Kumáresvámi 204
Kurdistan 70
Kurutaladam 134, 134, 140
Kusumbara 69, 113, 127, 141
Kusa, 229*
Kuvera 87, 97*, 180*, 204?

L

Laborde, referred to 71, 73
Lakshmesvara 136, 139 f.
Lakshmi 203, 210
Lakshmi 184
La Loubère, referred to 70 f.; quoted 17, 23
Land measure 133
Lanka 13
Latona 71
Linga 11?, 30, 34, 56?5, 96*, 107, 124, 126*, 127?, 159, 201, 210, 213, 214*, 218, 220?
Linga and Yoni 214
Lingavedi 214*
Lions 8, 104
Lotus posture 200
Lyons river 73

M

Mahalipuram, the name 111
Mackenzie (Colonel) 46 f., 60, 75
Mackenzie MSS. referred to 111, 116, 118 f., 125?, 127?, 133, 169
Mádhava 175
Madura 117*, 166?
Madura Country 220
Mahábali 47, 55, 311
Mahaballipura, the name 3, 53, 111, 165
Mahábhárata 1, 6, 13, 31, 60, 91?, 113, 220, 226 f.
Mahádeva 77, 80, 89?, 95 f., 107
Mahánualaipór, the name 111
Mahámalla race 127
Mahámantra 176
Mahámáyá 21*
Mahásuni 210
Maharshis 279
Mahendra Slate 129
Mahimalu or Marálanu 112*
Mahishamardini 200
Mahishásura 33?, 49, 77, 97, 99 ff., 100, 149?, 200, 208?, 209 f., 227 ff.
Mahishásura rock 100, 159, 210
Malabar Coast 163 f.
... alphabet 64?
Maharájika 104
Maléchoren 16
Malla 111 ff.
Malládbipa 180
Malla family 113 f.
Mallápuri 177 f., 181 ff.
Mallapuri, the name 165?
Mallápuri Máhátmya 178 ff., 185
Mallapuri or Mallapuri-kshetram, the name 111*
Malla-ráya 112?
Mallésvara 14*, 111*, 170

Mallervara 178, 180
Mâmallapuram, the name 111
Mâmallâ-puri 112[b]
Mâmallaipûr, the name 112
Mâmallai Perumâl 133, 141
Mandapa or Mantapa 200[*] et al.
Manmatha 57
Manu 97†
Maraga 70
Mârkandeyapurâna 99†, 101[*], 227 ff.
Mathus 130
Maundrel, referred to 70
Mâvaligangâ, origin of the name 3
Mâvaliparam, the name 3
Mâvalivanam 113
Mâvalivaram, the name 111, 163†
Mâvamalûr 113[*]
Mâvalivaram, its position 116
Max Müller, referred to 22[*]
Mâyâ 21[*]
Media 70, 74
Mercury 20 f.
Meru 175
Melûrâm 177
Monkeys 4[*], 76, 77†, 200
Monkeys' Rath 213
Moor's Hindu Pantheon, referred
    to 80, 95†, 46[*], 103[*]
Muir's Sanscrit Texts, referred to
    80†, 84[*], 89‡, 91‡, 97†, 101[*],
    107‡, 188†, 202, 214[*]
Makundanâyâr Kôvil 100†
Munis 175, 189 f.
Murelîdhara 94
Murray's Handbook, quoted 100[*]
Myæ Hormæ 162

N

Nâga-Maids 204
Nâgas 203, 154
Nahervabâ (Mahravlia) 96

Nakula and Sahadeva's Rath
    163†
Nakula's Vimâna 213
Namuchi 13
Nanda 5, 31†
Nandî 97, 104, 109†, 155†, 159,
    200, 205[*], 218
Nandivaram 112[b]
Nârada 175 f., 184 f.
Naradîyapurâna, referred to 98[*]
Narasimha Avatâra 12
Nârâyana 97†, 99
Narmadâ (Nerbuddah) river, 140
Nâyar (Nair) women 46
Nelatûr 198
Nelson's The Madura Country,
    referred to 230†
Nepaul 157†
Nowbold, quoted 149
Nowbold's Geology of Southern
    India, referred to 44†
Nowbold's Notes on the Coast of
    Coromandel, quoted 147[*], re-
    ferred to 149†‡
Nîlamangainâdâyâr 31[*]†
Nîlgund inscriptions 139
Nile 71
Nîpavana Mâhâtmya, quoted 220†
Nomius 5

O

Olakkannesvarasvâmi 210
Ootramaloor (Uttaramallûr) 115[v]
Orissa 114

P

Pâlâr river 113]
Pâli inscriptions 117 f.
Pâli language 9, 17 ff., 21, 61[*]
Pallava 126
Pallava Mardu 127
Pallavas 128

Palmyra trees 22, 78, 155[]
Pâmravaṭṭamn 214*
Pañchâgni 193
Pândavas 31*, 103*+, 200, 205, 212
Pându 46, 89, 151, 227
Pându princes 200+
Pândya kingdom 114, 166
Paramêsvara 208, 218
Paramêsvara Mahâvarâha Vishṇu 139 f., 141
Parasu 309
Paraghur 130
Pârvatî 21, 30+§, 39, 78, 80, 85, 96 f., 102*+, 107, 149, 157, 177, 208, 214*, 218
Pâm 100
Pâtupata 208
Pâtupatâstra 89, 91, 203
Pitâlie or Pîtâlaioka 67, 82, 204
Pavavakkâvan's choultry 124, 125, 128
Peacock 77
Ponnâr river 113
Periya Ârvâr 216;
Pôrsia 73
Prâm 71
Pharoah's Gazetteer, referred to 349§
Pihan 92
Pillaiyâr 76
Pillar in front of Shore Temple 91, 108 f., 158 f., 218
Fithâpûr 126
Pleiades 107;
Poodan 21
Porter (Sir R. K.) referred to 70
Prâbât 19
Pradakshina 216
Prahlâda 13
Pramathas 204, 309
Prem Sâgar, quoted 93†, referred to 94+

Prinsep, referred to 187§
Ptolemy 164
Pûduttâlvâr 217
Pulikara-nagara 136
Pulikesi 137*
Pundarîkapushkarini 217
Pundarîka pond 152 ff.
Pundarîka Rishi 170, 177 ff., 216
Pundarîkasuran 181
Pawyakôtivimâna 170, 211, 339

R

Râjamalla 127
Râja Râja Chola 138
Râja Râja Narendra 137
Râjendra Deva 132, 134, 138
Râmânujiyyar Maṇḍapa 962, 207, 223
Râmatâraka 187*
Râmêsvaram 137
Ranajaya 223 f.
Ranganâyaka 209
Rathas 7+, 8, 35, 52, 60, 71, 103 ff., 126, 147*, 155, 218, 214§
Râvaṇa 57
Rattakula 138 f.
Rattehalli 129
Râyala Gopura 92, 208, 212, 217
Rayala 208*
Raisonné, Dissertations, quoted 27
Remora 73
Renaudot, Anciennes Relations, quoted 84
Richie 90, 182, 204, 239§, et al.

S

Sadras (Sadurangapattanam) 1, 144, 163
Sahadeva 103+

Naladeva's Vimāna 215
Sala 71
Saivas 55f
Sakti 209, 211, 214 f.
Salsette (Sāshthi) 57*, 62
Salt-marsh 105, 213
Sāluvan Kuppam 69 f., 119, 140 f., 221, 226
Samana Kodam 17 ff., 21, 23‡
Nambbu 224
Sandutty 139
Ramavataua 181
Sani Bet
Sankara Bhārati 139*
Bhaskara 139*
Simhāsa... 208 ff., 209 f., 211, 213
Sanskrit, Ancient Alphabets of 60
Sanscrit language 54*
Sanscrit Sloka 15, 166, 220
Salavanian era 74
Sāsarahāran 99
Sadānanda 175
Baudhha 175
... finished state of 9 f., 150, 153 f.
Sea, The god of the 15
Son of Milk 177, 179
Semiramis 74
Snake 7, 33, 96, 159
Saihadharma, quoted 230
Setu (Bridge of rocks at Rameswaram) 140
Seven Pagodas, the name 2, 167
Shanmukha 162
Shaw's Travels, referred to 4†
Shanugar 73
Shore temple 10, 33, 51, 107 f., 156 f., 215 f.
Shanese 2, 17

Siamese priests 22
Sidon 70
Siddhas 204, 208
Sunha 7 ff., 31 ff., 33, 120
Simhanna or Singanna Nāyadu 70, 115c, 116d, 153, 207
Simhāsna 7
Simhikā 13*
Sind 73
Singalam 130*
Singbalser 23
Siva 10, 32, 34, 57 ff., 79 f., 80, 91‡, 97, 101 f., 104 ff., 140, 157, 170 f., 181, 188, 201, 204, 206, 214*, 215, 224
Siva's lake 70
Sivāi 140
Skanda 107‡, 187†
Skāndapurāna 90*
Smārta sect 139*
Soma 19†, 21†
Somesvara Deva I. 187 f.
Somesvara Deva Chalukya ...
Sonhapura ...
... of Bud...
... referred to 195, 207, quoted 21†
Southey's Curse of Kehama, referred to 66
Sphynx 94
Sramana Gautama 17*, 20‡
Srī Hanumān 217
Srī Mahā Vishnu 214
Sringeri 139*
Srī Rāma 211
Srīrangam 209*, 210‡
Srī Sailam 113
Srī Vallabha 137
Srī Vira Mārtanda 138
Steel, Indian 147*
Sthalapurāna 173 ff., 153, 215
Sthalasāyī 150, 196

Sthalasayana 160, 217
Sthalasayanavânî 153, 216
Sthalasayanoerâmî temple 160†,
   216
Sthalasekharasvâmî temple 205
   (see Sthalasayanasvâmî)
Stone coach 23, 90
Subrahmanya 97, 107, 218, origin
   of name 107‡
Suddhodana 174
Sukra 83
Sukrâchârya 18, 202
Sultan Ganj 204
Sumeru 176
Suras 220
Sûrya 203
Sûta 178, 181
Svarga 170, 180‡, 181
Syma 71
Syria 73

T

Tailapa Deva Chalukya 138
Tâlapât 23
Takkanga 171
Tamil alphabet 3, 126*; Ancient
   forms of 64*
Thadasuriya Mudaliyâr 138, 141
Tanjore (Tañjâvûr) 213, 139
Tanjore pagoda 165*
Tapta Mudrâ 183*
Târaka 183
Târakâ 184
Tai-et-mai 72
Toltingâna 113 f., 137, 141
Tôr of Arjuna 88*
Tiluvasam 183 f.
Tîrtha 152
Tiruvadandai 178*
Tiruvâkkari 191*
Tiruvalikkâni 214
Tiruvarâshi 134 f.

Tiruvirichilûr 126*
Tiyyattis (Tier women) 48
Todavera 121*
Tomara 209
Tondamandala 127
Ton-pô 204
Treta yuga 51
Tribhuvana Malla 123‡, 140
Tribhuvana Viradeva 141
Trichinopoly 117*
Trilochana Pallava 126
Tripalore (Tiruporûr) reef 143
Tripati (Tirupati) 69, 113
Triplicane 214†
Trisûla 203
Trivikrama 82, 202
Tulasi 214‡
Tulavâ 113
Tûngâ river 139
Turmeric 212*

U

Umâ 57, 102†

V

Vaigni river 220†
Vaikuntha 181
Vaishnava 204
Vikrama Avatâra 207, 82 f.
Varadarâjasvâmî 211
Vardha Avatâra 50, 55, 85 f.
Vardhakshetra 177 f.
Varâhasvâmî 178, 201 f., 210 f.
Varâhasvâmî temple 33 ff., 89,
   131 ff., 185*, 210
Varuna 219†
Varuna temple 219
Vedas 29
Vegavati 220
Yogidoman or Vengidoman 137, 140
Vellûra 113

Valloru (Velūr) 113, 135?

Vellagdivāru 115?, 153

Yalugoti Singama Nāyadu 40?

Venginādu 136

Venkatapati Srīlovarāya 112

Venus (planet) 53

Vidyādharas 204, 208

Vihāra 21, 87

Vijayāditya 126

Vijayanagara princes 205

Vijayanagaram 112?

Vijayanagaram dynasty 114 f., 117, 185

Vijayapāl 96

Vikāhas 136

Vikrama Deva 135

Vikramāditya 127

Vikramāditya II. 127

Vimāna 109?, 151, 210, 217?, 214 ff., 214 f

Vināyaka 201, 218

Viprachitti 13?

Vīra Chola Deva 135 f., 140

Vīragalam 80

Vīra Rājendra Chola 136 ff., 140

Vīrachōla 80

Vishnu 97 ff., 101, 105 f., 108, 149 f., 159, 170, 176 ff., 183 f., 202, 208 f., 211?, 216?, 218

Vishnu, Recumbent figure of 7 (See Nārāyana)

Vishnupurāna, quoted 98†; referred to 84, 97†

Vishwasarma 177

Vishnu Vardhana 127?

Vishnu's heaven 151?

Visvakarma 205

Vrishabhasvara 208

Vyāsa 89§

W

Wady Mokattab 73

Wardah (Varadā) river 139

Wheeler's History of India, referred to 89?

Williams' Indian Epic Poetry, referred to 80§

Wilkins, referred to 101

Wilkins' Hitopadesa, quoted 98†

Wilson's Rāmāyana, referred to 132?, 214?

Wilson's Meghaduta, referred to 182†

Wilson's Sanscrit Dictionary, referred to in the notes, passim.

Wilson's Vishnupurāna, referred to 84?, 97†; quoted 98†, 101?, 102?

Wōdan 81

Y

Yadava 177

Yakko 23

Yaksha 23?, 150

Yalamanganāfichāru 681

Yama 131†, 205?

Yamapuri Mantapa 208

Yamarāja 33, 140, 159

Yoga 176

Yojana 13, 106, 290

Yoni 214?, 216

Yudhishthira 6

Page 11, note †. *For* "Muro probably", *read* "Some here supposed it to be". (Cp. note† p. 158.)

Page 66. *For* "Mâhâmalaipûr", *read* "Mahâmalaipûr".

Page 96, note². *For* "Arûkknœœi ( ) temple", *read* "Urukkœwœi ( ) Îsvara temple"; and *for* "one o'clock (about 1½ gill)", *read* "one urakku (about 3 gills)".— (Cp. p. 210.)

Page 114. "Vijayanagaram ascendancy" appears to be a misprint in the original for "Vijayanagaram dynasty."

Page 118, note. *For* "Vellugâtâru", *read* "Velugôtivâru".

Page 118. *For* "a claw", *read* "as a claw".

Page 124, 126, 138. "Paraiakkâran's (prop. Paraiakkâran's) Choultry" signifies "Coral-monger's Choultry." (Korallanhândler-Schlösser—Graul.)

Page 126. *For* "Mahendra Shanta", *read* "Mahendra Sânta."

Page 128, note². With reference to Sir Walter Elliot's remark on the Tamil alphabet, it will be observed that the Grantha letter , not the Tamil letter , is used in the word "Adiyeshtavara," in the inscription referred to. (See p. 158.)

Page 128. [Tamil/Grantha text] is probably an error in the transcript for [Tamil/Grantha text].

Page 153. *For* "Mâhavarâha" *read* "Mahâvarâha.'"

Page 141. "56th year" appears to be an error for "57th year." (See p. 121.)

line 14 from the bottom. *For* [text], *read* [text].

Page 170, [illegible] [text], *read* [text].

Page 173, note². A [illegible] —

देवु सर्वामु च ततो मेरौ जिवबमेवुषा ।
संतुष्ट्वा घिचा तछ आमतो मुनिरेषम ॥

Page 174, Sloka 13. *For* [text], *read* [text].

Page 178. *For* "Hariadara," *read* "Harisekhara."

Page 181. "Pundarikasaranu", *read* "Pundarikasarnu."

Page 181. *For* Asrima, *read* Asruma.

Page 185. *For* "Sthalasayî", *read* "Sthalasayî".

Page 216, note². *For* "Purta", *read* "Purisa."

Page 217. *For* "Pundarikapuskarini," *read* Pundarikapushkarini."

Mr. Fergusson (*History of Architecture*, Vol. II., p. 502 ff.) thus describes three of the five *Rathas*:—

The Southernmost, No. 44 in the Sketch, he remarks "imitates a Buddhist monastery of five storeys. * * The time at which it was executed was very little removed from that of Buddhism in this part of India. There is little or none of the extravagance of later Hindu style in the sculpture. * Neither the Jains nor the Hindus introduced anything like a new style of architecture. They adapted the Buddhist style to their own purposes." * *

No. 41, Mr. Fergusson describes as being "the only free-standing monolithic representation I know in India of such a temple [Chaitya] as those excavated in the rock at Ajunta and elsewhere. * *
But in this, as in all more modern structures of this class, we find considerable confusion between the forms of the temple and those of the monastery. This is no more than might be expected when we consider that the original purposes to which these forms were applied had ceased to exist, and that in these late copies which employ subordinate ornamental ap-

And No. 45 the same author, "evidently belongs to the same system. * * There can be little doubt that it is the copy of a variety of the Buddhist temple or Chaitya, of which we have no exact representation in the caves—probably of a built Buddhist temple."

ADDENDUM.

Since the foregoing pages were printed, Mr. R. Bruce Foote, F. G. S., of the Geological Survey of India, has kindly favoured the Editor with the following:—

Note on the Geology of Mahávalipuram.

The rock in which the temples at Mahávalipuram are cut is a low ridge of quartzo-felspathic gneiss, an extension of which occurs at the [...] village of Padari, nearly three miles to north, and also at Collastór, three miles to the S. S. W.

The bedded character of the rock is but very rarely seen, hence it has often been described as a granite. The strike of the bedding is N. by 5° E.—S. by 5° W. and coincides with that of the grain of the rocks and with the general direction of the hilly ridges further inland. The dip of the beds appears to be westerly but is very obscure and nearly obliterated by excessive metamorphic action.

The texture of the rock suggests the idea of a coarse gritty bed having been exposed to severe lateral pressure, the quartz and felspar having an irregular flaky arrangement, and not forming distinctly continuous laminæ as in typical gneiss rock. The color of the [...] freshly quarried is a rich pinkish grey weathering to a [...] color. Where exposed to the sea spray, as in the walls of [...] the stone acquires a black color and decays far more [...] weather further inland. [...] quarried, as it splits very easily into blocks of useful size and shape, and has a decidedly handsome appearance.

The ridge of rocks to the East of the Shore Temple on which the fury of the surf is broken, consists also of gneiss, but probably belongs to another bed running in a parallel direction. The East foot of the Mahávalipuram gneiss ridge is covered by the beach or by blown sands, but at the West side are beds of sand and clay abounding in Marine and [...] shells of recent species, but in a subfossil condition. These beds are cut through in many places by the Coast Canal.

www.ingramcontent.com/pod-product-compliance
Lightning Source LLC
Chambersburg PA
CBHW060600030726
47498CB00005B/1472